Sin City Daemon

by

Rick Newberry

Sin City Daemon

Cover Art by *Debbie Taylor*

The Wild Rose Press, Inc.
PO Box 708
Adams Basin, NY 14410-0708
Visit us at www.thewildrosepress.com

Publishing History
First Black Rose Edition, 2016
Print ISBN 978-1-5092-1058-9
Digital ISBN 978-1-5092-1059-6

Published in the United States of America

I cozy up next to her

and slide my arms around her waist. "As long as that call can wait until tomorrow morning." I lean in and press my lips against hers, covering her mouth in a deep, penetrating kiss. I explore her velvety tongue and breathe in her perfume, sweat, and skin. My cheek nuzzles her brow, feeling her perspiration wet on my face.

Her breathing is heavy, like quiet panting. "The call can wait."

I'm still confused about the plan, the murders at Claremont, and their reluctance to tell me what my role might be. One thing, however, isn't confusing: my feelings for Dixie.

Primal thoughts enter my mind, calling me, pushing me closer. I kiss her cheek and move my hands across her body. She sighs, running her tongue over my ear. The sweet scent of her sex is more than I can stand.

I search for the zipper tab of her jeans, but her hand covers mine, stopping me in mid-zip.

"What's the matter?"

The gleam in her eye tells me it's a foolish question. "Is it okay if we continue this in my old bedroom?

"Of course."

She holds out her hand. "This way, Mr. Steel, and don't you dare forget where you left off. Promise?" All at once, she furrows her brow. "You have done this before, haven't you?"

The question takes me off guard. "No. Why, am I doing something wrong?"

Dedication

For Sylvia and Mike

Chapter One

Night terrors slap me awake like I'm on fire. Again. While wiping away sweat, I close my eyes and roll over. I'm sure the recent nightmares stem from one terrible thought: since I'm in prison for the rest of my life, there are things I'll never get to do. And as long as I'm up, I make a mental list of those things, putting them in order like numbered sheep: normal things like drive a car, eat a hamburger, or make a meal; simple things like comfort someone in need, drink a soda, or make friends; special things like study human faiths, watch the sunrise, or make love.

On the other hand, I've led quite a remarkable life and accomplished things most people can't even imagine. I've tasted the blood of my enemies, helped save the human race from extinction, and fallen in love with a Daemon. Dixie Mulholland, the Daemon I love, is the reason I'm in prison. I gave up my freedom on the promise of hers.

They call Wednesdays my "rest" days. I watch classic movies on television, read books, and draw. Most of my sketches are of Dixie, and I'm told they're quite good—at least the guards seem to like them.

On Thursdays, I have counseling: "Tell me how you feel today, Adam."

"Fine."

"Anything new to report, Mr. Steel?"

"Nope."

Fridays, I spend in the gym: spin bikes, treadmills, and free weights. I like Fridays.

Today is Saturday: clinic day. Doctors take samples of my blood and urine. Then it's off to the MRI, x-ray, and CAT scan machines. The routine has never changed in two years.

Today it does.

The sound of the door opening shoves me out of a pleasant dream. A whisper sneaks across my cell, "Wake up. I'm here to get you out."

Even though its inkjet black in my cell, I possess decent night vision and zero in on the man entering my room. With my heart thumping, I prop up on my elbows and remain silent. The man's face is still out of focus, but his voice—British accent, crisp, and military—stirs up memories I've fought hard to forget. I sniff the air. "What are you doing here, Colonel Dayton?"

"No time to explain. We have to go."

He turns on a flashlight and points it at my face, blinding me for just a moment. With a hand covering my eyes I ask, "Go where?"

"Las Vegas."

I plop my head back down on the pillow. The last time I heard his voice he called me a "mutt." Not a form of endearment. His presence tonight has to be a mistake, a cruel joke, or another in an endless series of attempts to make me transform. That's all they've ever wanted since bringing me here against my will—by Colonel Dayton.

He speaks in a confident tone. "C'mon, get up. Dixie's in trouble, she needs your help."

At the sound of her name, my feet hit the floor and

I sprint across the room to the door. "What's wrong? Is she in trouble?"

"I'll explain on the way."

All kinds of warnings go off in my head. I don't trust Colonel Dayton. Still, my interest is piqued, so I decide to see where this is going. I grab a few of my more recent drawings from a nearby table, fold them up quick, and tuck them into the pocket of my sweat pants. Colonel Dayton waves me forward into the hallway. The lights are dim, and I sniff at the air. "Where are the guards?"

"There are only two on duty at night. They're sleeping like babes with a little help from me." He raises a pistol in the air. "I gave them a dose of the tranquilizer I used on you two years ago, remember? No, of course you wouldn't."

I'll never forget. "What about the cameras?"

"Switched them all off. It's not a particularly sophisticated security system, despite what you may have thought. I'm surprised you never attempted an escape."

I ignore his criticism and concentrate on the surroundings. The cold tile under my feet and deathly silence in the hallway send chills through my body. I've walked this corridor almost every day for the past two years, but it seems foreign now. Another sniff at the air reveals the location of the two guards, their skin is free of sweat; they're peaceful and at rest.

A long forgotten ache in the back of my neck begins to throb, signaling the first sign of the oncoming transformation. The urge to change into a canine and tear the colonel apart is strong. Are the cameras really off? I stare into his eyes. "How do I know I can trust

3

you?"

"You don't. But that's the wrong question then, isn't it?" His voice is steady and calm as he explains, "I'm standing within easy reach of someone who can rip me apart. The real question is: how do *I* know I can trust *you*?"

My answer to his question races out in no uncertain terms, "Because I'm not a killer."

He smiles. It's a taunting smile, like he's goading me on, and that makes me think my hunch is right: this *is* a trick to get me to transform. But I'm not biting—literally.

"And because I'm not going to let whoever's watching see the wolfhound." With little effort, I force the ache in my neck to subside. I'm in complete control of the change.

He tucks the pistol into a holster under his armpit and glances at his watch. "Good to know. And for the last time, there are no secret cameras watching us. The day shift will be here in about three minutes, so we don't have much time. I suggest you either come with me now, or, if you feel more at home in a cage, crawl back into yours. But just to be clear, however, Dixie is expecting you."

He sounds convincing. "Lead the way."

Colonel Dayton continues down the hall, and we pass an open door. Inside the darkened room, two guards dressed in black uniforms lean forward, their heads lying on a metal desk. The monitors on the wall are blank—the cameras *are* out.

Quickening my pace, I catch up to the colonel at the exit. When he opens the door, I expect alarm bells to greet us. Instead, the only sound I hear is crickets chirping. What I see, however, stops me cold. The night sky is lit up like the Starry Night painting. Millions of tiny lights fill the sky—a sky I haven't seen in two years. I'm so grateful to be able to see the world as any other human would at this exact moment of my life: in color. The smell of clean, outdoor air sends adrenaline pulsing through my body.

Footsteps echo down the hall behind us. In a tight whisper, the colonel says, "C'mon, they're changing shift. Let's move."

He tugs at my shirt and pulls me outside. I'm standing on dirt—real dirt. My senses drink in the sensations of freedom in one big gulp: cold wind bites at my face, the smell of fresh, unventilated air intoxicates me, and a strange, almost alien-like silence fills my ears. I'm dizzy with the lack of boundaries and want to sprint across the open field ahead.

Colonel Dayton eases the door shut and motions me forward with a wave of his hand. "If we don't hurry, they'll be on us, and you'll be back in that cell for good."

Fleeting thoughts of my list and all the things I've never done race through my head as I follow him. We clamber down into a small ravine and jump over an old wooden fence. I can't help but risk a glance back at where I've been held for the past two years. The sight of my prison stuns me. "It's nothing but an old barn."

"Designed to look like that," Colonel Dayton says as he yanks on my shirt again. "It blends with the countryside. No questions about a barn way out here, and no need for anything larger; it's a prison built to hold just one: you. C'mon, I've a car at the base of the hill. Let's keep moving. Double time."

"Then what?"

"We get as far away from here as fast as we can."

Dayton throws the "we" word around pretty freely. I find it unsettling. It makes me think he told me the truth which is not good—that means Dixie really is in trouble.

The car he has stashed away is a brand new, jet-black Camaro. I've seen the advertisements for this particular model on the TV in my cell. It looked super-fast in the commercial. When I shut the passenger side door and the colonel hits the gas—it is.

****

Miles stack up as Colonel Dayton keeps his foot mashed on the accelerator.

The morning sun paints a hazy shine on the mountains ahead of us and muted colors begin to define the landscape. The biting chill in the air gives way to a cool, but comfortable, temperature. Being raised in Las Vegas, I've never seen so much green grass, trees, and shrubs all in one place; spending the past two years in prison didn't help either. The snow-capped peaks take my breath away. Even though Mount Charleston, back home, is covered with a dusting of snow much of the year, I can tell (by the color of the sky, the frost on the ground, and the eerie silence) we're nowhere near home.

"This isn't Kansas, anymore," I say to Dayton; a reference to a line in a movie I like.

He gives me a sideways glance—no hint of Oz-recognition. "It's Colorado."

Important questions need answers (why does Dixie need my help is first on my mind), however, I can't help but ask, "Why Colorado?"

"That barn—your prison—is a facility built especially for you by the UN, the perfect spot, right out in the open. As they say, hidden in plain sight. Besides, who would think the United Nations has any holdings in Colorado? I didn't"

"You still work for the United Nations?"

The colonel grins. "I suppose I just tendered my resignation." We swerve down a steep grade, and he struggles to keep control of the wheel. Some might consider the road paved, not by my standards. "You want to know why I'm helping you."

I nod, then realize his eyes are fixed straight ahead and not on me. I shift my glance to him and grunt. "Uh-huh. The last time I saw you, we weren't exactly on friendly terms."

Dayton eases off the accelerator and straightens his back against the form-fitting bucket seat. "I'll be honest with you. I never put much belief in the paranormal, Daemons, werewolves, and the like. Then I met you. Your ability to shape-shift from human to canine opened my eyes—changed my view of the world. At first, I blamed you for everything: The Disaster in Las Vegas, the incredible loss of life, but most of all I blamed you for dragging me into your world."

"My world? What's that supposed to mean?"

"The existence of supernatural creatures, I suppose. Sure, I travelled the world in search of them—part of the job—but I'd never verified anything remotely close to being paranormal, not until I found you. And the very night that happened, I lost Jean."

"Major Ransom."

"And I blamed you." He gives me a quick glance. "A few months ago, I received a call from Dixie on my mobile. She asked me to return to Las Vegas—said she needed my help; that it had to do with The Las Vegas Disaster. I nearly hung up, but I was struck by an odd thought: how did she call me?"

"It's pretty clear why she called you. She knew you were some kind of paranormal hunter for the United Nations and—"

"No, not *why* she called me, but *how* she called me. How did she know my number? Only a handful of people in the world know what I do, let alone have access to my personal number. When I asked her about it, she told me the most incredible thing."

The road flattens out a bit, enough to let me concentrate on what he just said. *Is he waiting for me to ask him what the incredible thing was*? "What was it?"

"She said Major Ransom gave her my number."

"But, Major Ransom is—"

"Dead." He brakes hard, hits the gas again then turns onto a smooth highway. "Jean is a very gifted person." He chuckles. "She'd laugh when I called her abilities mind-reading. She insisted I use the term telepath. But she was more than that; she was an empath, one who can feel what others feel. I believe the major's paranormal gifts were much greater than even she understood. I'm convinced Dixie obtained my number from the major—how else could she have gotten it?"

"Major Ransom is alive?"

"You're not listening to me." He sucks in a large gulp of morning air. "Don't ask me how, but I'm convinced Jean spoke to Dixie from the other side."

"Are you even listening to yourself? What you're saying is—"

"I know very well what I'm saying. Major Ransom is using her abilities to communicate with Dixie Mulholland."

I'm quiet for a long time. None of what he said makes any sense. Communicating from the other side? What other side? The major is dead. At first, I didn't trust Colonel Dayton because he's my enemy; now, I'm convinced he's insane. I saw a movie once where the hero was cornered in a room with a crazy person. The hero played it cool and talked his way out. Since I'm basically trapped with a crazy person, I try the same trick. "What does Major Ransom want?"

"When Dixie first contacted me, she told me what she and her Aunt Rose were doing. She explained everything in detail, and I decided to have a look-see. At first, I was dead set against what they were doing, but the more I became involved, the more their plan made sense. In principal, I suppose, it's the most decent course of action. I decided to put my activities at the UN on hold and help them; now they need your help as well."

"I don't follow; you're not making any sense."

He smiles, the first sign of any honest human emotion. "I couldn't agree more."

Chapter Two

The colonel said Major Ransom insisted on my presence. I barely knew the woman and have no idea what "problem" they're working on in Las Vegas. I try to make some sort of sense out of what he said, but I can't. "I've been out of circulation for two years. What does Major Ransom think I can do to help?"

"According to Dixie, Major Ransom seems to think you're the only one who can."

All at once, his words usher in a ray of hope; even though he thinks the idea came from Major Ransom (which isn't possible), the words themselves are straight from Dixie. *She* wants me in Las Vegas, and that lifts my spirits. Still, it's strange Colonel Dayton offered his help. The last time I saw the man, he threatened to kill us both.

But he speaks with such conviction, I start to feel like I'm missing something; as if I've skipped a few episodes of my favorite TV show and have to catch up on what's happening. So, I decide to keep him talking—after all, I'm still cornered in a high-speed car with a crazy person at the wheel and talking seems like a logical plan. "The last I heard, Dixie worked for a network in New York; I can't remember which one, CBS, NBC—"

"How could you possibly know that? Any news about Dixie or The Las Vegas Disaster was censored."

"A few of the med techs talked about her when they thought I wasn't listening. They all spoke openly around me, as if I didn't even exist, like doctors do with their patients."

The colonel smirks while he shifts gears. "Shoddy security, if you ask me."

"There's something I need to ask you." The answer has always eluded me, and this seems like the perfect opportunity to ask. I wait for him to look my way, or grunt, or give me some kind of sign to continue. He doesn't, so I ask anyway. "The last time I saw Dixie, that night in the penthouse, there was a gun to her head. You told me if I came with you, you'd arrange a network anchor assignment for her—like she always wanted."

"Wrong. I said I would let her live. The rest was entirely up to her. Besides, that's not a question."

"Something's always bothered me about that night. You know I gave up my freedom on your promise."

He changes lanes and speeds up. "Still not a question."

"Why did you keep your word? I mean, while I was in prison, the only thing they wanted was to witness my transformation into a wolfhound. They tried everything, but I wouldn't give them the satisfaction. I would have cooperated in an instant if I thought Dixie was in danger. Why didn't you use her to force me to cooperate?"

The colonel smiles. "You don't know me very well."

I shake my head. "That's your answer? You're a man of honor?"

He shifts gears, and we race down the freeway in

silence. The sun pops up through gaps in the mountaintops as we wind our way down to the open flatland ahead. The highway widens and a few other cars appear. Dayton keeps a sharp eye on the rearview mirror. He's going just fast enough to head west at a good pace, but not so fast that we'll stand out to the local cops, or whoever else might be looking for us.

"So, Dixie called you and—"

"Listen, my main concern is to get you to Vegas. Dixie can answer all your questions."

He's pressing the accelerator hard—too hard. Blue lights flash behind us.

"Damn. Make sure you're buckled in."

"Oh, I did that as soon as we got into—" The words stick in my throat as he jams on the gas, and I'm sucked back into the seat. The blue lights fade into the distance. So does everything else. I'm afraid to look at the speedometer; I know I won't like what it says.

Even though my captors let me have a television, drawing supplies, and books to read (they laughed about it—called it "creature comforts"), they never let me have a video game. I've seen them in commercials, however, and can only assume zooming across the road this fast is what they must feel like. Everything flies past us as if we're standing still, or vice-versa. Unlike a video game, however, we have no do-overs.

Dayton's eyes dance back and forth between the road ahead and the rearview mirror. It only takes the slightest turn of the steering wheel to swerve past slower vehicles.

Two patrol cars speed across an overpass ahead of us. We zip under it and I turn around in my seat, watching them hug the entrance ramp and race onto the freeway behind us.

"We're not going to outrun their radios," Dayton says.

"So that's it? We give up?"

He sets his jaw. "As I said, you don't know me very well."

He hits the brakes, spins the steering wheel, and shifts gears. We wind up on the other side of the freeway as the patrol cars zoom past us. The officers strain their necks and stare at us as they rocket by in the opposite direction. Dayton exits the freeway, spins the wheel left and we dash across the same overpass the two patrol cars had occupied no more than a few seconds ago.

With his foot glued to the accelerator, the Camaro responds, speeding away from the freeway. We're on a two-lane road heading north.

"That'll slow 'em down a bit, wouldn't you say?"

"Do you know where we're going?"

"I haven't a clue, no." He makes a right onto a dirt road, a plume of dust filling the sky in our wake. "But it's better than where we were."

We're going about fifty miles an hour now, and my insides bounce around like I'm trapped in a speeding blender. An orange warning sign zips by, Road Closed Ahead.

As far as signs from the universe go, this is a bad one.

****

Colonel Dayton brakes hard and parks. He pulls a cell phone out of his shirt pocket.

"Who are you calling?" Even though I know the colonel, I still don't trust him; now he's calling someone I don't know, and that makes me even more nervous than before.

Instead of answering my question, he concentrates on the small screen of the smart phone; swiping his fingers across it, tapping on it, and turning the device sideways. After studying the information for a few seconds, he swipes it again and types out a message, his thumbs working furiously. He's focused on the screen as I peek over his shoulder at the screen.

In one sudden movement, he whips around and glares at me. "What the hell are you doing?"

"Just wondering what you're texting." I'm more interested in *who* he's texting.

He finishes typing and stares at me again. "It's plan B," he says as he tucks the phone back into his pocket, pulls out a handkerchief, and wipes down the steering wheel, shifter, and anything else he might have touched.

"You have a plan B?"

Without missing a beat, he says, "There's always a plan B."

As soon as he says this, I detect the sound of helicopter blades. Dayton scurries out of the vehicle and pops open the trunk. He grabs a large flashlight (more like a car headlight with handles) and sets it on the ground. He shines a brilliant white light into the air, turning it on and off, as the chopper closes in.

"Who's that?"

"You are a curious canine, aren't you?"

"Do you have a plan C if this doesn't work?"

Without hesitation, he says, "Absolutely." He has to shout the word as the helicopter touches down next to the Camaro. Grabbing my elbow and the flashlight, he guides me to the chopper. I can't hear anything but the whooshing of blades cutting the air. Dayton shouts something like, "Climb in," or, "Pile in," or, "Dive in." There's no time to interpret the phrase as he shoves me onto the chopper, then jumps in himself.

The pilot turns around and gives the colonel a thumbs-up signal. Locks of bright red hair show at the sides and back of the man's helmet. The mirrored face shield conceals his face.

My stomach stays on the ground when the machine rises at a crushing speed. In a few moments, we're miles away from the Camaro, zipping through the sky. Colonel Dayton doesn't seem a bit concerned that we're in a metal, dragonfly-like contraption hovering high above the ground. I wish confidence were contagious.

"You all right?" the pilot shouts to Dayton over his shoulder. "Everything go okay?"

Dayton pats the man on the top of the helmet. "Thanks for the lift."

"I wondered if you were gonna try and make it all the way to Vegas in the Camaro. Man, she's a sweet ride. Too bad you had to leave her behind. Sweet ride."

The pilot's red hair and tone of voice are familiar. I sniff the air to confirm the identification. He's the man who held a gun to Dixie's head as Colonel Dayton took me captive two years ago. Now there are two men I don't trust helping me escape.

The familiar cold ache gnaws at the back of my neck, and I have to do something—say anything—to keep it at bay. "Why use a car for the get-away if you had this helicopter?"

Dayton smirks at my question and shakes his head, as if I should know what he's thinking. "They would have heard it coming a mile away at the prison. Just lean back and enjoy the view. We'll be in Las Vegas in no time."

Even though Colonel Dayton broke me out of jail, I still feel like a prisoner. I glance at the colonel's watch. It's six a.m., the time I'm normally awakened by the guards on Saturday for my medical exams. I wonder if the technicians will miss me. Two years of rigid routine are hard to shake.

Dayton folds his arms, leans back in his seat, and closes his eyes.

"You're taking a nap?" I'm still in fight or flight mode (not to mention struggling with trust issues), but he's taking everything in stride, like it's just another day at the office.

"Relax," he says, popping one eye open, "I'm tired. I've been up all night planning your escape. I suggest you grab a few winks as well. I have no idea what may be waiting for us in Las Vegas. This is the perfect time to take a break—trust me."

Did he just say that?

Glancing out the window at the world sliding by, I see a thin black ribbon. It's a highway and tiny flashing blue lights race across it in both directions. They're still hunting for our get-away car. They'll probably find the abandoned vehicle soon, but have no idea where we've gone. I close my eyes and allow my mind to wander over the last two hours—that doesn't happen. As usual, my thoughts display blatant disobedience and carry me back two years.

Dixie Mulholland told her Aunt Rose she loved me. I overheard the conversation and confessed I felt the same. Dixie knew what I was then: a Giant Irish

Wolfhound with the ability to transform into a human. That same night, we both found out Dixie was a Daemon. But none of those little details seemed to matter at the time; we were in love, and love is what it is. Like a red rose, its red because it has no choice.

"Hey, wake up."

My eyes shoot open. The sound of the helicopter blades, their beating rhythm that lulled me to sleep, are silent. I look up and see Colonel Dayton staring down at me.

"Let's go, we're here."

"Las Vegas?"

Again, he shakes his head and smirks. Again, I'm supposed to know his thoughts. "C'mon, follow me."

I jump out of the helicopter and feel the instant crush of desert heat squeeze my body. Miles of white sand meet my eyes. A black sedan, its engine revving, is the only sign of life in this desolate landscape. Colonel Dayton grabs me by the elbow once again and rushes me toward the vehicle at a fast trot.

"Get in the back. Say hello to Paul Cuthbert, our helicopter pilot and driver. Settle back and relax, we're still a couple of hours away from Vegas."

"Hey man," the driver says, "glad to meet you. Call me Cutty." He tosses a duffle bag into the backseat next to me. "Here's some clothes—shoes, too. Picked 'em out myself. I hope everything fits."

Dayton jumps into the passenger seat. Cutty accelerates down a sandy road for about a mile. He guides the sedan onto blacktop then turns onto a highway, and we join a line of other vehicles. A sign rushes by—Las Vegas 185 mi.

"Then what?" I ask.

"Then what, what?" Dayton says.

"Where's Dixie?"

"Not so fast. There's something we have to do first."

"But—"

"Then we'll go see Dixie."

"But what if she—"

"Listen, Adam. There isn't a script for any of this, it's all improvised. Just settle back and relax."

I push against the seat. For the first time ever, Colonel Dayton called me "Adam." It's a minor victory, a small indication he acknowledges my humanity, and that carries a lot of weight with me. "Thank you."

Dayton wrinkles his brow. "For what?"

Silly question, this time he should know what I'm thinking. I change into my new set of clothes, making sure to hang onto my drawings of Dixie, and close my eyes, hoping for another dream of her.

Instead, I get a nightmare: hundreds of Giant Irish Wolfhounds running wild on the streets of Las Vegas, slaughtering humans. I feel claws dig into my back and teeth rip through my flesh. The smell of death, the screams, and the blood make me shake—like scenes from a horror film on television looping over and over. I can't turn it off.

Chapter Three

Dixie Mulholland parked her faded maroon Hyundai on Seventh Street; no more colorful, recognizable vehicles for her anymore—all low profile now. She walked a half block and turned right onto a small, tree-lined avenue. The long row of houses with neatly trimmed front yards and "water-smart" landscaping put a smile on her face. Thoughts of her old neighborhood always brought a rush of happy memories: childhood friends, freezing nights filled with Christmas lights, and the endless dog days of blistering summers.

A truck rushed by, pulling her back to the current realities of life: parking a few blocks away from home, keeping her eyes open for strangers, and trying to hold that ever present, anxious feeling under control.

Her world had changed, transformed radically, since meeting Adam Steel: the man with the ability to shift into a Giant Irish Wolfhound; the man she loved.

Only 9 a.m. and already ninety-five degrees. Another long, hot day lay in wait. Her steps were sure and steady as she glanced straight ahead, then across the street, then behind. This careful scrutiny of her surroundings was yet another reminder of who she'd become, but more importantly, who might be watching. Sweat coated her brow and her breathing labored under the early morning sun as she continued her trek through the old neighborhood.

A small garage sale attracted her attention a few houses ahead. She'd never seen anyone outside the red brick house before, so she decided to stop and linger over the offerings. A 4 x 8 sheet of particleboard propped up on two sawhorses held the bulk of the items: a varied mish-mosh of knick-knacks, paperbacks, and clothing probably one step away from the garbage.

"How much for this?" Dixie held up a faded Las Vegas 51's baseball cap.

The homeowner, a lady in her sixties wearing a colorful muumuu, smiled, revealing a row of missing front teeth. "Quarter."

"I'll take it." She fingered other items on the makeshift table and grinned at a few of the unclaimed treasures: a bag of runes, a deck of tarot cards, and a miniature crystal ball. Apparently, the homeowner had seen nothing in the crystal but the error of her ways at trying to look into the future. Dixie smiled. Humans placed so much weight in divinations.

"What do you want for this bag of runes?"

"Two dollars, only 'cause they're ivory. But if you take 'em off my hands, I'll throw in the cards and glass ball for nothing."

Dixie gave the woman two dollars and took the items.

"Hope they work for you," the woman said, "didn't do a damn thing for me. You want a bag for all that?" Not waiting for an answer, she produced a plastic bag and carefully placed the items inside. "Have a nice day."

Dixie thanked the woman and returned to the sidewalk. The bill of the 51's cap shaded her face from the sun, a few strands of blonde hair sneaking out from under the brim.

In a few minutes, she stood in front of Aunt Rose's 1950s green and tan bungalow. Memories of the night everybody now called The Las Vegas Disaster flooded her mind; the night she discovered she was a Daemon; the night she confessed her love for Adam Steel.

"C'mon, a little farther," a voice prodded. The words were so clear, so real, Dixie turned back to the red brick house, wondering if the homeowner, too, heard the voice. The old woman busily boxed up her items.

I know, Dixie thought, *don't you think I remember where I used to live? I just don't know who might be watching.* Furtive conversations with Major Jean Ransom were now in Dixie's nature, a part of her life. Those discussions with the other side, however, were not always congenial. *I'm just being cautious, that's all.*

"You're being slow is what you're being. Hurry along then."

"Dixie? What are you doing standing out there? Come inside." The screen door creaked open and an elderly woman—white hair, glasses, and a beaming smile—stepped out onto the porch. She wore a blue print dress and dark shoes.

Dixie marched up the walkway. "Hi, Aunt Rose. Sorry I'm so early. I'm just a little anxious."

"Don't be silly, today's the big day." They hugged on the porch. "Shopping so early in the morning? What have you got in the bag?"

"No, not shopping. There was a yard sale down the street, and I picked up a couple of silly things. Got this hat, too."

21

"Good for you. How environmentally enlightened of you, my dear. Well, come on in, I've got the air on."

What Aunt Rose called "the air" was nothing more than two portable circulating fans in the living room. The house had been built without central air conditioning, and even the noisy swamp cooler, attached to the kitchen window by rusty bolts, had long since given up the ghost.

Standing in the living room, intoxicated by the familiar aroma of baked goods wafting in from the kitchen, brought back so many mixed memories. She glanced at the fireplace and remembered Christmas stockings hung with care. At the same time, she recalled the green flame in the hearth the night of The Convergence—the night evil Daemons ravaged Las Vegas.

The lies the government spread about that night sickened Dixie. Over thirteen hundred people died in the attack. The official report cited solar flare-ups, underground earthquakes, and a dozen other natural phenomenon, including rumors of roaming packs of wild wolves. The public never learned the real truth about that awful night; the truth about Giant Irish Wolfhounds created and trained by evil Daemons to kill humans. Dixie tried to reveal the facts on national television and got fired for her efforts. Fired? Humiliated and blacklisted was more like it.

"Can I get you some tea, my dear?"

"Oh, no, don't go to any bother."

"No bother at all. Have a seat," Aunt Rose said, a twinkle glowing in her bright eyes. "I'll be right back."

Dixie lifted the crystal ball from the plastic bag and positioned it on the mantel. She stepped back and smiled. The item seemed to add a bit of magic to the room—quite appropriate. She set the bag on the floor and eased onto the comfortable old brown couch. Removing the baseball cap, she closed her eyes and let the warm breeze from the fans rush across her face.

"Here you go, sweetie. Just the way you like it." Aunt Rose returned to the living room carrying a pot of steaming tea and two cups on a silver tray.

"That was quick."

Aunt Rose bent over, hugged Dixie, and nodded. "I had a feeling you would be here early; call it a hunch, so I prepared tea and a bite for brunch."

Dixie stared at her aunt. "Something's going on— you're rhyming."

"Well, this *is* the big day, isn't it? The return of Adam Steel. If the colonel has done his part, and I know he has with all my heart, then everything will soon be well. I'm a bit excited, can't you tell?"

"Yes, I can," Dixie said with a grin. "It's been a strange few months, hasn't it? Like the participants say on all those reality TV shows: an amazing journey. And now Adam's coming home. I hope he's okay."

"Of course he is. He's strong and fit—"

"I don't mean physically. I mean, I hope he doesn't think I've forgotten about him, or worse, he's forgotten about me." She held out her hand and drew Aunt Rose down onto the couch next to her. "We've all been working so hard, and it wasn't until Major Ransom insisted on his presence—"

"She also insisted on Charlie Nguyen. Don't forget about that."

"You're really worried about Nguyen, aren't you?"

"With good reason—and so should you.

Remember, Nguyen was on the side of the evil Daemons during The Disaster."

"Why do you say Disaster? Why don't you call it what it was: The Convergence?"

Aunt Rose frowned. "We needn't give that word any more power than it already has. If The Las Vegas Disaster is good enough for the humans, then it's good enough for us."

"Major Ransom doesn't seem concerned about Nguyen."

"Ha. Once a viper, always a viper, and Nguyen was quite the snake. You can't change your stripes just like that."

Dixie grinned and snorted. "Adam and I once discussed changing stripes. I'm so worried about him, Rose; about what he'll think of our plans—about what he'll think of me."

"Nonsense, my dear. You have nothing to fear. He gave up everything for you. Besides, we didn't even know where he was until Major Ransom told us. Without her, we still wouldn't know if Adam was alive or—" Aunt Rose shifted her gaze to the fireplace. "I'm sorry, sweetie." She touched Dixie's cheek and stared into her eyes. "Stop all the negative thinking. We have more pressing problems."

"For instance?"

"I believe Gorgeous and her ilk may very well be at the root of our problem."

"Gorgeous?" Dixie felt the air in her lungs escape in one big whoosh as she said the name. "But Gorgeous is dead."

Once again, Aunt Rose avoided Dixie's inquisitive eyes.

"You killed her, didn't you? Tell me she's dead."

"We stopped The Disaster. We succeeded in driving the evils from Las Vegas, but," Aunt Rose looked down and whispered, "I could not kill her.

"Couldn't, or wouldn't?"

With a sigh, she said, "It's complicated."

Dixie bolted up and marched to the fireplace, staring at the framed photo of her parents. Without turning around, she said, "Tell me what's so complicated about killing that witch."

"Daemon, my dear, she's a Daemon."

"What does it matter?"

"Oh, it matters a great deal. You see, there are very strict rules in our world—the world you are now a part of; rules I should have told you about long ago." Aunt Rose smiled. "Why, if Gorgeous were a mere Witch, I could have killed her with ease; or a Muse, a Succubus, an Imp—"

"What are you talking about?"

"Oh, I'm just getting started, my dear. None of us can directly destroy each other: a Daemon may not kill another Daemon, a Muse may not kill another Muse...you get the idea. Now, most of us cannot directly harm humans, but a Devil may kill a Daemon and a human, although a Witch cannot touch an Imp, but a Devil—"

"Stop." Dixie rolled her eyes. "How do you keep track of all that?"

"Yes, it is a bit complicated, but you'll learn."

"How? How am I ever going to learn who can do what? You just said a Daemon can't kill another Daemon, right?" Dixie twirled away from the fireplace and stared at Aunt Rose. "Gorgeous had no trouble with that. She killed my parents."

"She lit a match. The fire killed your parents."

Dixie shouted, "What's the difference?"

"We may not kill directly; end of argument. The evil Daemons have learned to use intermediaries to do their bidding: Humans, Devils—"

"Giant Irish Wolfhounds."

Aunt Rose nodded.

Dixie moved away from the fireplace and stood across the room from her aunt. "So you're saying we have no power at all."

"Nonsense. Together we are strong, a force to reckon with." She chortled, "I'd like to see a Devil try to tele transport. But the others, the evil Daemons, they are cunning, and quite determined to rid the world of humans. They found methods—call them tricks of the trade—to achieve their goal without directly breaking the rules. Believe me, my sweet, if I was able to end Gorgeous, it would be a treat."

Dixie came back to the couch and plopped down, her head resting on Aunt Rose's shoulder. "There are so many rules. How am I ever going to learn them all?"

Aunt Rose kissed the top of Dixie's head. "I've neglected your education far too long, that much is obvious, and I was wrong. I shall arrange your Suffering at once."

"My suffering?"

"A formal education, that's all—nothing to worry about."

"Suffering?"

"It sounds worse than it is, believe me. A rite of passage, nothing more."

"Aunt Rose, I don't think I'm ready for—"

"You'll be fine. All of your questions will be answered." Aunt Rose stroked Dixie's hair and hugged her. "Perhaps then you'll understand why Gorgeous lives, something I really should have told you long ago. Am I forgiven?"

Dixie nodded.

"Now then, tell me again why Major Ransom insisted on the help of that beast, Charlie Nguyen?"

"I don't know. She said Nguyen's involvement was vital. Besides, I'm not too worried about Nguyen. It's Adam I'm concerned with right now."

"Sweetie, you have nothing to fear: his love is unconditional, he told you as much two years ago."

"That was two years ago."

****

My eyelids slide open just a bit as my hands and feet twitch. I'm still trapped in the nightmare; blurred visions of what they call The Las Vegas Disaster. I've had this dream so many times in the past two years, I know it by heart—racing through the backstreets of the city in the form of a Giant Irish Wolfhound; ripping through canine fur, and human flesh; being bitten and pawed; blood and screams. Mikael, my brother, chases after me, grabbing my hind legs with his claws. I paw at the ground, but can't escape his hold. His mouth springs open, fangs gleaming in the moonlight as he drags me back for the kill.

Reality pours in as the sound of tires racing across the road and cold air blasting through A/C vents, jerk me out the nightmare that will always be part of my life.

Just as my heart rate evens into a steady rhythm, I glance through the window at the scene ahead. Once again, my pulse kicks up a notch and sweat coats my brow.

"Oh my God." I can't believe what I see; the reality of The Las Vegas Disaster hits me. The Daemons reduced the city to just a few hotels and some outlying structures surrounded by miles of desolate sand dunes.

Colonel Dayton turns around in the front seat. "What's the matter?"

"Are you joking? Look around. Is this all that's left of Las Vegas?"

Both the colonel and Cutty snicker.

My hands ball into fists. "How can you laugh at this?"

"Relax," Colonel Dayton says, "this isn't Las Vegas. It's Prim. We've still got about an hour to go before we reach Vegas, depending on traffic."

Prim: a familiar name.

"I'm kinda munchy," Cutty says, "mind if we pull over?"

"Good idea. How about you, Adam?" Colonel Dayton grins. "Are you *munchy*?"

"I don't know what that means."

"Are you hungry?" Cutty says as he flips on the turn signal and steers us off the freeway. "I'm starving, you?"

"I could eat."

Cutty parks the sedan on a gravel lot in the shade of a scraggily pine tree. To the left, paved parking lots lead to a large casino. On the right, a small pet area and a lot reserved for campers. Just behind us is a combination convenience store, fast food restaurant, gas station.

"C'mon." Cutty is out of the vehicle, looking back

at us from the front door of the restaurant. "You guys coming, or what?"

Colonel Dayton chuckles. "That boy can eat almost as fast as he can talk." He opens his door and glances back. "At least get out and stretch your legs if you're not hungry."

I do as he suggests, but can't seem to shake a strange sensation. Humans call it déjà vu; the feeling you've been somewhere before, but can't remember when. On the heels of my nightmare, this feeling is just plain eerie.

I hurry and catch up to Colonel Dayton at the front door of the restaurant. He holds it open for me, and I step inside. My nose works double time, taking in the aromas of meat and cheese and bread and lettuce, even the condiments make my mouth water.

We join Cutty at the counter.

"Let me have two double cheeseburgers, two regular hamburgers, large fries, a cookie, and a vanilla shake." Cutty turns to us. "What about you guys?"

Colonel Dayton grins. "Chicken sandwich and a small coffee. How about you, Adam?"

I study the menu, but don't know where to begin. I want to try everything. "I definitely want a hamburger, that's for sure." The girl behind the counter rolls her eyes and huffs. A line grows behind us.

"He'll have the same as me," Cutty says.

"C'mon, Adam." The colonel puts his hand on my shoulder. "Let's find a place to sit down. Cutty can bring us our order."

I follow the colonel to a booth, and we sit. The establishment is noisy, but I like it. I've almost forgotten what a crowd sounds like. Not counting

29

doctors and guards, I've lived alone for two years. My spirits are lifted even higher when Cutty arrives holding a tray crowded with food. He places it in the middle of the small table and we all dig in.

The first bite of hamburger stirs up more strange feelings—more déjà vu. The tastes, smells, and sounds hit me hard, but that doesn't deter my appetite. I'm onto the second hamburger before Colonel Dayton has eaten half his sandwich.

"This isn't a race," the colonel says.

Cutty laughs between bites. "If it was, you'd lose."

"Sorry," I say, "I guess I was more munchy than I thought."

After a few minutes, I decide if this *is* a race, Cutty is the winner. He finishes his meal long before I do, slurping down the last of his milkshake.

"Man that was good," he says with a grin, wiping his mouth. "Didn't know if you liked milkshakes so I got you a soda instead. You haven't even touched it."

"He'll get to it." The colonel wags a finger at Cutty. "If you want another drink, order one. Let Adam eat in peace."

"I never had a soda," I mumble through a mouth full of fries, "but I always like to try new things."

"Groovy." Cutty stands up. "I'm gonna get one for the road. Anything for you, Colonel?"

Colonel Dayton dismisses Cutty with a wave of his hand. "The lad sure can eat. I don't know where he puts it. Must be his wooden leg."

I watch Cutty, but can't detect a limp; he hides his loss well. I grab my soda and follow the colonel outside. Cutty catches up to us, and we pile back into the scorching sedan.

Cutty starts the engine and turns the air conditioning up all the way. "That's what I'm talking about. It'll cool down in a little bit. Man, I hate this heat."

"You drive pretty good for a man with one leg." Colonel Dayton greets my compliment to Cutty with an unexplained laugh.

Chapter Four

"So, what's our next move?" I say from the backseat. I gulp down some soda through a straw and burp, the first time that's ever happened. I like it.

"Our next move?" Colonel Dayton repeats.

"Sure, I mean, you must have a plan. You told me you always have a plan, right?"

Cutty clears his throat and speaks quietly. "Are we ready to show him?"

My ears perk up. "Show me what?"

Dayton gives Cutty an odd look, then turns around to stare at me. "Yeah, there's a plan, not a very solid one, but a plan. When we get to Las Vegas, we have to pick someone up at The Tropicana. Dixie said Major Ransom insisted on it. I've never met the gentleman, so…" He let the words, and his apprehension hang in the air. "Before that, however, there's something you need to see."

My heart catches in my throat. He's so serious and I imagine the worst: did something happen to Dixie?

We jump on the freeway and head north. The highway cuts a path through endless miles of white sand and dry, open flatland. Las Vegas, the world's playground, is straight ahead, hidden in the misty haze of the desert heat. A never-ending line of vehicles crams the road ahead of us, all melting together in a shimmering mirage.

Before long, a familiar sight looms in the distance. A small peak juts up out of the valley floor about ten miles south of Vegas: Claremont Estates—the place where everything began, where I was born. I close my eyes, hoping Cutty drives past it as fast as he can. Instead, the car slows down and the turn signal blinks.

Cutty takes the Claremont exit and drives to the base of the small hill. The road changes from blacktop to gravel and rises steadily upward, winding its way through tall pines, slender palms, and short Joshua trees. Memories skitter through my mind. I think of my family—my pack. I recall when Dixie drove me here and later saved my life. I remember The Las Vegas Disaster.

"What are we doing here?"

"You'll find out," Dayton says.

"No. Tell me now."

Dayton puts a hand on Cutty's shoulder, and the sedan's tires crunch to a stop. The engine keeps running and Dayton swivels around to face me. "Hundreds of Giant Wolfhounds were brought to Las Vegas the night of The Disaster. Most of the wolfhounds were killed by the military. Some survived."

A form scampers across the road in front of us. It moves so fast I can't tell what it is.

Dayton continues, "Aunt Rose, Dixie, myself, and Cutty have tracked down most of the survivors and settled them here. They're off the radar, so to speak. Without the Daemons or Alphas guiding them, they live quietly in the surrounding houses.

"Dixie said Major Ransom insisted I help with their relocation. I agreed, reluctantly at first, but soon saw the merit in what they were doing. These

33

wolfhounds were unwilling pawns in The Disaster. Once their bond to the Alphas ended, they were lost; homeless and hungry."

My hands start to sweat.

We continue climbing the hill and park in the cul-de-sac outside my old house. This is the last thing I want to do; the last place I want to be.

Cutty rolls down his window and honks the horn twice. The door to my old house creaks open, and a girl steps out. She wears a white sleeveless blouse and blue jeans. A big dimpled smile accompanies a friendly wave. Her gait is quick and light down the driveway to our sedan. She leans into the open window, her arms folded across the door.

"Hi, Cutty. Hi, Colonel. Who's that in the backseat?" Her dishwater blonde hair hangs in curls around her freckled face. Her manner is open and trusting. I don't trust her.

"Tina, meet Adam Steel. Adam, this is Tina."

"He's cute." She sniffs the air. "He's one of us. Are you dropping him off?"

"No." I can't get the word out fast enough. "They're not dropping me off, and I'm not one of you. I'm human."

"Okay, okay." Tina frowns. "In denial."

"Colonel." I lean forward and place my hands on the front seat. "We need to leave. I don't know why you brought me here."

"Sure."

Cutty turns off the engine.

My heart races. "What are you doing?"

"Need to unload the stuff we brought." Cutty steps out and grins at Tina. He calls out, "Hey, Adam, want to give us a hand?"

"No."

Tina giggles. "Suit yourself."

Cutty makes two trips to the house and back. Tina helps him carry in cases of bottled water and bags of ice. Another person scampers out of my old house to help with the supplies.

"Hey, Jake," Cutty says, "thanks for the hand."

"Oh boy," I hear Jake say, "Pop Tarts. Ciminum, my favorite. Yuminum."

The joy in his voice makes me smile.

Dayton clears his throat. "I thought you'd want to know, you're not the only one of them left alive."

I don't know what he means. I'm no longer one of *them*.

"At one time, I wanted them all put down," he says, "including you. I've done a complete one-eighty. Obviously."

I don't say anything back right away. The trunk slams shut and Cutty and Tina make small talk and laugh.

I lean forward and put my arms on the front seat again. "How many of them are here?"

"About seventy."

Cutty slips back in behind the wheel. Tina leans through the window. "Come back when you're ready, Adam."

Glancing over her shoulder, I see faces staring through the windows of my old house. We drive down the hill and hop back on the freeway heading north. I guess I'd always thought about survivors, but never dwelled on it. The night of The Convergence, I witnessed hundreds of them slipping into the shadows and running off to the desert. "You say there's only about seventy of them?"

The colonel nods. "I imagine the rest died in the desert. Some tried to assimilate in the city as humans, but they weren't very good at it, not like you. That's where we found most of the ones we relocated."

It's hard to get my mind off the wolfhounds. They were brought here to kill humans. Why should the colonel care about what happens to them? Why should I? I have to change the subject. "Who is this guy we're picking up?"

Colonel Dayton swivels around. "His name is Charlie Nguyen. Dixie said Major Ransom insisted on his presence."

My mind races. Who is this Charlie Nguyen guy? How long has he known Dixie, and how well do they know each other? I wrestle with an emotion humans call jealousy, but I don't know why. Of course, I have feelings for Dixie, but it's been two years. She's been out in the world able to mix and mingle with all sorts of people. It's unreasonable to assume she still has feelings for me.

Sure, one time we kissed, we hugged, and she confessed her love for me, but that was a long time ago and circumstances were much different. Times change—people change.

Colonel Dayton turns around again. "You're pretty quiet back there, are you okay?"

"Yeah, fine." A white lie, acceptable in the human world.

The enormous structures of the Las Vegas casinos loom ahead like giant castles rising from the desert. Cutty takes the Tropicana exit and crosses Las Vegas

Boulevard. The Tropicana Hotel and Casino towers over us on the right. Cutty parks the car near the main entrance.

"I won't be long, Cutty. Keep the engine running and wait here."

"Will do, Colonel."

Dayton gets out and enters the casino leaving me alone with Cutty.

"So," Cutty turns in his seat, running a hand through his wild red hair, and stares at me, "what'd ya think about seeing Claremont?"

I don't want to answer.

"That's okay, you can tell me. We're on the same side now. You know, I jumped ship with the colonel. He's a helluva guy. Oh, sure, the UN was a pretty good gig and all, but I think what we're doing now is more important, you know, good against evil and all that. Plus, Aunt Rose sets a mean table; I mean she can cook anything you want. What more does anyone need? Great food and a good cause. I mean, it doesn't take a genius to figure out that those dogs—"

"Canines," I blurt out in an effort to stop him from saying another word. "They're not dogs, they're canines: Giant Irish Wolfhounds."

"Sure, sure, I'm sorry. You know I've never talked to a dog, er, I mean, a canine before we started bringing supplies up to Claremont. They seem like a nice bunch, really friendly, you know? At least Tina is. It must be fun, barking and running and stuff."

His constant prattle annoys me at first, but it doesn't take long before I realize he's genuinely interested. Cutty has an open, honest face, even though his eyes tend to narrow a bit when he's on a roll, like now.

"I mean, from what Tina says, life is so much less complicated in her world. You know where you stand with the pack. And man can they run! I've seen Tina tear down that hill and race back up in no time. Man, what I wouldn't give to be able to do that."

"It has its moments." He stares at me and I need to ask him something, now, while I have his attention, and while we're alone. I've wondered about it for two years. "Tell me something, Cutty, when Colonel Dayton ordered you to hold Dixie at gunpoint, did you ever question his motive? I mean, after all, she was trying to stop The Disaster."

"No way. I just did what he told me to do. He gave me a gun on the way up to the penthouse in the elevator and told me what to do. That night was so crazy, I didn't even know who the hell she was then."

"And you did it, just like that?"

"Sure." He has a funny laugh: Yuk-yuk-yuk. "But it didn't matter. I mean, the gun wasn't even loaded."

My eyes bulge. "What?"

"That was okay with me, man. I mean, I'm not a killer. I've never shot anyone in my life, hope I never have to. I'm a great driver, a decent pilot, and I can get you almost anything you need—but a killer? No way, man." He laughs again. "Besides, I talked to Dixie about it, and she doesn't hold a grudge. She's cool about it." The car shudders, and Cutty is instantly distracted. "Damn, I hope the A/C doesn't quit. I hate this heat, don't you?"

Before I can agree with him, the door opens and Colonel Dayton gets in. The door across from me opens and a woman wearing red shorts and a black tube top sidles in next to me on the bench seat. Her gold platform shoes are outrageous: at least ten inches tall, sprinkled with glitter—the most impractical footwear I've ever seen anyone wear (outside a cartoon character, of course).

"Gentlemen," Dayton says, "meet Charlie Nguyen."

I smile at her. Charlie Nguyen is a girl. My smile widens. "Nice to meet you."

She ignores my hand. "So, you're the dog."

"Canine," Cutty says. "He prefers canine."

"Whatever," Charlie Nguyen says. "Let's get going."

I notice Colonel Dayton and Cutty exchange a quiet glance, and realize it's not just me who feels uneasy with our new passenger.

"C'mon," Charlie Nguyen barks, "are you deaf? Let's go."

****

Maxwell Sullivan tipped the valet in exchange for his keys. The twin turbo-charged V-8 engine purred under the parking canopy. Max knew the jet-black luxury car was a bit over-the-top, but what the hell, he could afford it. Besides, why not greet the end of the world in style? It wasn't his world.

"Thank you, sir," the valet said as he pocketed the c-note tip and held the door open. "Be safe out there, sir."

Max pushed his shades down over the bridge of his nose and studied the young man through sparkling green eyes. "Why?" With that, he slammed the door, shifted the Mercedes S-Class into first, and painted black tire tracks on the gray pavers of the Palazzo Hotel and Casino porte cochère. He caught oncoming traffic at just the right moment and powered onto The Strip.

Things couldn't have been going better. The past two days, he spent acclimating to the Vegas lifestyle: gambling and hookers. As far as gambling was concerned, he'd just about broken even; the hookers were a different story. They hadn't performed to his liking so he'd given them permanent reminders the customer was always right. When their pimps knocked on his door, he knocked harder on them.

The nights, however, belonged to Gorgeous.

He blew through the red light at Sahara Avenue and glared back at the blue lights in his mirror. "Shit." He eased the Mercedes to the curb and stopped.

"Do you know why I stopped you?"

"No, I haven't a clue, officer. Why don't you enlighten me?" Max squinted up at the blond-haired kid behind the badge. This prick was gonna make him late.

"You failed to stop at a red light."

"Fail to stop, my ass. I pushed on the gas—big deal." He held two hundred-dollar bills out of the window toward the officer, as if he were at a drive-through.

"Sir, step out of the car."

"No."

The officer un-snapped the holster strap securing his pistol.

Max laughed. "Are you going to shoot me?"

The officer drew his pistol. Max raised a hand, twirled his fingers, and a dark blue Mustang veered toward the patrolman and clipped him, sending him to the pavement in a heap. Max reached out and dropped the bills onto the injured officer.

"I'm letting you off with a warning this time."

Max raced up The Strip and jumped on the 95. At almost twice the posted speed limit, it took only fifteen minutes to reach the Sky Pointe Drive exit. He turned left on Moccasin Road and pulled off onto the Paiute Indian Colony land.

He turned off the car and sat with the windows rolled up, in the middle of a burning desert under the late afternoon sun. After lighting a fat cigar, he puffed smoke rings at the windshield.

In his side view mirror, he caught billows of sand rising in a straight line a mile or so down the road. An approaching vehicle. Glancing at his Rolex, he smiled. She was right on time.

She parked the white Lexus next to his car and got out. Her ivory-colored, full-length, dress danced in the wind.

Max exited the Mercedes and strode forward to greet her, his white hair tousled by the breeze. "Gorgeous, how you doing? What gives with a daytime meeting?"

"Maxwell Sullivan. What part of low-profile do you not understand?" Gorgeous spit the words out in sharp contrast to her unwavering smile; the mask he knew so well. "You know, I had my doubts about involving you. However, you gave me your word you'd behave, and I trusted you."

"Behave?" He grinned. "I don't think I'm familiar with that particular *human* word." He pinched the lit end of the cigar with his fingers until the fire went out. "Besides, since when can a Devil's word be trusted?" He snickered. "Oh, come on, Gorgeous, I'm just having a little fun. After all, this is what the humans call Sin

41

City. A little tame for my tastes, but still—"

"Two prostitutes in the hospital, their procurers in comas, and a Las Vegas Metro officer hit by a car in full view of the public, on Las Vegas Boulevard for Hell's sake. And all this in just three days." Gorgeous glared at him.

Max thrust out his chest, smiled, and nodded.

"You do realize I'm not praising you. I need you to keep doing your job, which has been excellent, thus far. Beyond that, I want you invisible. Do you understand?"

"Oh, but listen honey, that policeman deserved—" His throat constricted. He dropped the cigar and stared at Gorgeous through blurry eyes.

Gorgeous's smile grew just a bit as her brows came together. "Do you think I enjoy driving like a human, through miles of desert just to see you?"

Maxwell shook his head, his hands pawing at his throat.

"That's right, I don't. But, unfortunately, I am not able to tele transport onto sacred ground. The good news is meeting here, your father cannot listen to our conversation; a fact you should appreciate given your brazen disregard of my commands. Listen well my young Devil, I may not be able to kill you, but endless torture is well within the scope of my terms for your use."

Sullivan nodded and allowed a breath. He raised his hands to his throat. The word shot out like a cough, "Sure."

"Sure, what?"

"Sure, I understand. Do my job, but keep a low profile. Invisible."

Another plume of dust rose from the dirt road

behind them. Gorgeous and Sullivan watched the vehicle approach. A brown Toyota Corolla shuddered to a stop, and a woman stepped out. She handed the keys to Gorgeous, bowed, and backed away.

"Your new ride is here," Gorgeous said, offering the keys to Sullivan.

"What? That piece of crap? Oh, please honey—" His throat closed again.

"The vehicle is nondescript," Gorgeous said, "practically invisible, but most reliable."

Max nodded and took the keys. He sucked in a large breath. "Okay, okay. I'm sorry. No more luxury sedans."

"And I've gotten you a very nice room at the Wild Joker Motel on Fremont Street."

"The wild what?"

"And no more gambling, and especially no more prostitutes. Is that understood?"

Max scanned the surrounding desert. He may have gotten a bit out of line and Gorgeous simply reeled him back in, that's all. He might have done the same if he were her, maybe worse. But no more hookers? That was just mean. He swallowed and nodded.

"Good." Gorgeous lifted her head and gazed toward the sun, as if her next words required solar assistance. "I like you, Maxwell, I really do. In fact, normally, I find it quite amusing when you misbehave. You've got a real style about you; a genuine penchant for perverseness." She lowered her head as well as her voice. "A quality that reminds me of your father."

"My father is old. He's lost his edge."

Gorgeous stared at him, her eyes burning like miniature suns. "I couldn't agree more. This is your chance to effect real change…perhaps a regime change. If you perform well, your stock will rise in his eyes. He might be more willing to rely on your council, perhaps take you back into the fold, as it were."

"I like where this is going."

"Max, my darling, all I'm saying is I have a lot on my hands, and I'm counting on you to do your part. Crawl into the woodwork and become invisible when you're not working. If all goes as planned, it will soon be over."

"And after that?"

"Why, after that you can do whatever the hell you want."

Max glowed. Gorgeous was a woman of her word. Whatever the hell he wanted sounded like heaven. He marched to the Toyota and hopped in. "Your wish, my command—all of that. I guess you know where to reach me then, my sweet. I'll be poolside at the Wild Joker."

"Oh, sorry Max, there's no swimming pool. But they do have free HBO."

Chapter Five

I can't believe my eyes. I knew we were going to Aunt Rose's house; still the sight of Dixie standing on the front porch takes my breath away. I make a mental note of this moment; I always want to remember it. Two long years melt away, replaced by an excitement I've never experienced before: desire.

I dash out of the car and race up the walkway to the porch, my arms folding around her in an instant. Her body feels warm and welcome. Her arms wrap around me as well, and we stand motionless in an embrace that blocks out everything else. The scent of her fills my lungs and I ease back, just a bit, so I can look into her eyes. Cupping her face in my hands, I cover her mouth with mine. She kisses me back with animal hunger. For two years, I've dreamt of this moment; dreams are over-rated.

"Okay you two," Colonel Dayton says, slapping my back, "let's get inside. You don't need to give the neighborhood a free show."

Even though I'm still kissing Dixie (or she's kissing me, who can tell anymore), I open my eyes and see Cutty amble up the steps behind Colonel Dayton. He laughs, yuk-yuk-yuk, "Right on, dude."

"This is just not right," Charlie Nguyen says, following Cutty into the house, "Daemons and dogs. Not right at all."

Now, I'm certain I don't like Charlie Nguyen.

"Adam," Dixie says when our lips part, "I've missed you so much." She takes me by the hand. "Come inside so we can all talk. There'll be time for us later."

I shake my head. "No. Are you sure?"

"Oh, I'm sure." The smile she gives me is more than just words: it's a promise.

After a deep breath, I follow her inside, wanting to hold her in my arms again, but I have to behave. It wouldn't be fair to the others.

"Are you two quite done? I was about to fetch a bucket of water."

"You must be the Daemon Charlie Nguyen," Dixie says. Her face is still a little flushed, but her voice is smooth and even; she's in total control of the situation. "Have a seat."

"Where's Rosalyn?"

"Out," Dixie says in a flat tone.

Charlie Nguyen glances around the living room, finally narrowing her gaze on Dixie. "When you see her, tell her I hope nothing bad happened to keep her away."

"Okay," Colonel Dayton says, "enough of that. We're all here, now would somebody please tell me why the bloody hell we need this Daemon—"

"Language, Colonel." Dixie waves to the couch, and Dayton sits down. "You know how Aunt Rose feels about that kind of talk."

"You said she's not here."

"It's still her house. Everybody, please sit down. I'll get some tea. Aunt Rose has it in the kitchen. Colonel, would you help me please?"

Cutty and I sit on the couch. Charlie Nguyen strolls around the living room like a cat examining unfamiliar territory, as if taking note of quick escape routes. Finally, she decides on the rocking chair near the entrance hall.

The grandfather clock bongs twelve times. I lean toward the kitchen, trying to hear what Dixie and the colonel are talking about. I only catch a few words of their whispers: Dixie asking, "How did he take it?" and Colonel Dayton answering, "Not well."

"Now then," Dixie says as she and the colonel return from the kitchen. He carries a silver tray with an enormous teapot, milk, and sugar. Dixie places some cups down on the coffee table. "Major Ransom brought us here. She arranged for you to be here Miss Nguyen."

"Charlie Nguyen, if you don't mind."

"But she didn't tell me the reason for your presence."

"Isn't it apparent, even to a good little Daemon like yourself? You need my help. Duh. What I want to know is why she chose this particular dog." She turns to me. "We could have used any of the dogs on Claremont— why you?"

I glare at her. "Stop calling me the dog."

"Ha!" Charlie Nguyen giggles. It's a nasty, high-pitched snicker. "You may have the others fooled, even Major Ransom, but not me."

"Wait a minute," Dixie says, "how do you know Major Ransom?"

Charlie Nguyen smirks at the question and takes her time to answer. "Major Ransom speaks to me."

Dixie reddens and takes a deep breath. "I thought—"

"You thought you were the only one she communicated with? You thought you were special? Ha! I am key to this plan. Why else do you think I'm here?"

"What's that supposed to mean?" Colonel Dayton says. "How is Jean Ransom even remotely acquainted with someone like you?"

Through a sly smile, she says, "Who has not heard of Charlie Nguyen?"

"Major Ransom told me you were an evil Daemon," Dixie says. "She said you were a major player in The Las Vegas Disaster."

"The Las Vegas Disaster? That was no Disaster— that was a joke; one of the reasons I'm done with the evils. I remember what it was like in The Pit, and why I climbed out with The Legion, my dignity intact. We were going to clean up the mess the humans made of this world, and the only way to do that was to clean up the humans. But the plans and plots to eliminate them became so ludicrous, I felt ashamed to be a part of it. Ha! Gorgeous and her ridiculous schemes. How comical. So, I quit The Legion; jumped ship, as it were. I'd rather be known as one of the good little Daemons rather than embrace a plan to take over the world using talking dogs."

I stand up ready to tell her off.

"Down, Fido." Charlie Nguyen furrows her brow at me. "I'm on your side now, remember? The humans are truly ruining this world, but maybe, just maybe, there's a better way to stop the disease than killing the patient."

Dixie sends me back to the couch with a nod of her head. I don't want to sit down, but I can't help it, it's as if I were nudged by an invisible hand. Apparently,

Dixie has been practicing her powers over the past two years. She scowls at the Daemon. "Listen Nguyen, just because Major Ransom wants you here, doesn't mean I do or Aunt Rose for that matter."

"Ha. Why don't you ask your aunt Rose about The Pit? I doubt if she's ever told you bedtime stories of that little amusement park."

"Enough," Colonel Dayton says. "This bickering has got to stop. We were all brought together in this house for a reason." His gaze turns to Dixie. "Is there any way you can simply ask Jean what her plan is? What she wants of us—especially her?"

"I can try, but it usually works the other way round. I generally have to wait for Major Ransom to contact me."

"Well, I don't."

All eyes turn to Charlie Nguyen. Dixie plops down in a leather armchair as if punched in the stomach.

"Major Ransom is a strong one," Charlie Nguyen says with a smirk, "for a human that is. She's a determined soul. Her voice is clear and on point. I can talk to her whenever I want."

I swallow hard. Suddenly, it hits me: if Charlie Nguyen has been in contact with Major Ransom, then my presence here did not come from Dixie; that also means I have to re-evaluate my opinions of what the humans call *the other side*.

Dixie shakes her head. "Major Ransom instructed me to have Colonel Dayton pick you up. I don't understand the roundabout way of getting us all together."

"No?" Charlie Nguyen says with a sneer. "Isn't it obvious? Are you not cautious in your movements? I know I am. The evil Daemons are always watching. Your major Ransom is a smart one. She told you to come here, asked me to wait at the Trop, made arrangements for the colonel to pick me up and, voila, we all meet here. Don't you see? She did her best to mask our travels from them."

Dixie nods.

"There's just one thing she did not confide in me," Charlie Nguyen says.

"Oh?" Dixie asks, "And what's that?"

Charlie Nguyen stares at me and lowers her head. "Why the dog?"

****

I can't stand the constant squabbling and raised voices, and so I get up. If Dixie's going to nudge me back in my seat again, she better use a damn strong push. "I agree with Charlie Nguyen." That shuts everybody up. "Would somebody please tell me what I'm doing here—what we're all doing here?"

"They didn't even explain to you what's going on? How rude." Charlie Nguyen sneers. "Your doggie pals are being put down…one by one, and your human pals didn't even tell you about it? Quite rude, indeed."

Her words take a few seconds to sink in. What does she mean by my doggie pals? "You mean the survivors at Claremont?" The silence in the room is my answer. "Somebody's killing them? Who?"

Charlie Nguyen huffs. "They probably wouldn't tell you even if they—"

"We don't know," Colonel Dayton says, stepping over Charlie Nguyen's words. "At first, we thought it random. You know, hunters out and about looking for coyotes, or kids shooting target practice; something of that sort."

"They're being shot? Deliberately?"

Charlie Nguyen smiles. "One by one."

"Shut up," Cutty chimes in. He turns to Dixie. "Look, I thought Major Ransom was trying to help us. Why'd she want Miss Freak-show here involved? I'm pretty good at reading people, and I don't like her, not one bit."

"Listen to me, ginger-boy." Charlie Nguyen points a finger at Cutty. "If I wanted to, I could—"

"You could what?" Dixie says.

Charlie Nguyen scowls, lowers her finger, and says nothing.

"That's what I thought." Dixie turns to me. "I was going to tell you, Adam. It's so awful." She shuffles to the center of the room. Even though she speaks loud enough for everyone to hear, her words are directed at me. "Aunt Rose and I started locating survivors a few months ago. They seemed so lost, their spirits crushed; no direction, no hope. They didn't know how to live in the human world, and they would have perished in the desert—many of them did. So we began finding them and re-locating them to Claremont Estates where we thought they'd be safe. The first murder took place three nights ago."

The colonel stood up and continued the story. "The next night, another murder. The next night, another. That's when Major Ransom suggested we bring you in. We need to do something to stop the killings."

"How touching," Charlie Nguyen said, "your pity for that pack of hounds brings a tear to my eye. It really does."

Colonel Dayton points a finger at Nguyen. "Your

people made them what they are. In any case, they're no longer controlled by evil Daemons. They're lost and afraid. They need help. I wouldn't even treat—"

"A dog that way?" Charlie Nguyen spits out.

Colonel Dayton aims a cold stare at Charlie Nguyen. "I was going to say: I wouldn't even treat *you* that way."

"You can't treat anybody that way, man." Cutty raised his voice. "I mean, it's not their fault they got caught up in this. They're like refugees, and that's who the UN is supposed to help in times like these, right? But they won't. Look at what they did to you, Adam. The police ain't gonna help either, and forget the military. I figure it's up to us to take care of them, teach 'em how to get along in the human world, then let them make their own choice: self-determination, right? I always been a self-determining kind of guy myself."

"Good for you, Cutty," Dixie says.

"But the murders have thrown everything out of whack." Colonel Dayton shakes his head. "We've got to find out who's at the bottom of it, and put an end to it."

"Yeah, okay, we get it." Charlie Nguyen says. "Somebody's got it out for these wolfhounds, and Major Ransom thinks you can find out who."

I stare at her, realizing the *you* she means is *me*. There are secret thoughts in this room, words unspoken. Everyone stares at me now. I don't like the feeling that everybody knows something I don't. "How am I supposed to do that? What can I do to stop the killings?"

A voice drifts in from the kitchen. "Hello, everybody." Aunt Rose appears and smiles. Her smile fades. "Nguyen."

"Rosalyn," Charlie Nguyen says. "I thought something terrible happened. I'm so glad to see you're okay."

"I'm quite well, thank you. Your concern is touching. How is everyone else? Do we need refreshments?"

"Aunt Rose." Dixie crosses the room and hugs her aunt.

Aunt Rose beams at me. "Adam Steel, as I live and breathe. How are you, my boy? Did you have any trouble in your escape? No, of course you wouldn't, Colonel Dayton is a very capable man."

The colonel winks at Aunt Rose. "Thank you, mum."

"Well then." Aunt Rose takes Dixie's hand in hers and clears her throat, "what has Adam been told about his part in the plan?"

The silence in the room crawls across my skin. Why don't they just tell me?

"Nothing yet," Dixie says.

"You guys are starting to worry me," I say. "There's something going on here that—"

Aunt Rose holds up her hand for quiet. She turns to the rocking chair. "And you, Nguyen? Are you prepared?"

Charlie Nguyen nods. "Of course. Charlie Nguyen is always prepared."

"In that case, I have a suggestion." Aunt Rose steps to the front door. "Colonel, and Mr. Cutty, would you please escort this back to wherever it is she came from."

Charlie Nguyen jumps out of the rocking chair.

"How dare you—"

"Be still. I merely think Adam should hear about his part from someone he feels comfortable with." She turns to me and smiles. "Therefore, he and Dixie will remain here, I'm sure they have much to discuss."

"Oh my," Charlie Nguyen says with a grin, "so that's what they're calling it now."

Dixie sidles next to me and places a hand on the small of my back. Her touch is comforting, but does little to ease my apprehension about the plan.

Aunt Rose opens the door. "And I will return to Claremont, where I've been keeping an eye on things. We'll all meet back here tomorrow—say noonish?"

"Cutty and I will drop by to give you a hand at Claremont," Colonel Dayton says. "After, we drop *this* off."

"I've never been so insulted in all my life." Charlie Nguyen marches out of the house and down the walkway to the street.

Aunt Rose winks at me. "Yes, she has. She just doesn't know it."

"I heard that, Rosalyn," Charlie Nguyen's voice sails back from the sidewalk, "don't think I didn't. Charlie Nguyen hears everything."

Chapter Six

Five o'clock in the afternoon and the sun starts sliding behind the Spring Mountains, the hottest part of the day. After re-confirming our rendezvous tomorrow, the others leave the house, and Dixie and I finally find ourselves alone. The only sound is the grandfather clock tick-tocking in the entry hall, and the whoosh of air from the circulating fans. I hardly notice any of it; my full focus rests on Dixie.

"Will you tell me what's going on?"

She kisses me. "I promised you there'd be time for us."

Her arms around me feel comfortable and warm. She presses her body into mine, her head resting on my chest. "There's something I need to ask you."

I put my arms around her and kiss her. If she wants to make sure how I feel about her, this is the best way I know to answer.

She pulls away a few inches. "It's about Marco Ramirez."

Now it's my turn to back up a little. "What do you mean? I don't follow."

"Something Cutty said earlier." She turns around and steps toward the fireplace. "He said we can't rely on the military or the police to help us. I agree, both bound by protocols and procedure. The last thing we need is their involvement, but Marco's different. He knows the truth about The Disaster, about the wolfhounds and Daemons. I didn't want to get him involved, but we sure could use his help."

"Why are you telling me this? Why don't you just call him?"

"I want to know if it's all right with you."

"I don't understand. Of course, it's okay with me. I can't wait to see him."

She frowns. "Are you sure?"

I cozy up next to her and slide my arms around her waist. "As long as that call can wait until tomorrow morning." I lean in and press my lips against hers, covering her mouth in a deep, penetrating kiss. I explore her velvety tongue and breathe in her perfume, sweat, and skin. My cheek nuzzles her brow, feeling her perspiration wet on my face.

Her breathing is heavy, like quiet panting. "The call can wait."

I'm still confused about the plan, the murders at Claremont, and their reluctance to tell me what my role might be. One thing, however, isn't confusing: my feelings for Dixie.

Primal thoughts enter my mind, calling me, pushing me closer. I kiss her cheek and move my hands across her body. She sighs, running her tongue over my ear. The sweet scent of her sex is more than I can stand.

I search for the zipper tab of her jeans, but her hand covers mine, stopping me in mid-zip.

"What's the matter?"

The gleam in her eye tells me it's a foolish question. "Is it okay if we continue this in my old bedroom?

"Of course."

She holds out her hand. "This way, Mr. Steel, and don't you dare forget where you left off. Promise?" All at once, she furrows her brow. "You have done this before, haven't you?"

The question takes me off guard. "No. Why, am I doing something wrong?"

She answers me with a kiss. "Follow me," she says, leading me down the hallway.

Mating in the canine world is nothing more than a physical act, pure and simple. There's no emotion involved, and even less thought. Pheromones are a powerful force, attracting a mate and ensuring the survival of the species. The act itself takes no more than a minute or so, if that, and when it's over, it's over. No "call you later," no breakfast in bed, and definitely no commitment.

Humans, however, put a little more stock in it than that. First of all, they call it *making love*. The term alone carries a certain aura about it. It's usually planned, seldom with a random partner, and more than likely ensures some type of bond. To a certain extent, I'm familiar with the various rituals surrounding the act itself. I've seen enough movies to know when two people are in love.

Here's what I've learned so far: two people meet and, by their expressions, mannerisms, and speech, it's understood they are, or will soon be, in love. Moviemakers call this moment the meet-cute. After that, there's a period of absence or anger, whichever best moves the plot along. This period of loss has a way of making the heart grow fonder; eventually, the two people get back together and kiss (usually at the end of the film) and we fade to black.

The movies I like the most are old black and white classics, filmed in the forties and fifties. Censorship was more than just customary then; it was the law. I have never seen what happens after the film fades to black, although I have a pretty good idea, but can only use my imagination (as the censors preferred).

We get to the end of the hall and turn into her bedroom; the room she grew up in. All at once, I know why she wanted to make love here. This isn't just a room. This room *is* Dixie: the dark shades on the window for privacy, soft linens on the bed for comfort, and the pictures on the wall for memories. The shaded lamp on the nightstand emits a soft, warm glow. This room is special to her. Now, it's special to me.

I ease her onto the bed and lie on my side next to her. My breathing is slow and heavy as my hands continue their exploration. I lightly kiss her cheek, her neck, and her shoulders, my lips leading me on to new, unexplored territory. Her hands run through my hair and over my back.

Under my breath I mutter, "I've always loved you, Dixie Mulholland."

"I know." She hugs me tight, her legs crossing over mine.

More than animal desire surges through my body. I find, in her, what's always been missing: I'm no longer acting on natural instinct, this is pure human nature.

"Would you mind turning off the light?" she says with a smile. "Believe it or not, I'm a little bit shy."

I reach across to the nightstand, fumbling with the lamp. The room fades to black.

****

"I'm here tonight with the Chief Executive Officer

of The Sterling Gaming Group, Mr. Thomas Coleman." Carol Melody smiled into the KLVA camera lens, a dazzling mix of excitement and wonder playing in her voice. The cameraman gave her a thumbs up. She faced Coleman, holding the microphone equal distance between them. "Mr. Coleman, we're standing here tonight just below the enormous new marquee erected outside The Sterling International Resort. I must admit, I've attended many casino openings in the past two years, each one more spectacular than the last— fireworks, music, celebrities—but this is a first for me: the grand opening of a marquee. Can you tell us why this is so significant?"

Hundreds of people circled Melody and Coleman, the color of their faces washed away to stone white in the harsh glare of camera lights. Thousands more onlookers stood on The Strip, held back by police lines.

Thomas Coleman, gray hair, goatee, immaculate suit, shouted above the din of well-wishers. "Well, Carol, this is more than just a marquee. This is a tribute. I'm sure, by now, everyone's heard of The Mystic. He's performed at The Sterling International Resort for almost two years, selling out every performance. He's a legend, and tonight we pay tribute to that legend."

The camera panned up and pulled back to wide angle, taking in the full scope of the marquee: a crystal obelisk standing six-hundred feet tall. A shimmering glow visible inside the structure lit up the form in a pallet of ever-changing colors. Huge letters etched into the precious stone spelled out The Mystic in a bold gothic font.

"They tell me this is now the tallest obelisk in the world," Carol Melody shouted over the noise of the gathering, "surpassing the Washington Monument. The cost of this structure has been a closely guarded secret. Mr. Coleman, would you be willing to hint at what it cost to—"

"Worth every penny," Coleman said with a wink at the camera. "But I've got even bigger news than our marquee."

"Bigger than this?" Melody nodded at the obelisk.

"I am thrilled to announce tonight The Mystic has been offered a long-term, exclusive contract to perform at The Sterling for the next ten years. And believe me when I tell you, Carol, the cost of this marquee is nothing compared to the cost of that contract."

"Wow, you heard it here first," Carol Melody said, turning to the camera and beaming, "a ten-year contract for The Mystic; virtually unheard of in Las Vegas."

"Unheard of anywhere in the world," Coleman shouted. "And, of course, The Mystic, in keeping with his principals, has announced he will donate a large portion of his salary to local charities."

Carol Melody flashed her trademark smile. "Wow. Unbelievable. The Mystic truly does practice what he preaches." She turned away from Coleman and faced the camera. "Pete, I don't know if you've had a chance to catch The Mystic's performance yet, but let me tell you—"

"I've seen several of his performances," the voice of Peter Hudson, live from the KLVA news studio, boomed over hers, "and I can tell you the man is amazing."

"Yes, well, I just wanted to point out—"

"We've got several cameras located at strategic positions around the ceremony tonight, Carol," Hudson said, "and we'll let the pictures speak for themselves. What a spectacular night for Las Vegas."

Views from across the street, adjacent rooftops, and helicopter cams projected on a portable Jumbotron screen set up specifically for this celebration. Peter Hudson's voice described the scene for viewers at home, "Thousands are on hand for this remarkable event. Nearly every celebrity appearing on The Strip is here tonight for the festivities. Of course, as you may have heard by now, President Walker, who was scheduled to arrive for the ceremony earlier this evening, has been forced to land in Dallas due to mechanical problems with Air Force One; problems which had earlier been foreseen by The Mystic. Quite an incredible story. I'm sure once the repairs are made, the president will want to shake The Mystic's hand in thanks for the heads up."

"Pete," Carol Melody roared into the mic, "as you know The Mystic does not allow anyone to touch—"

Her cameraman slipped a finger across his throat and turned off the flood light.

"The fireworks are now being launched from the rooftop of The Sterling," Hudson went on, his voice booming from speakers lining the resort's façade, "an incredible show of light and color in the night sky. As I said, President Walker will probably have a few kind words for The Mystic as a possible tragedy was averted today with quick action by Las Vegas's very own super-psychic. Let's watch and enjoy this marvelous spectacle for as long as we can."

Thomas Coleman's bodyguards formed a human wedge and pushed through the spectators, escorting him back to the casino entrance as fireworks exploded overhead. The crowd roared its approval with every burst in the sky. Huge blossoms of color filled the night sky as music blared from outdoor speakers. The downtown congregation erupted into chants of "Mystic...Mystic."

Chapter Seven

Deputy Chief Marco Ramirez examined his notes for tomorrow's meeting. He wanted to arrive well prepared for the budget talks, and if a few hours in the office on Sunday morning helped so be it. Last year took him by surprise. He wasn't ready for the onslaught of department in-fighting and petty squabbling, all too new to him then. But he'd been Deputy Chief for two solid years now, and by God he'd be ready for anything this time.

He concentrated on the monitor in front of him, ignoring the cell phone chirping on his desk. He didn't have time for anyone right now; he had to focus on the spreadsheet. The chirping stopped then started again a few seconds later. Ramirez winced and scooped up the cell, his eyes still focused on the computer screen. "This isn't a good time. Give me a call back on Monday and—"

"Marco?"

His gaze darted away from the monitor; budget talks, spreadsheets, and numbers all fading into a distant memory. Nothing but the familiar voice on the line mattered. "Dixie? Dixie is it really you?"

"Marco, I need to see you."

He held his breath, clutching the phone in a death grip. He hadn't spoken to Dixie in almost two years. She'd gone to New York after The Disaster while he stayed behind, going through the motions of trying to fix a broken city. He'd attended so many funerals—too many: Sheriff Gale Hendrickson, FBI Agent Ed Miller, Major Jean Ransom, and all the others taken by a war they knew nothing about.

To try and move on, he applied for the Deputy Chief position, and buried himself in work. His refusal for an interview with Dixie was the final wedge that drove them apart; at least that's what helped him accept her silence.

He kept an even tone. "How are you? How long have you been back in Vegas?"

"A few months."

The words cut at him. *A few months?*

"I need your help."

He didn't say anything.

"Can you meet us, at Aunt Rose's house?"

"Us?"

"Yes. Aunt Rose, Colonel Dayton, Cutty, myself and...and Adam."

Ramirez' pulse missed a beat. His thoughts flashed back to the night of The Disaster: Daemons and wolfhounds, death and destruction. It was all covered up by the government, but he knew what really happened. "Adam's here?"

"He asked about you."

"What did you say?"

"He wants to see you, Marco. He misses you."

Ramirez cleared his throat, his mind racing. After two years, there was only one reason for this call. "Dixie, things are different now. I'm Deputy Chief. If something's going to happen in this city—something like last time—I have a duty, a responsibility, to bring it to the sheriff so we can stop it before it begins. No more wars in this city. Too many lives are at risk. I can't let anything like that happen again, no matter who's involved."

"That's why I'm calling you. I want you involved."

He eased back in his chair and gazed through the window, south across The Strip, toward the Stratosphere with its amusement park rides in full motion eight hundred feet above the ground. The tourists were finally coming back to Vegas.

Physical reminders of The Disaster had been removed. Fresh new casinos rose from the rubble of The Las Vegas Disaster; taller hotels with larger neon signs. Amazing adult playgrounds erected: The Phoenix, featuring the world's only underground water park—*come for the sun, stay for the fun;* The Lone Mountain Hotel and Casino proclaiming Lucas Knight the greatest magician of our time—*performing twice nightly at seven and ten;* The Sterling International Resort with its six-hundred-foot obelisk—*home of The Mystic.* But the emotional scars, enemies made and bonds formed would never be forgotten, no matter what changes a new city skyline promised.

Ramirez swiveled around, turning his back to the window. "Tell me what's going on."

"I'd rather not explain over the phone."

"Why?" He waited, listening to her breathe.

Her voice broke as she said, "I've been in contact with Major Ransom—"

"What the hell are you talking about? Is this some kind of a joke? You know as well as I do Major Ransom is dead."

"Listen to me, please, Marco. I know Major

Ransom is dead. I can't explain how she communicates with me; she just does. There's a situation and—"

"A situation?" He felt his face flush. "So help me, Dixie—"

"Marco, please listen. We need your help. More to the point, Adam needs your help."

"Is he okay?"

"Yes. It's hard to explain over the phone. We need to see you."

What could he say to that? He understood now why she called: he was one of Clark County's top cops, and the only one at Metro who would understand what she was talking about. She needed his assistance, his support—the kind of support human codes, regulations, and laws didn't cover.

"What do you want me to do?"

"Meet me at Aunt Rose's house. We need to discuss our options. I've always trusted you, Marco, and I still do. Nobody knows strategy better than you."

"If I recall correctly, Colonel Dayton seemed to understand strategy pretty well. I'm surprised he associates himself with Adam or with you, for that matter."

"Colonel Dayton has changed. He loved Major Ransom, and he's willing to do whatever she says. Besides, Colonel Dayton doesn't have Metro at his command."

At last, she decided to be direct with him. Sure, she wanted his help, but she also wanted the army that came along with that help. His mind raced. He didn't want anything to do with the supernatural, the paranormal, or whatever else anyone called it—that wouldn't make it go away.

Another part of him desperately wanted to see Adam. The union formed between them two years ago was more than just a magical spell—it was a true connection. "When and where."

"Tomorrow, about noon at Aunt Rose's?"

He hung up, swiveled around, and continued his slow inspection of The Strip. He could see the tops of six or seven hotels from his vantage point. He also saw the face of his old friend Sheriff Gale Hendrickson whenever he closed his eyes, an innocent victim of an unearthly war.

Ramirez would not allow another supernatural battle in Las Vegas—not on his watch.

****

The room at the Wild Joker sucked. Not only was it the smallest motel room Maxwell Sullivan had ever occupied, it smelled old, the sheets were spotted, and the free HBO came in all squiggly. Not to mention an A/C system in name only. "This is bullshit."

Max grabbed the room key and flung open the door, throwing his hand over his eyes against the sun's ungodly glare. "Total bullshit."

He decided it wouldn't be the worst idea to leave the Toyota at the motel and walk the six blocks west to downtown Las Vegas. It wasn't as if the car held any creature comforts—its air conditioning was as effective as his room's. "Bullshit."

He trudged along, each step taking him closer to the action downtown; action he sorely missed. Empty lots, vacant shops, and an endless parade of street people gave way to the welcome sight of tourists smelling of sunscreen, searching for the same thing he was: stimulation, excitement, and something different.

He ached for a cocktail, and hungered for a hooker.

His mood improved as he stood under the canopy of the Fremont Street Experience. He strolled inside a chilly casino and grinned at the empty bar.

One bourbon, straight up. After four more tall glasses of the golden liquid, he felt almost normal. What nerve Gorgeous had to put him up at the damned Wild Joker? Sure, she had the right to dictate his moves; after all, she *had* negotiated for his services, so she essentially owned him. But that didn't mean he had to suffer at a fleabag motel, did it?

Now, this place—downtown Vegas—he liked; money changing hands, cigar smoke, and good-looking women. He threw back his head, tossing down another soothing bourbon. The liquor burned his throat, bringing a smile to his face.

He ordered one more and sauntered through the casino, keeping his eyes open for a nice pair of legs. Even though his vision was blurry, no doubt due to the clouds of cigarette smoke, or maybe the six bourbons, he knew what he craved and she'd be easy to spot. She was here in the crowd somewhere; a blonde, maybe a redhead, willing to sell her soul for a few pieces of gold.

He trundled to the pool area and leaned against a post, watching the girls in their cheap sunglasses, shimmering lotion, and string bikinis.

The last swallow of bourbon went down hard; burning his throat and making him cough. He placed the empty glass on an unoccupied blackjack table before easing outside to Fremont Street.

Fate. A tall blonde in a short blue dress caught his eye at once. The white belt wrapped around her waist accentuated her hips. Her tanned legs glistened in the sun as if freshly waxed. Perfect.

He picked up his pace and followed her at a close distance. The black pumps on her tiny feet accentuated the muscle tone of her calves. He grinned, remembering the name of those particular shoes back in the day: come-fuck-me-pumps.

His words came out a bit garbled, "Excuse me, miss."

She turned, offering him a gleaming smile.

"I'm kind of lost. I'm staying somewhere on The Strip, but I don't remember how to get back there. I'm from out of town. Can you help me?"

"My pleasure. What hotel is it?"

Reaching a hand into his pocket, he mumbled, "I've got the room card here somewhere." He brought out a fistful of hundred dollar bills. "Whoops, my mistake. Got lucky at the tables last night."

Her smile grew. "Wow, you sure did."

Her skin flawless, smooth, and inviting. He put a hand on her soft shoulder. "I'm kind of looking to get lucky again, if you know what I mean."

"Really?"

"Sure thing." He swayed a little as he counted out five hundred-dollar bills and placed them in her hand. "How about you come with me to my room? In fact, we could both come in my room."

"Are you paying to have sex with me?"

"You catch on real quick. Where you from, darling?"

The woman slipped her hand into her purse and pulled out a shiny metal object, her smile vanishing. "You're under arrest for soliciting."

"What the fuck? You bitch." He reached out to her. She stepped aside and he fell forward, face first. Things got real fuzzy after that.

Vague images crowded his alcohol soaked brain: lifted off the sidewalk by two Metro officers; his hands cuffed; a breathalyzer test in the back of a patrol car; a stinky holding cell; piss dribbling down his legs.

"Get up, sunshine." Someone led him out of the cell, escorted him down a gray hallway, and placed him in a small room. His hands cuffed to a metal ring on the table in front of him. Voices shouting from the hallway caught his attention.

"I want him released at once."

"Sorry, sir, but he's been booked for—"

"I don't give a rat's ass what he's in here for, I want him released now. You know who I am, right?"

"Yes, sir, but—"

"But nothing, patrolman. I'm Deputy Chief Marco Ramirez and that man's a CI in an ongoing investigation. We need him on the job now. Do you understand? No time to waste."

The door to the small room opened, and Max put faces to the voices. A uniformed officer, face white as an egg, held the door open for a brown-skinned man in a suit.

The brown-skinned man rushed in. "Take those handcuffs off him. That's an order, son."

"Sir, I don't know if—"

"Let me ask you something, you like working here?"

"At the jail?"

"On the force."

The patrolman took a key from his belt and

unlocked the cuffs.

"I'll be back later and tell your supervisor you did the right thing. Don't worry, son, you might even get a bump for this. Now let's go, Sullivan. Move it."

Max stood up and scrunched his eyebrows together. He shook his head, trying to clear his vision, and stared at the man in the suit.

"I said let's go—now."

He lumbered into the hallway and turned right. Ramirez grabbed his elbow, turning him to the left. "Other way."

Max whispered, "Who are you again?"

"Deputy Chief Marco Ramirez."

"I don't recall—"

"Shut up and move." Ramirez put his hand on Max's back, forcing him to pick up the pace. They strode to the elevator foyer and waited.

"Do I know you?" Max glared into the man's eyes.

The elevator arrived and both men stepped into the car. The doors slid shut. He kept his gaze on Ramirez. "What's going on?"

Ramirez turned to him. A bright flash illuminated the elevator. Gorgeous stared back at him, her stone-faced grin firmly in place. Max trembled. Another bright flash and the form of Deputy Chief Ramirez reappeared.

"What's the matter with you?" Gorgeous said. "I'm risking everything to get you out of this mess, and right after our little talk yesterday. When your father finds out—"

"I'm so sorry. I just thought—"

"That's the trouble, you didn't think. Listen to me, it's almost twilight and I have a car waiting for you

71

outside, a vehicle more to your liking—a black Continental. Go back to the motel and do whatever you have to do to sober up, but be quick about it."

He felt shivers run down his back. He thought about the pain she could inflict for disobeying her orders to keep a low profile.

"Not just pain," Gorgeous said as the elevator bottomed out, "endless pain. I'll check in with you tomorrow. Now get a move on, you must get to Claremont by sundown."

Chapter Eight

The cool, dark, quiet space cut a sharp contrast to the constant bright lights, endless chatter, and pervasive heat of The Strip outside. Soothing sounds of water trickling down a massive glass wall echoed like soft whispers in the shadows.

The Mystic sat motionless, his head erect, eyes closed, and hands clasped in his lap. His breathing came in an unhurried, measured rhythm; he could have been asleep.

Two United States Secret Service agents hovered over him, their movements anything but calm; their voices far from whispers.

"How did you know about Air Force One?" an agent asked. "Tell us who you work with."

The Mystic remained silent. If anything, his breathing became slower, even more serene.

"Look, pal," the other agent said, "this is your last chance to level with us before you find yourself in federal prison. How'd you know about the president's plane?"

The Mystic's eyebrows rose and he smiled at the sound of the door opening. His eyes remained closed as he spoke. "President Walker. Welcome to my home." A lyrical voice, quiet and childlike.

"Sir," an agent said, turning to face the president, "we're not finished with him."

"Relax, boys. I wanna speak to him alone." President Walker's voice exuded Southern drawl, minus the charm. "Go on, now, leave us be."

The Secret Service agents eyed the president, then each other before being shoed away with a final wave of the president's hand. "Go on now. I'll be fine."

Walker approached The Mystic and held out his hand. No hand offered in return. "I wanna thank you for the heads up. They tell me a slow leak in the hydraulic system almost did me in."

The Mystic cocked his head. "Oh. The warning about your plane. You're quite welcome." The Mystic motioned to the chair next to his.

President Walker undid the button of his tailored coat and sat down in the armchair facing The Mystic. He grimaced. "My men want to know how you knew about a problem with the jet. To be honest, so do I."

The Mystic's lips widened, his eyes glowing. "And I, as well."

"What'cha mean?"

"Visions come to me. I have little control over what I see, its importance, or its overall role in the grand scheme of things."

"Come again?"

The Mystic crossed his legs in his chair, lotus position, and continued, "At the very moment I received the image of your plane crashing, I also received a very striking and clear image of a little girl— six-year-old Wendi Culver of San Jose, California. She dropped her chocolate ice cream cone."

President Walker leaned forward. "I don't have a friggin' clue what you're talking about."

The Mystic smiled again. "I had a choice to make,

you see: warn Wendi about her ice cream, or warn you about your plane."

Walker chortled. "Well, I hope to shout you made the right choice."

Looking at the waterfall, The Mystic sighed. "I wonder."

"What the hell does that mean?" President Walker stood and glared down at The Mystic.

"Please, no offense. Your life is as important as little Wendi's, I'm sure, but in the grand scheme of things—"

"Listen here, Mystic. I may not know much about the grand scheme of things, but there are a few people who happen to think I'm pretty goddamned important compared to a chocolate ice cream cone."

"Yes, I agree. You may have more worth than a scoop of ice cream."

The president chortled. "Damn straight."

"Wendi Culver, however, reached down for the ice cream and lost her balance. She stood on a second floor balcony. The railing collapsed. She fell to her death in the street below." The Mystic closed his eyes.

President Walker said nothing. He dropped back into the armchair and lowered his head as well. In a quiet voice, he said, "You still made the right choice."

"Life," The Mystic said as he stood up and walked toward the waterfall, "is about choices. I chose to warn you about the plane. You chose to heed my warning. Your pilot chose to land immediately. A tragedy averted. As a result of those choices, Wendi Culver is dead."

The president straightened up in his chair. "You could have warned us both."

"I had no time to warn you both. Let me ask you," The Mystic smiled. "Do you think I made the right choice?"

President Walker stood. "Hell yes, I do. If I had died today, our enemies, all around the world, would have cheered—grown stronger, maybe tried an attack. The economy would have faltered, the nation thrust into mourning right now. If I had—"

"You're saying you are more important than a six-year-old child?"

Without hesitation, he said, "Damn straight."

"The child had potential. The two most wretched words in the world are: what if."

"But...but you chose to warn *me*. You know you made the right decision. Admit it."

The Mystic said nothing. He shut his eyes and sighed, deep in meditation. For the next few moments, only the sound of water trickling down the glass wall filled the room.

Three sharp raps on the door shattered the silence. A man in a dark suit entered. "Sir, you're wanted on the phone."

The Mystic opened his eyes, stood, and smiled at the president. "Thank you so much for your visit. I'm sorry we had to meet under these circumstances. I trust your stay in Las Vegas will be productive. I'm sure it will be."

President Walker leaned forward and whispered, "The press would have a field day if they knew about my belief in the paranormal. Ha, and the damned Republicans would probably talk impeachment. In any case, I want you to know I'll never forget what you did for me today. Thank you."

A gentle nod.

"Come and see us at The White House, anytime. Trudy would love to see you again."

"That will never happen."

President Walker's upper lip quivered "What do you mean by that? Is something going to happen to her? To you? To me?"

The Mystic sat down, crossed his legs, and closed his eyes. "I'm sorry, Mr. President, but I must prepare for a television interview. I despise the press, don't you?"

"Son of a bitch, tell me what you see."

The president's aid approached. "Sir, the Secretary of State is on the phone."

The Secret Service agents rushed inside, put their hands on the president's shoulders and led him from the room as he continued to yell over his shoulder, "What's gonna happen?"

****

The Mystic waited patiently, eyes closed, breathing calm and measured. He sat in a cross-legged position on a white couch in the green room, waiting for the summons to the studio. Two bodyguards (one with a blond mustache, the other with no neck) dressed in black business suits stood on either side of him. A knock on the closed door brought them to attention, while The Mystic remained unflustered.

The door opened, and a young man popped his head in. "They're ready for you, sir."

"Ah, splendid," The Mystic stood. "And what is your name?"

"Who, me? Oh, I'm no one, sir. Just a gopher."

"You are a gopher? Surely, even gophers have

names. What is yours?"

The young man hesitated, then grinned. "Simon Quail, like the bird."

"Tell me, Simon Quail, like the bird, do you enjoy your work here?"

Simon produced a raw laugh and shrugged his shoulders. "I'm just an intern, but yeah, I like most the stuff I do around here. Meeting good people like yourself is always fun. There's something new happening every day. I mean, Vegas is just that kind of crazy city—always hopping."

"Well said, Simon. Tell me, what are your goals?"

"I don't follow, sir."

"Your dreams, ambitions. What do you enjoy?"

Simon paused for a moment, then beamed. "Singing. I love to sing."

"You hesitated before you answered."

"Sorry, it's just that no one ever really talks to me around here."

The Mystic grinned. "Not yet, but they will."

"Uh, anyway, sir, they're ready for you—right this way." Simon turned and marched down a narrow hallway, stopping at a door marked "Studio C." "Right in here, sir."

The bodyguards entered the room first, scrutinizing the layout, then nodded to The Mystic. He sauntered into the brightly lit room. The three-point lighting system and two television studio cameras whirred in the background giving the room a futuristic atmosphere.

"Well, there you are—ugh..." Peter Hudson became the meat of a bodyguard sandwich the moment he rushed into the studio.

"Walter, Fabian...relax. This is our host, Peter

Hudson. We are guests in his domain."

Walter, the one with no neck, stepped back, pulled an index card from his pocket, and placed it in Hudson's hand. With a slight European accent, he said, "These are questions you will ask. Any deviation from card and interview will terminate. This is not conversation; it is question and answer. If Mystic gives answer, you listen. If Mystic does not, you ask next question. Understood?"

Hudson nodded and glanced at the index card. He furrowed his brow and shook his head. "What kind of questions are these? *What performers do you most enjoy on The Strip? What is your favorite city? What do you think of the weather in Las Vegas? Do you have any hobbies*? These questions are lame. This isn't what my viewers want to know. They don't—"

"Right, mate," the bodyguard with the blond mustache stepped into the conversation, his nasal voice echoing through the room. "These terms were agreed upon. A lot of money has changed hands and you're bound by the provisions in the contract. Now, if you'd like to renege on the—"

"Fabian, Walter, please." The Mystic put his hands on the bodyguards' shoulders. "Relax. Everything will be fine." He turned to Hudson with a sheepish grin. "They protect me a little too much." He held out his hand.

"I was told you didn't like to be touched," Hudson said.

"Ha, I will never know how that rumor started. Who doesn't enjoy the human touch? So soft, so supple." He grasped Hudson's hand and held it. "Ah, you must relax, Mr. Hudson. Calm yourself and think happy thoughts."

Hudson wrestled his hand free. "We'd better sit down and get ready. This is a live feed, after all, carried to almost all of our network affiliates. A lot riding on the next twenty minutes."

The Mystic sat down and got comfortable in the soft leather chair. He noticed Hudson pulling an index card from his pocket, not the card Walter had given him. "I have enjoyed meeting some of the staff here at KLVA."

"We're live in thirty," the director yelled.

"Thirty," Hudson echoed. A bell rang in the background.

"Especially Simon," The Mystic said, "he is such a fine young man. So open and honest. A true pleasure to talk to."

"Ten," the director said.

"Ten," Hudson repeated. "Simon?"

"Yes, so much potential."

"Live in five, four, three..." The director counted down in silence then pointed at Hudson. Camera one's red light came to life.

"Good evening." Hudson's voice lowered an octave as he faced the camera and beamed. "My guest tonight..." He drew out the introduction, waiting a beat, then said in an even deeper voice, "The Mystic." Hudson swiveled in his chair and leaned forward. "Welcome. I'm honored you chose KLVA for this very rare glimpse into your private life."

"Not my decision, to be honest." The Mystic chortled. "I'm sure your network gave The Sterling Group an exorbitant amount of money for this brief interview. Ah well, no matter. What is important is I am here and here we both are."

Hudson furrowed his brow and clamped his lips shut like a vise.

"There it is, Mr. Hudson," The Mystic said with a grin. "I love that look when you're reading the news. It makes you seem so important; so in control, you know?"

A brief smile flashed across Hudson's face as he turned to The Mystic. "I'd like to start by asking you a direct question: what is your real name?"

"Excellent question. You know, there are so many. I can't really decide which one I like best: Clint, Bobby, or Don. But I'd better not say because I might forget the one I truly like."

Hudson glanced at the index card. "Well, I'll keep it Mr. Mystic then. I'm sure our viewers would like to know where you were born."

"Ah, another superb question. Let me see, I suppose I'd better say Las Vegas." The Mystic smiled. "If I don't say Las Vegas, I would never hear the end of it, don't you think?"

"So, you're a local? Born in Las Vegas?"

"Of course I could do without the heat, Pete. Ha, ha. Heat, Pete. But there are times when I enjoy the sun and, of course, the winter does bring rain, and sometimes even snow."

Hudson turned to the director who signaled for a commercial break. "We'll be back in a few moments. Don't touch that remote." The camera lights dimmed.

"Mr. Hudson," The Mystic said with a chuckle. "Didn't Walter explain the rules of the interview? You were given a card with questions. Instead, I believe you are using a different card. Normally, a breach of this magnitude would terminate the interview, and invalidate our contract, but I will agree to continue, if only for Simon's sake."

"Simon?" Hudson pulled an index card from his pocket and placed it side by side with the one he held. "You're answering the questions on your card. No matter what I ask, you're answering—"

"Back in twenty," the director barked.

Hudson glared at the cards in his hands.

"Fifteen, fifteen," the director yelled.

"Fifteen," Hudson whispered. The director pointed to Hudson. "Welcome back. We're chatting tonight with The Mystic." Hudson faced his guest and leaned forward. "Mr. Mystic, I'm sure my viewers would love to hear how you knew about the problem with Air Force One."

"Well, Pete, that's simple. I enjoy flying very much." He chuckled. "But then if you've seen my performance you know what I'm talking about. Ha. Seriously, flying gives me such pleasure; the freedom to go anywhere with no restrictions, and that must never be compromised."

Hudson hunched his shoulders and shook his head. With a hard sigh, he asked the final question, "Can you tell my viewers if Elvis is alive?"

"Elvis. That is the most interesting question of all. How many times have I been asked that question during my performance? So many times, I've lost count. But let me give you the answer I truly believe, in my heart, to be correct: yes."

Hudson's eyes widened as he leaned forward. "You think Elvis is alive?"

"Of course. There has been so much speculation

about life and death, living and dying—I believe they are the same. The more relevant question is, are *we* alive? How do we know? Can we prove we truly exist? There is a spectrum of existence, you know, and to be on one level does not disprove the existence of the others. It is really a matter of perspective. In that sense, we are all alive, and we are all dead. Time is relative; the choice is ours. You see, Pete, this world is not what it seems. There are things happening you can't even imagine. It takes a very gifted person to deal with the truth."

Hudson cocked his head and glanced at the director who waved his arms in the air, signaling the arrival of yet another commercial break. Hudson smiled at the camera. "We're going to take one more short break. Please stay with us for the conclusion of my exclusive interview with the very talented Mystic of Las Vegas."

"And out," the director said.

Hudson turned to The Mystic. "Mr. Mystic, I want to—"

"Thank you for having me here tonight." The Mystic unclipped his microphone.

"But we've still got six minutes."

"As I've said, time is relative. Now listen to me, Mr. Hudson, I came here tonight for two reasons. One, because I am bound by contract to do this interview. But the main reason I am here is to warn you."

"Warn me? About what?"

"Dark forces are at work in this city. Some on your station have taken an interest in these forces."

"Who?"

"Well, not you, that's for sure. Look, your station must turn a blind camera eye to the magicians, psychics, hypnotists, and illusionists on The Strip. If you don't, I cannot be held responsible for whatever happens."

"What could happen?"

The Mystic stood and glanced down at Hudson. "I'm leaving you with six minutes to fill. If you are strong, dedicated to your craft, you will fill that time like a professional. If you need help, may I suggest you introduce Simon Quail. He loves to sing." He turned for the door and spoke over his shoulder, "I've never had time for self-professed know it all's, Mr. Hudson, especially when it's obvious they know nothing at all. Let me be clear, don't stick your nose where it doesn't belong. Good evening and goodbye."

Chapter Nine

Lucas Knight held the sword over his head before leveling it, aiming, and running it through a sandbag hung by a thick rope in front of him. Heaps of silver white sand poured out of the bag creating hourglass-like piles on the stage. The audience stared in trance-like astonishment, some gasping when the blade ripped the heavy canvas bag as if made of the finest silk.

He held the sword up and addressed the audience, "The *katana* sword. Quite possibly the most elegant instrument of death known to man. First used by the samurai of feudal Japan; characterized by its distinctive curved blade, single-edged and razor-sharp. Made of the finest tempered steel, the katana is my particular weapon of choice.

"Sharp enough to slice through a soft tomato. Ahem…" Knight held out his hand, palm up. "I said, sharp enough to slice through a soft tomato." He waggled his fingers as his eyes stared straight ahead at the crowd.

An assistant shouted, "Oh," and ran forward placing a tomato in Knight's hand. The audience offered nervous laughter.

"Thank you, Gwen." Lucas deadpanned to the audience, "Believe me, ladies and gentlemen, it was better in rehearsal." A few chuckles drifted toward the stage.

Knight tossed the red fruit in the air and slashed at it with deft precision. The tomato fell to the stage in two pieces. He sneered at the audience members lucky enough to sit in the front row of the sold out amphitheater. "Shall we try a watermelon? It would make, I believe, a bigger impression. No? Right, then. Mr. Cameraman, follow me please."

Knight backed to center stage, all the while smiling into the lens of the portable close-up camera carried by a man dressed in black. He turned and faced his hapless assistant, Gwen, lying face up on a metal table. After placing the sword in a scabbard, he secured his assistant's ankles and wrists to the table with shackles.

Most in the audience followed Knight's every movement on stage closely, hoping to spy the moment he switched the deadly sword for a plastic one. Others kept their eyes glued to the large screen above the stage. The camera lens never left the sword.

"Now then, ladies and gentlemen," Lucas Knight bellowed, "shall we see how the sword fairs against an apple?" He secured a shiny red apple from another assistant and placed it gently on Gwen's stomach. "The shackles that bind my lovely assistant, Gwendolyn, are constructed of hardened steel; the table upon which she lies is composed of stainless steel, and you've just seen a demonstration of the capabilities of this most excellent sword." He drew the weapon from the scabbard and held it high above his head with both hands, Samurai position. "Gwendolyn, my sweet, do you have any final words for our audience before I release you from the bonds of this world, and send you to the next?"

She screamed, and the apple rolled off her belly to

the stage.

"Please lay perfectly still, my pet." Knight scooped the apple off the floor and replaced it onto Gwen's tummy. "Not a breath, my lovely." He raised the sword again. "Be still. Not-one-single-breath."

Knight swung the sword down, parallel to the table, catching Gwendolyn's midriff, cutting through the apple, and slicing her in half. The metal sword clanged on the table. Shrieks sounded from the crowd. Blood spurted in the air. The stage went dark.

In an instant, a brilliant white light flooded the stage. A lively, and quite alive, Gwendolyn stood next to the very table she occupied seconds before. A line of red crossed her white stomach showing exactly where she'd been "cut in half." She held up half an apple. Standing on the table, in a hand-on-hip pose, Lucas Knight grinned at the audience, holding high the other half of the apple. He jumped off the table and took a bite.

As if with one mind, the audience banged their hands together. Whoops, whistles, and cheers added to the deafening roar. Shouts of "Amazing" and "Unbelievable" were directed at the stage.

Knight took Gwendolyn by the hand. Together they bowed. The curtain came down. The applause continued until the curtain rose and they bowed again. They waved at the audience and bowed one more time as the curtain fell for the final call.

"Shit, that stings each and every night," Gwendolyn said, rubbing her hand across her stomach and flinging the apple to the floor.

Knight grinned. "I can only imagine."

"You have no idea."

"Listen to them out there. They love a good murder."

"If those idiots only knew the truth—"

Knight grabbed Gwendolyn's arm and squeezed tight. "They never will." He returned her stare with blazing eyes. "Right?"

"No…that's right, they never will. Please let me go, Luke; that hurts."

He released her arm and turned to the approaching stagehands. After spitting out the bite of apple, he tossed the rest on the floor. "Clean up this mess."

Knight led the way off stage, Gwendolyn following close behind.

"The humans think I'm the greatest magician of all time, and that's the way it's going to stay until we hear otherwise." He stopped and faced Gwendolyn. "Look, Gwen, so I kill you every night—I bring you back in a wink, don't I? So it hurts for a little while—that's the price of fame, isn't it? We've got a good thing going here. Nobody can figure out the ruse. We're exactly where we're supposed to be, exactly where Gorgeous wants us. So for now you better just suck it up and—"

"Did I hear my name?"

Knight spun around at the sound of the voice and faced the woman in white standing just behind him. "What are you doing here?"

"Quite the greeting. I wanted to see my favorite magician, and you make it sound as if it's a crime."

"I'm sorry. Please," Knight said as he held his hand out, "will you join me in my dressing room? Please, this way."

"Much better." Gorgeous drifted across the stage.

****

I yank open the door, almost ripping it off its hinges. I thought I'd never see Marco Ramirez again, so I haven't prepared for this moment. I consider Marco the only man I've ever loved. He led me into battle two years ago, and under his guidance and quick thinking, we both made it out alive. Shivers of pure joy zip through my body. He's taking way too long getting out of his car, so I jump off the porch and scamper down the walkway to greet him.

"Adam." Ramirez beams at me, his arms open wide.

I charge at him and throw my arms around him in a bear hug. His breath whooshes out with a, "ugh."

"Hey, settle down, big fella. Stand back and let me get a good look at you." He keeps his hands on my shoulders, moving his gaze over my face, across my chest, and down to my shoes. "You haven't changed a bit."

I rub my belly and grin. "Put on a few pounds."

"Nah, that's nothing." He pats his own stomach, and we both laugh. "I did everything I could to find you: missing person alerts; posters; even called in a few favors in Cali, Utah, and Arizona, but it's like you disappeared off the face of the planet. Where were you?"

"Colorado."

He cocks his head. "Really? You'll have to tell me more about that when we get a chance. C'mon, let's go inside, I want to say hello to Dixie and Aunt Rose."

I nod and keep my arm over his shoulder as we march back to the house. I understand what's going on with my emotions—why I'm so giddy. Even though Aunt Rose created a magical bond between us on the night of The Disaster, this is the closest thing I've ever felt to truly belonging to someone (except Dixie, of course). He's my friend, my mentor, and the only Alpha I will ever accept.

"Marco," Dixie says, stepping out onto the porch and smiling at us. "Look at you two. Almost like old times, isn't it?"

Marco slaps my back and enters the house, closing the door behind him. "Dixie." He holds out his hand, and they shake. "I guess we have a few things to talk about."

The two people I love most stand on either side of me. I clutch Dixie's hand in mine, and do the same with Marco, a huge grin glued to my lips. Marco wriggles free of my hold and steps back. A strange expression moves over his face. I can't tell if it's a grin or a frown, maybe both.

"Oh, no," he says, "don't tell me."

"Tell you what?" I ask.

"You two didn't sleep together, did you?"

Dixie lets go of my hand and glares at Marco. "That's none of your business."

I can't stop beaming. This is truly a great day. "We sure did."

"Adam." Dixie stares at me. "That's not something anybody needs to know about. Whatever we did, or didn't do, doesn't concern him, or anyone else."

"Doesn't concern me?" I can't tell if he's angry or annoyed. The subtleties of human emotions are sometimes hard to decipher, even for other humans. "Did you tell him about us?"

"No, why would I? There isn't any us, not anymore. That doesn't concern Adam."

"What's going on?" I look from Marco to Dixie and back again.

"She should have told you that we used to...you know...date," Marco says. "She broke it off for some reason," he snaps his fingers, "just like that. And now—"

"And now what, Marco?" Dixie's voice grows louder. "That was a long time ago. Things are different now. I'm different now; we all are."

"I know. Everybody's different...except me."

"And just what is that supposed to mean?" Dixie says.

"I'm still human," he says as if it's a bad thing. "You're a Daemon, he's a—"

"I'm human." My voice is small. Dixie and Marco speak over and around me, like I'm not even there, the way the med techs used to talk in prison.

Dixie marches to the living room. "What's your problem?"

Marco closes his eyes and rubs a hand across his forehead. "I'm sorry, you're right. It's just that I haven't heard from you for so long. I apologize. Can we start over?"

Dixie turns from her position in front of the fireplace and faces us. Her shoulders relax and she grins. "Of course. Why don't you come in? Do you want something to drink?"

Marco shakes his head, puts his hand on my back, and we step into the living room while Dixie waves her hand and shuts the front door.

"How did you do that?" My gaze is glued to the doorknob. "How did you close the door from over there?"

"I don't know." Dixie's worried appearance turns into a beam. "The door needed to be closed and I...I don't know, I just did."

The grandfather clock in the entry hall chimes eleven times, its deep gong reverberating in my chest.

"Where's Aunt Rose?" Marco says as we sit on the couch.

"Well, in order to explain that, I have to tell you the whole story. I hope you're comfortable."

The grandfather clock strikes twelve times when Dixie finishes telling Marco about my escape from jail (thanks to Major Ransom and Colonel Dayton), the murders at Claremont, and Aunt Rose's distrust of Charlie Nguyen.

"I don't like her either," I say. "She keeps calling me *the dog*, very condescending."

Dixie laughs and aims her comment at me, "I guess she doesn't understand how someone can change their stripes. If anyone should understand that concept, she should. I mean, she was on the side of the evils when they attacked Las Vegas. Now she claims to want to help us."

"How can you be so sure she's changed her stripes?" Marco says.

"Major Ransom is convinced, and that's good enough for me."

Marco rubs his chin and stares at her like he's a teacher about to explain a difficult concept. "We only knew the major for a few hours before she died."

"She didn't die; she was killed, ripped to shreds because of the evil Daemons. I don't think she would side with them under any circumstance. I wish you could hear her the way I do. She's so calm and at peace.

She sincerely wants to help us."

Marco nods. "In that case—"

A knock turns our attention to the front door.

"The others are here," Dixie says.

Both Marco and I stand up as Dixie unlatches the deadbolt and pulls the door open. A lone figure stands on the front porch: Charlie Nguyen.

Dixie asks, "Where's Colonel Dayton and Cutty?"

Charlie Nguyen stares at her through dark eyes. "They're both dead."

Chapter Ten

Dixie's hand trembled as she covered her mouth, her face draining of color. "What do you mean the colonel and Cutty are dead? How? What happened?"

"Let me inside and I'll tell you," Charlie Nguyen fanned her face. "You may not be aware of the fact that I tend to overheat quite easily, or you may not even care. Either way, if you let me in right now I may forgive—"

Dixie grabbed Nguyen's arm and yanked her inside, slamming the door shut as she turned to face the Daemon. "Tell me what happened right now, or so help me—"

"So help you what?" Nguyen smiled, a misplaced grin, an expression she may have forgotten how to use, or never quite understood. "You can't do anything to me, little Daemon—nothing at all."

Marco Ramirez leaned over Dixie's shoulder. "She may not be able to, but I sure as hell can." He took a step forward.

Nguyen shouted, "*Imobili.*"

Ramirez froze in place. Under the spell, his eyes remained alert and functioning, his breathing normal, but any overt physical movement ceased.

"And who is this?" Charlie Nguyen brushed past Dixie. She inspected Ramirez as a cat considers a mouse. "He's spirited." She licked her lips. "I like the spirited ones, up to a point."

Adam vaulted over Dixie and leapt at Nguyen. He reached out, falling to the ground with the Daemon in his hands.

Ramirez shuddered, free from Nguyen's spell, and fell down, becoming part of a growing heap of bodies on the floor. Dixie joined the pile, shoving her elbow into the Daemon's stomach, trying to knock the wind out of her lest another spell be spoken. Charlie Nguyen's breath rushed out in a steady whoosh, her face turning purple. Mission accomplished.

A bright green cloud circled around the donnybrook. "Terminum!"

Dixie looked up, searching for the source of the command. Aunt Rose, hands on hips, loomed above them like a rugby official standing over a scrum. "What is going on here? Why are you fighting? More importantly, why is this happening in my house?"

"Charlie Nguyen killed Colonel Dayton and Cutty," Dixie said.

"She was about to kill Marco, too," Adam said.

Charlie Nguyen's mouth moved, but no sound came out. She put a hand to her tummy and scowled at Dixie.

"Calm down, Nguyen," Aunt Rose said, "I'll get to you in a moment. Marco, you should know better than to fight with a Daemon. What's your excuse for such childish behavior?"

He pointed at Nguyen. "Well, she started it."

"Deputy Chief Marco Ramirez," Aunt Rose said, followed by a loud tsk-tsk-tsk. "Stand up and meet Charlemagne Nguyen. She is here as my guest to help us with our problem. Nguyen, you may now speak.

Explain yourself."

"Explain myself?" Charlie Nguyen stood, brushed herself off, and stepped toward Aunt Rose. "How dare you ask me to explain myself."

Aunt Rose folded her arms.

"Very well then, if you insist. I came here at noon, as we agreed, and they attacked me for no reason."

Dixie scrambled to her feet. "You said you killed—"

"I never said I killed anybody."

Adam sprang up and put his hand on the small of Dixie's back. "She's right; she never said she killed anyone. She said, 'They've been killed.'"

"Well, at least the dog heard what I said."

"Stop calling me *the dog*."

Aunt Rose raised her hands and asked for silence. She turned to Nguyen. "Suppose you tell us your side, and tell the truth if you've nothing to hide."

Charlie Nguyen's gaze fell on each face, but came to rest on Aunt Rose's. "Very well. I'd like to start by addressing you, Rosalyn. You seem to think I've never fully turned away from the darkness. Have I done anything to make you question my loyalty?"

Ramirez leaned into Nguyen. "Quit stalling and tell us what happened."

Charlie Nguyen raised an eyebrow at Ramirez. "As you are the only human in this house, may I suggest you remain silent and let the gifted ones speak?"

Dixie bit her lower lip. "Aunt Rose. If she doesn't tell us what happened to Colonel Dayton and Cutty, I'm going to turn her into a pile of lint and vacuum her up." She wagged a finger at Nguyen. "Don't think I can't do it either, Nguyen. I've been practicing."

Charlie Nguyen attempted another smile, but failed. She turned to Aunt Rose. "Is your niece aware of the fact she can't—"

"Unfortunately, my niece is unaware of what she can or cannot do. She has yet to experience The Sufferings. I would tread lightly if I were you."

Charlie Nguyen threw a brief glare at Dixie. "Very well. Colonel Dayton arrived at the Tropicana as arranged. We walked to the parking lot and he opened the door for me. The English are always so polite, ugh. At that point, a supernatural force kept me from entering the vehicle. Instead, Colonel Dayton was pushed into the car and the door slammed shut. Clearly, to me, the driver, the one you call Cutty, had absolutely no control over the vehicle. It sped off by itself. It's obvious to me they met with foul play."

"You expect us to believe that lie?" Dixie said. *Believe her, she's telling the truth.* "What?"

"What do you mean, what?" Adam said.

"It's Major Ransom. She said Nguyen's telling the truth."

Charlie Nguyen raised her eyebrows and grinned. "Was there ever any doubt?"

"This is ridiculous," Ramirez said, "she's obviously trying to save her own neck."

"Hush." Aunt Rose held her hand up. Nobody said a word while her hand remained in the air. "Look for what?" She glanced about the living room, moving from couch, to easy chair, to fireplace mantel. "Who put this here?"

"I did," Dixie said. "I bought that crystal ball at the garage sale yesterday. I thought it would look nice on the—"

Aunt Rose slammed it to the floor. It burst into a green flame and vanished.

"What's the matter?" Dixie rushed forward.

"Our every word in this house has been projected...somewhere. I hadn't even noticed it. My dear, you've got to be careful. The evil Daemons are clever."

"Oh my God, I had no idea. I'm so sorry."

"Calm yourself, sweetie. There's no way you could have known. I, on the other hand, should have kept my eyes open for such nonsense. You too, Nguyen."

"Me? It's not my house."

"Honest," Dixie said, "I feel just awful about—"

"Shhh." Aunt Rose held her hand up again.

"We're wasting time," Adam said. "We've got to try and find the colonel and—"

"Hush." Aunt Rose cocked her head and closed her eyes. Her face brightened. "I'm told the situation is being dealt with. I've also been instructed not to interfere as that may endanger Colonel Dayton and Mr. Cutty. We are to wait here." She clasped her hands together. "So, that's that. Please come in and have some biscuits and tea. Come on, then, follow me."

"You expect us to eat?" Adam said.

"There's nothing to do now but wait. Please, go in the kitchen and grab a plate."

****

Gorgeous glanced around the small dressing room, keeping her hands clasped together waist high, as if touching anything in the dimly lit space would cause illness. She stared at the ceiling then ran her gaze along the dirty walls. "The end of days will soon be upon the humans." Her voice rose, but the grin she wore, like a mask, stayed constant. She waved Lucas and Gwendolyn to the small settee near the makeup table while she remained standing, a position of authority.

"You honor us with your presence, my queen. Two nights in a row, this is such a treat," Lucas said, turning his lips up.

Finally, after what seemed a full minute, she made eye contact. "You amaze the humans with your magic."

Lucas broke into full Cheshire-grin. "You are too kind. I merely—"

"Quiet." Gorgeous turned and strolled from him to the other side of the room, using precise, measured steps. "You've done well, playing to a packed house each and every night. The humans are a curious lot, enjoying your special brand of dark magic from their safe, padded seats. And, as I suspected, one human in particular is quite taken with you."

"The president."

Gorgeous twirled around. "He has a penchant for the paranormal; an insatiable curiosity for the supernatural." She offered a smile. "But let's not get ahead of ourselves. He will attend your performance in two nights. The Secret Service has already secured his luxury box and sealed it off." She snickered. "But they cannot seal his mind."

Lucas grinned. "Will you melt it, my queen? Or steal it? Or—"

"You're a formidable Daemon, Knight, but a bit short-sighted. I was thinking more of a long-term possession. The very thought excites me."

Lucas gave her a respectful nod. "And what do you wish of me?"

"You can start by keeping your mouth shut." She

spun and faced him. "Simply continue doing exactly what you've been doing. Magic." She paused and furrowed her brow. "Something is on your mind, I sense it."

"There's nothing, my queen. I have nothing to hide."

"Hide?"

"Wrong choice of words, my lady. I'm an open book; an honest soul."

Gwendolyn stood up. "He's so right; we're both open books—"

"Shut up, you idiot," Lucas said. He turned to Gorgeous. "I apologize for my assistant's lack of social etiquette." With a venomous glance at Gwendolyn, he said, "Go."

She exited the dressing room without another word.

"She's such a bother. I only keep her in the act because the humans seem to think her klutziness is part of the show. It amuses them. And besides, it's so hard to find good help."

Gorgeous narrowed her eyes on the magician. "I couldn't agree more. In any case, we must make do with what we're given. Still, I would keep an eye on that one if I were you. The other side can be quite cunning. In any case, you impress me, Lucas. You possess the power over life and death, quite an unheard of gift for a Daemon. Indeed, your abilities are reminiscent of the *Sangre di Real*."

Lucas Knight shook his head. "No, my lady, surely you don't think I could be a part of that abhorrent faction. They were imprisoned behind the Gates of Hell for a reason. I assure you that I—"

"Calm down, magician." She extended her hand and uttered, "*Imobili.*"

Lucas Knight froze, still as a block of ice.

"Simple spells have no effect on True Bloods." She circled him, caressing his cheek and staring into his eyes. "Still, it never hurts to check." She stroked the side of his head; an act she thought gave the process a personal touch, allowing him to regain movement.

He tested his limbs and shook his head. "My loyalty is only to you."

"Your thoughts are not clear to me, either, and that, too, gives me pause. How you've acquired such precious gifts concerns me."

Lucas Knight bowed his head. "My queen, I do not know. However, I will prove my allegiance to you tonight."

"How?"

"You've told me before about that horrid Daemon Rosalyn Chase. Through a fortuitously placed *objet d'art*, I managed to acquire two of her human miscreants. They'll be featured in my next performance. I would consider it a great honor if you'd attend."

Gorgeous smirked. "I already have Rosalyn on a red herring hunt far from The Strip. She knows nothing of my plans. Still, your invitation intrigues me. Tell me more."

"I arranged a special illusion, just for you. If you have any doubts about my loyalty, your fears will be put to rest. Please allow me to prove my devotion."

"Devotion?" Gorgeous stepped to the door. She turned back to Lucas, giving him a sly grin, an even larger smirk than usual. "I do enjoy devotion." With that, the mask faded for just an instant, a quizzical expression taking its place. A moment later, the Mona Lisa smile returned and Gorgeous evaporated in a blue mist.

Gwendolyn cracked open the door and tiptoed inside. She waved her hands through the blue vapor Gorgeous left behind. "What did she say?"

Lucas turned away from her and glanced into the large makeup mirror. He stroked his chin, rubbing at the sides of his face. "You tell me. You were obviously listening at the door."

Gwendolyn put her hand on his sleeve. "I would never think to—"

He tore his gaze from the mirror and glanced at her hand. "That's the very nature of your problem, sweet Gwen. You never think."

"You're so right, sir, but I would never listen to your private conversations. Honest. Please tell me what she said. Please?"

"And why would I do that? What makes you think you deserve to know?" He turned back to the mirror. "I can't even look at you right now. I heard you could follow orders and keep your mouth shut. It seems you have trouble with both. Go away and come back when you're ready to apologize."

"Apologize for what?"

"For complaining every night when I cut you in half. Your whining infuriates me. You're a Daemon, for God's sake, act like it."

"I'm so sorry, Lucas."

He turned from the mirror and grabbed her by the throat, kissing her hard on the mouth as he compressed her windpipe with his thumbs. "You know, that is the one human word I cannot stand—sorry—it's pathetic and cowardly."

Gwendolyn's eyes widened. She struggled, but Lucas held tight. Through a constricted throat, she squawked, "What are you doing?"

"You know very well what I'm doing. What I'm thinking is quite a different matter." He spoke offhanded, as if her struggle for air had nothing to do with him. "I think I need to freshen up the act a bit. Perhaps a nice, slow hanging would thrill the audience; watching your feet kick as you struggle to breathe. Cutting you in half is far too quick."

A muffled cry echoed from the small wardrobe in the corner, seizing his attention. "Lucky for you, my sweet girl, it seems your pretty little neck has been spared just in time." He released his hold.

Gwendolyn coughed, gasping for air, her shoulders heaving. She backed away from him and took several deep breaths. "What do you have in the closet?"

A broad grin crawled its way across his face until his lips formed a thin line from cheek to cheek. "Call it a gift. A little surprise for Gorgeous."

"Gorgeous will be in the audience again tonight?"

"Go now." He marched toward her, his hand shooing her away. "Prepare yourself for the performance. It will be spectacular. Right now you're of better use to me alive than dead." He tapped the closet door. "More than I can say for these two. Hurry and get ready. The show begins in thirty minutes. Tell Sebastian I want to see him. Go."

Chapter Eleven

The audience entered the theater by ones, twos, and small groups; the typical Vegas show crowd: excited, boisterous, and enjoying the effects of several cocktails too many. Most would have already called it a night in their own hometowns. Towns with names like Chicago, Miami, or San Francisco, but Las Vegas—Vegas never slept.

The ten o'clock show at the Lone Mountain Hotel and Casino sold out, as usual for a Lucas Knight performance. The nosebleed seats were snatched up earlier in the afternoon. VIP box seats had been booked weeks in advance, or comped by the hotel to high rollers and guest celebrities.

The cool air, usually scented with a fresh coconut bouquet, had been replaced tonight with a unique blend of cinnamon and roses. The lights dimmed and the crowd came to life with a rousing chorus of applause.

"Ladies and Gentlemen," a deep voice boomed across the theater, "it's Knight-time!" A generic rock and roll riff was greeted by applause. "Lucas Knight's illusions are performed with adult audiences in mind. Those with small children, or those offended by material, which include life and death situations, may wish to leave the theater. The use of cell phones and photography of any kind is strictly prohibited. We hope you enjoy tonight's performance." More music, the volume increasing with each beat.

"And now, he's been hailed as the world's pre-eminent magician, the foremost illusionist of our age...ladies and gentlemen, Lucas Knight!"

Some in the crowd stood, some whistled, but all banged their hands together in wild applause as the black curtain concealing the stage lifted.

Lucas Knight, caught in a bright, white spotlight, grinned from center stage and bowed. The noise in the theater rose with each bow. He stretched out his hands, asking for quiet. The applause died as the audience obliged, settling into their seats.

"Ladies and gentlemen, my name is Lucas Knight, and I personally want to welcome each and every one of you to the Lucas Knight Theater at the Lone Mountain Hotel and Casino in fabulous Las Vegas, Nevada." Another brisk, but brief, round of applause followed his greeting. He stretched out his hands again then shielded his eyes from the glare of the spotlight. "I'm glad to see most of you have remained after our brief disclaimer about adult themes. We have to do that, you know, for two reasons. One: the lawyers insist." Quiet laughter came from the crowd. "The other: because this ain't your momma's old rabbit out of the hat magic act." Wild applause followed. "In fact, most of the rabbits we use in the show retire after just a single performance." Nervous laughter greeted his statement. "No need to worry about them, however, their retirement is quite enjoyable...for me. A little salt and pepper; they taste just like chicken."

The audience broke into laughter as a snare drum began a slow cadence in the background. The spotlight illuminating Lucas Knight went dark and the drum grew louder. Knight's voice rolled across the theater. "Tonight, I have something very special planned for you—an illusion so unique, so exceptional, it will leave you breathless."

Dark shapes ran back and forth on the stage; workmen carrying flashlights, erecting metal rails and assembling props, their footsteps masked by the drum. The audience sat still, quiet, and focused. In a gush of lights, the stage came to life. Dancers dressed in colorful costumes paraded about in a choreographed routine. The drum never missed a beat during their dance. One by one, the dancers exited. Lights bathed the stage revealing Lucas Knight standing between two guillotines. He smiled at the crowd and gave a quick wink. "Ladies and gentlemen, I give you...The Execution."

Two figures dressed in black, their heads covered by hoods, hands tied behind their backs, appeared on stage in step to the drum.

"Tonight, ladies and gentlemen, you will witness an execution—Lucas Knight style. Now, we don't know much about our two...ahem, volunteers. Perhaps, they're cold-blooded killers and the punishment is deserved. Maybe they work for the IRS and they deserve much worse." Brief laughter. "In any case, the time has come to pay the piper. So, sit back, relax, and enjoy...The Execution."

The audience roared its approval. Lucas Knight stood behind the first criminal, and with the help of his assistants, placed the man on a table, face down, his hooded head hanging over the edge above a basket. Leather restraints held the man in place. Knight rushed around to the other criminal and performed the same operation. The two men struggled, but could not move.

"Ladies and gentlemen," Knight raised his arm, "may I introduce my lovely assistant, the fair-haired Gwendolyn." A smattering of applause greeted her arrival on stage. Some in the audience chuckled. "Oh, you've seen my act before," Knight deadpanned. "Gwen, there is a rope just to your right. No, your other right. Please reach out and grasp it. On the count of three, pull down on the rope. Don't be shy—pull hard. That will release the two blades and..." Knight swiped a finger across his throat. "The blades will, in turn, release two souls."

"One." Shadows covered the stage. "Two." The lights dimmed. "Three." Gwen pulled the rope and both blades raced free. A crisp "chop-chop" sound filled the theater as the two heads tumbled into baskets. The audience, with one mind, drew in its breath.

Bright light washed over the theater. Stagehands rushed out and released the restraints from the legs of the criminals who lay motionless on the tables. The two criminals stood, under their own power, and faced the crowd. Gwendolyn appeared as the criminal on the right, Lucas Knight on the left. Both waved their arms and smiled.

The audience roared in approval. The switch had been seamless, unnoticed by anyone in attendance...except Knight. He peered into the basket at the base of the guillotine. A severed head, mouth gagged, stared back through cold, dead eyes. Not the head he expected. He spun around and glanced into the other basket.

Lucas Knight stood beside Gwendolyn and grabbed her hand. As they bowed, he shouted above the applause, "Where are they?"

"Who? What do you mean?"

One more bow. "You're the only one who knew about the humans in the closet." When they stood, Lucas glanced to the rafters at the lighting technician and pointed—the signal to kill the spot. The curtain came down, and Knight grabbed hold of a stagehand. "The Samurai illusion is next."

"But, sir, that's the show closer."

Knight turned an evil eye toward Gwendolyn. "Exactly."

****

"Adam, come here and listen very carefully." Aunt Rose is so serious; I almost think I've done something wrong; broken one of her many rules. I follow her into the kitchen while the others remain in the living room.

"What is it?"

"Dixie, you too. Come in here as well. Hurry up, on the double, young lady."

Dixie rushes into the kitchen.

"My dear," Aunt Rose takes hold of Dixie's hand, "I've put it off far too long and feel like such a ding-dong. You need specific skills before we proceed, of that I am certain; almost guaranteed." She turns to me. "I want you to go with Dixie to this address." She hands me a piece of paper. "Dixie, both of you, memorize the address, hurry now."

Dixie cozies up next to me and glances at the scribbles on the paper. "Got it," she says. "But I don't get it."

Aunt Rose takes the paper from me, tears it up, and throws it into the sink. It ignites and burns away in a green flame. She stares at Dixie, lowers her voice, and raises an eyebrow. "The Sufferings. I made a call and arranged it all. You are expected."

"Oh, I don't think I'm ready for—"

"Not ready? My dear there are things you simply must know, and I blame myself for putting the whole thing off far too long."

"But—"

"Enough hesitation. Adam will be with you every step of the way. Now off with you both, and don't delay. Now then," she turns away, "Marco, you come with me. We're going to meet my contact. She's at the Lone Mountain Hotel on The Strip."

"And what of me? Have you forgotten about me?" Charlie Nguyen says.

"You're so right. I can't leave you here. Come with us. Better to know what you're doing than wonder what you're up to."

"Unbelievable. When are you going to accept the fact that I'm—"

"Well?" Aunt Rose turns to us. "What are you still doing here? Go."

We leave the house and venture down the walkway to the street. The others soon come out behind us and pile into Marco's car. I wave as they drive past.

Dixie tightens her grip on my hand as we stroll down the sidewalk. She keeps her eye on a red brick house not far from Aunt Rose's. "That's where I bought the crystal ball."

A young woman steps out of the house leading a small terrier on a leash.

"Excuse me," Dixie calls out, "did your mother or grandmother have a yard sale here yesterday?"

The woman appears caught off guard and pulls

back on the leash. "You've got the wrong house." The small Schnauzer starts yapping.

"No, this was the house. I bought some things here."

"No, *you're* mistaken. We don't have yard sales."

Dixie tightens her grip on my hand. "This *is* the house, and I bought—"

I pull back on Dixie, my arm over her shoulder, and lead her away. "It's no use. She'll never admit it. We'd better just go."

Dixie relaxes. "You're right. Evil Daemons probably set up the sale while she was away from the house. I'm so stupid."

"Not your fault." We walk away from the red brick house and cross the street.

"I'm glad you're coming with me. I don't think I could face this alone. The very name, The Sufferings, gives me the creeps."

Her anxiety buzzes through her hand and crawls up my arm. "What exactly is The Sufferings?"

She shrugs her shoulders. "It's something all Daemons go through. Of course, most experience it when they are much younger. Aunt Rose said something about her wanting me to have a *normal* life, so she never arranged it for me. I guess it's too late to be normal now. I'm also supposed to get my color."

"Color?"

"Sure, every Daemon has its own color. There are as many Daemons in the world as there are colors. We also get a scent; like Aunt Rose's is fresh baked bread."

"That explains Charlie Nguyen's funky odor."

"I hear some of them are just awful. I hope you don't hate me if I get a bad one."

This makes me smile. "C'mon, are you kidding? I'm a canine; we love to sniff all kinds of stinky stuff." It's just a joke, but she doesn't laugh.

"You're not making me feel any better. Anyway, The Sufferings are also where we learn exactly what our skills are and what we can or cannot do, you know? The rules."

"Doesn't sound so bad. I wish something like that existed for me."

"I don't know. You seem pretty good at figuring things out for yourself. At least you were last night."

This makes me blush. We walk a couple of blocks. "Where's your Hummer?"

"Traded it in for something a little less conspicuous." She stops and points at a dirty compact car. "Nobody gives this thing a second look, not even me."

The address is on the west side of town, near a section of Las Vegas known as The Lakes. Dixie takes her time negotiating downtown traffic until we hit the 95. She stomps on the accelerator and zips along in the fast lane, barreling around slower vehicles. The car complains, but she ignores it. We take the Summerlin Parkway and exit at Durango.

"I sold my house when I came back to Vegas, to make ends meet. I bought a condo not far from here. I'd like to show it to you after we're done."

"Absolutely."

When we stop at a red light, she gives me a quick glance. Her tone is calm, almost hesitant. "There's something I need to tell you."

I feel my skin tingle. She's so serious. "What is it?"

"Aunt Rose and I have been making inquiries. We think …"

"Tell me." Now I don't know if I want to hear what she has to say. "Just say it."

"We think Lucy's alive."

Memories of my sister rush in. "What do you mean? We saw her killed."

"No, we didn't. We heard her fighting with Bane. Her body was never found."

My breathing is shallow, my voice weak. "Have you asked Major Ransom? If anyone should know—"

"Of course, but she doesn't. Aunt Rose is doing what she can to look into it. She has connections all over town. She says—"

Dixie keeps talking, but I tune her out. The thought that my sister may be alive drowns out everything. I considered Lucy and Ivan the only real family I ever had, and I know for a fact my brother is dead; he died saving my life.

Dixie's voice fades in, "So she could have gotten out of the house, away from Bane. Then The Disaster started and who knows what happened after that. If she's still alive, which we think is a real possibility, she could be anywhere. I didn't want to tell you and get your hopes up, but I can't keep it to myself anymore."

Dixie turns left onto Fort Apache from Sahara Avenue. She makes another left on Lake South Drive. The road winds through and around small parks and ponds with shallow waterfalls. Geese and ducks scamper across the road.

"I'm glad you told me." My thoughts are mixed, my emotions on fire. "In a way, Lucy was *my* Sufferings."

"What do you mean?"

"She taught me how to transform, the secret to it. She gave me hope. I thought I was the only one of my kind who wasn't a cold-blooded killer, until I talked to her. She saved both our lives that night, remember?" The houses and streets rush by; I'm only half aware of them—my mind is on Lucy.

Dixie gives me a sideways glance after she parks the car. "Are you okay? I shouldn't have told you. Are you sorry you came with me?"

I rest my hand on hers. "Not a chance. I'll ask Aunt Rose about Lucy when we get back later. Let's go." A smile appears for her benefit. "Time to start suffering."

"Gee, thanks."

The houses are modern cookie-cutter stucco homes, no different from the thousands of others on the west side of town. I get out of the car and glance at the row of brown, beige, and tan homes lining either side of the street. Palm trees tower above our heads and different kinds of cactus fill many of the front yards.

Dixie points to a house across the street, a tan one story on the corner. Rocks and Joshua trees spread out in front of it leaving no discernible walkway to the front door. We step across the rocks and skirt around cactus on our way up the grade. The door opens when we arrive at the porch—perfect timing, as if we were being watched.

A small voice calls out, "Are you Dixie?"

Dixie nods.

"Who's that with you?"

"His name is Adam Steel. He's a friend."

The door opens wider, the owner of the voice still concealed in darkness. "Only you."

"But Aunt Rose, er, I mean Rosalyn Chase said—"

"Only you."

Dixie turns. "Please wait for me. I left the keys in the car if you want to listen to the radio. It'll be okay."

"No. I'm sticking with you."

"It's gonna be all right. Aunt Rose sent me here, and she would never put me in harm's way." Her arms wrap around me in a big bear hug. I bear hug her back, not wanting to let go.

"It's too hot in the car. I'll wait right here, just outside the door, okay?"

She nods and gives me a peck on the cheek. "I shouldn't be too long." She turns around and steps into the house.

The door slams shut.

Chapter Twelve

The pungent odor of things unseen forced Dixie to cup a hand over her nose. She stood as still as a sculpture until her eyes adjusted to the darkness. The form of a small person materialized in front of her. Was it a child?

"Follow me."

"Why can't my friend come in, too?"

"Follow me." Ignoring the question, the small figure turned and strolled down a long hallway, sometimes disappearing as it blended into the shadows.

Dixie followed, taking small, tentative steps. "Wait for me." No response. "Will you wait, please?" She used her hand against the wall as a guide; one step after the other, feeling her way down the hallway. "Please wait for me. Please? Why won't you answer?"

"Stop." The voice was calm, cool—almost indifferent. "Wait here."

Dixie heard no air conditioning unit, but shivered against the freezing temperature. She wrapped her arms around herself and watched, or imagined, the small figure scurry away. The cold, the darkness, and the silence unnerved her. If Aunt Rose hadn't insisted on her coming, this was the last place she would want to be. *If only I hadn't bought that damned crystal ball.* There were so many things to learn.

"Dixie Mulholland, welcome." A new voice—

older, deeper, and almost cheerful. "Welcome to The Sufferings."

Dixie strained against the blackness, but saw nothing. "Where are you?"

"You're older than I expected. Nice head of hair, though, and a good complexion. A little on the thin side. Don't you eat?"

"I eat. Why can't I—"

"You've only known for two years. Why?"

"Known what? I don't understand what's going on."

"Known you're a Daemon. What's the matter with parents these days?"

"My parents are dead."

"Sorry. Ah yes, Rosalyn. Your aunt is your guardian. Still, she should have told you ages ago. Most Daemons endure The Sufferings in their teenage years."

"So I've heard, countless times. Can you please tell me what's going on?"

"Sit down."

Dixie bent down and felt for a chair in the darkness. "Where? I can't see a damn thing."

"Language," the voice admonished. A spotlight snapped on, illuminating a red velvet easy chair. "Sit."

Dixie sat down. The spotlight turned off. "Why can't I see you?"

Whispers darted across the room followed by unseen giggles. "Your aunt didn't tell you much, did she? Ah well, we work with what we're given."

"Aunt Rose said I needed to learn a few things, learn what it means to be a Daemon. I assume you'll teach me."

Another round of snickers. "You are so green for

your age. Ah well, I suppose we'd better begin at the beginning, work through the middle, and get to the end."

"Who's here with us?"

No answer.

"How long is this going to take? I have a friend waiting for me outside."

"Ah yes, the dog. Shall we begin?"

Dixie's eyelids felt like lead. When they closed, she fell into a sudden sleep—no dreams, only darkness as deep as death.

"There you are then, how do you feel?" The voice sounded cheerful.

Dixie rubbed her eyes and shook her head. She cleared her throat. "Did you drug me?"

"Ha, nothing as crude as that." The voice now sounded hesitant, lacking the power it once carried. "We entered your mind." Another pause. "There's greatness in you, Dixie Mulholland. More than you know."

"We? I don't understand."

"Someday perhaps, not today."

A different voice—deeper, older than the first— purred somewhere in the distance. The purring sound evolved into a croon, and settled into a chant:

The sunshine has returned,
In truth the secret lies.
The night it must be burned,
In love the body dies.

The lines repeated as Dixie closed her eyes. "I don't understand."

"Someday perhaps, not today." The speaker cleared her throat and continued in a businesslike tone,

"In any case, we conveyed to you all the knowledge you may, or may not, want to use: performing spells, translucent teleportation, shape-shifting, and the like; all the Daemonology you could ever wish to study. Do you have any questions?"

Dixie sucked in a deep breath. Her question wasn't really a question, rather a command, "Show yourself."

A harsh light bathed the room at once which wasn't a room at all, but more of a cavernous hall—much bigger than the house she'd seen from the outside. In attendance, hundreds crowded together, their eyes all fixed on Dixie. Just as fast, the light flickered and died, throwing everything into darkness. Dixie's heart raced. She was sure the image of the multitude was an illusion.

Giggles, chortles, and snickers drifted through the shadows.

She wrinkled her brow and sniffed the air. The light, exotic scent of jasmine made her smile. "Is that my scent? I suppose it could have been worse," she said, recalling Charlie Nguyen's wretched smell. Thoughts filled her mind; new thoughts—recent memories of things she'd never done, places she'd never been. Everything she wanted to know about being a Daemon, and it had only taken a few minutes.

Laughter filled the darkness.

"Why are you laughing? Stop laughing at me."

The same calm voice that led her into The Sufferings answered, "Two days have passed."

"Two days? Oh my God, where's Adam?"

"Ah yes, your companion banged at the door repeatedly, quite annoying. In any case, The Sufferings have concluded."

118

Dixie bolted out of the chair, fell down, threw up, and winced in pain. "What have you done to me?" Her head felt heavy and thick, as if she'd been put through the spin cycle.

"You have not been harmed," the voice said. "A common side effect of The Sufferings."

"But, where's my friend?"

"I'm sure I don't know. At the end of the second day, he got in your car and drove away."

"He drove my car? But he can't drive."

"Truly. He motored right through the stop sign at the end of the block. Curious, not a drop of rain in sight, yet he turned on the windshield wipers."

Dixie stood up and bent over as a wicked cramp churned through her stomach. "What's the matter with me? I'm going to be sick again."

"The Sufferings, my dear. No need for alarm."

"But I've got to find Adam, to know he's okay. There's no time to be sick."

"Then may I suggest you simply...go. You know how."

Dixie closed her eyes, doing her best to ignore the pain, and rummaged through her new found knowledge. Yes. Imagine a place; imagine the journey, close your eyes—deep breath and just...go. Silver mist swirled around her feet, rising until it covered her completely. In an instant, the room vanished.

****

I've experienced so many feelings as a human: love for Dixie Mulholland, and hate for Sonny Russo; delight at being human, and fear when I thought I was the Werewolf Killer. There are, of course, so many more emotions that cover the spectrum of being human;

119

they come and go as my life unfolds, but the worst of them all (at the very top-of-the-bad-list) is panic.

Panic makes me feel useless—even worse, hopeless. Dixie has vanished from the face of the earth. I thump on the door, bang at the windows, and yell until a woman across the street promises to call the cops. I give her my word I'll keep it down, and I do for about a minute. I kick the bottom of the door until my foot hurts, pound on the side of the house, and run around to the backyard to see if there's another way inside.

Black drapes hang at the windows hiding everything inside from view. As I make my way back to the front, I hear a car drive down the street. It's a Metro cruiser, so I duck down low behind a prickly bush and watch it come to a stop. The woman across the street scurries out of her house and talks to the officer in the patrol car. She points in my direction, and the officer looks my way. I'm certain neither he nor the nosy neighbor have any idea where I'm hiding so I remain still.

The officer parks at the curb and walks through the maze of rocks and cactus to the front door. I hear him knock. "Metro." He waits for a minute, knocks again, then walks back to his car.

"House is empty," he barks at the nosey lady. "Give Metro a call if there's another disturbance. I'll be close by—here's my card." The officer drives away, and the woman goes back into her house.

Maybe I *should* make another disturbance, wait for the cops to show up, and tell them about Dixie being kidnapped. But that could get messy—they'd probably ask for my ID, my relationship to Dixie, the nature of our business here, and I'm not ready for those kinds of questions. The worst part is I have no idea what's going on inside the house. Dixie called it The Sufferings. It seems the only one suffering right now is me. Panic is an emotion I can do without.

I decide to sit in the backyard with my back to the wall and wait, listening for something—for anything. The house, the neighborhood, even the sky is still, no birds, no wind. When the sun starts to fall, my panic rises. Standing up, I turn around and put my palms on the stucco wall. It's still warm to the touch after baking all day.

With my eyes closed, I try to contact Dixie telepathically. It's almost the silliest thing I've ever done, but with all the talk of communication with the other side, I give it a shot. I even try to communicate with Major Ransom, hoping she can get a message to Dixie. *That's* the silliest thing I've ever done.

Time to stop trying silly things and start taking action. After backing up several steps, I reach down and grab a good-sized rock. Looking left, right, then straight ahead, I throw the rock at the window. It bounces off. I pick up another rock and throw it harder. It bounces off faster, ricochets back at me, and makes me jump. The windows are thick, probably bulletproof panes of glass. This house is an unsolvable puzzle.

Running around to the front, I attack the door again with both fists. The lady across the street opens her door, and I high tail it out of there to avoid a confrontation. It doesn't take me long to sprint down the street and hide in one of the parks we'd driven by earlier. The sun settles behind the Spring Mountains, and I wait for a while before returning to the house. I have no choice but to find a comfortable hiding place in the backyard and dig in for the night ahead.

Funny how time races by when it's spent doing something enjoyable; like the night I spent with Dixie. Tonight, however, will crawl by like a bug. I sit in the backyard, never moving, never closing my eyes; listening, watching, waiting until the stars come, then go—and *that* takes forever.

The lady across the street is up early, watering her front lawn with a garden hose. Groups of children lugging heavy backpacks hurry down the sidewalk, probably on their way to school. Overhead, a jet cuts through the clear, blue skies leaving white smoke lines in its wake. Everything is as it should be, another peaceful day in The Lakes except for the Daemon house holding its dark secrets—holding Dixie prisoner.

I sneak back to the front of the house, planning to try one more assault on the main entrance. Assuming it'll take the lady across the street a minute or two to get through to the police and five more minutes for them to respond, I have six, maybe seven, minutes of noise to make.

Thanks to Colonel Dayton, I've already formulated another plan in case this one fails. The back-up plan makes me nervous, but at least I have a Plan B. In my best imaginary British voice, I say, "There's always a Plan B."

I pick up another rock and pound on the windows. After stepping back a few paces, I throw the rock, full force, against the stubborn door and shout, "Dixie." No answer. "I know you're in there." Nothing but silence.

The lady across the street appears, phone in hand. "Yes, that same man is back. He's trying to break in. Please hurry."

Time for Plan B.

The keys are indeed in Dixie's car. My heart races as I turn the ignition and hit the gas. The car doesn't move. What am I doing wrong? That's right! I have to put it into Drive. I pull the shifter-stick-thing, but the car doesn't move. With a glance across the street at the lady in full voice, I step on the brake pedal and try the stick again. This time it slides into D and the car lurches forward. The engine dies. I turn the key again, but it won't start.

I have to calm down. I've seen people drive before and know what pedals they step on to go and stop, but there are so many knobs and buttons and levers and switches and gadgets and gizmos. I should have paid closer attention. *How do they do it?*

I push the shifter back into P and turn the key again. With my foot on the brake, I pull the shifter into D, and press down on the gas pedal. The car moves forward. My hands grip the steering wheel so hard it makes me think more of my fear than what I'm doing. I definitely have to calm down, so I take a deep breath and turn the wheel, pushing down the gas pedal a little harder. The speedometer needle climbs, reading about twenty miles an hour. It feels like flying. When I get to the corner, I spin the wheel to the right. My hand touches a lever and the windshield wipers scratch against the window. I'm too busy trying not to crash to worry about how that happened.

There's a red stop light up ahead, and I've got to do something quick. I mash on the brakes and the car stops, lurching me forward in my seat. The car dies about a hundred yards from the intersection and somebody honks a horn behind me. I turn the key and hit the gas, then stomp on the brakes. Another honk. It's going to be a long road trip to Aunt Rose's house.

Chapter Thirteen

Clouds of blue mist faded as Gorgeous materialized. She glanced about the cavernous room, nodding a silent approval of the décor. Her flowing white gown stood in sharp contrast to the murky walls surrounding the chamber. She turned toward the sound of water trickling down a large wall made of glass. The water illuminated by the glow of a fire pit behind the glass.

"Cinnamon and roses, what a delightful aroma." His voice, soft and sweet like music, drifted across the room.

Gorgeous stepped toward a plush armchair near the wall of water. The speaker, The Mystic, faced the wall, his back to her. She tried penetrating his thoughts, but they were blocked. He couldn't be human; she could always penetrate their frail minds. He seemed to know who she was by her scent. If that were true, if he knew her identity, he kept quite calm about it. "There's no fear in your voice."

"Fear," he said smoothly, "what is fear?"

Gorgeous glided next to The Mystic and stared down at him. He looked smaller than she imagined. Maybe the black robe he wore had something to do with that. His hands were pressed together under his chin, as if in meditation or worse yet, prayer. He sat in lotus position, barefoot, and relaxed. He did not return her gaze. She raised her voice, "Fear: defined as an apprehension; concern for what is not known."

At last, his gaze, gray and cold, turned up to her. "You quote Webster; one of my favorite books. Concern for what is not known. And how does Webster define that which is not known?" His voice remained smooth, even, and direct as he answered his own question. "The unknown: something not yet discovered. I believe the fear of what is yet to be discovered is a waste of time, a waste of energy, nothing more. One must simply not worry about the unknown. To paraphrase another one of my favorite books: an anxious heart weighs us down."

"Proverbs? I come to you for truth and you give me fairytales?"

"You did not come for truth."

Gorgeous scowled and stepped in front of The Mystic, blocking his view of the glass wall. She placed her hands on her hips, and cocked her head. "You don't even know who I am. You have no idea why I'm here."

"I do know you. You've come for my advice." He waved to the chair next to him. "Please, sit down and make yourself comfortable."

Gorgeous took a deep breath, exhaling slowly. The Mystic was too patient with her, too calm; the virtues of a Saint—she had no use for Saints. Still, she stood by the adjoining armchair and collected herself, deciding to change tact. "I like the *feng shui* in this room; a sort of modern medieval isn't it? It's quiet and dark, reminds me of a cave."

The Mystic bowed his head. "It reminds me of a church."

"Bah." She kicked off her white sandals and sat

down, mimicking his lotus position. The Mystic reached down and turned her sandals over, making sure their soles lay flat on the floor.

She chuckled. "I see you adhere to the old superstitions."

"Souls must always be prepared."

With a glare, she said, "Enough word play. They say The Mystic knows all."

"Indeed."

His calm unnerved her. She'd tried being nice, but nice didn't cut it with him. "Listen to me. I don't know who or what you are, but I've had you watched. The things you say during your *act*—how can you possibly know all those things? Are you a wizard? A prophet?"

He smiled. "A prophet of God?"

"Is that what you are?"

"You know," he said, tapping his fingers together, "a new school of thought has recently emerged regarding the Creator."

Gorgeous gave him the rope. "Why don't you enlighten me?"

"Very well. Some believe the Creator was created by the humans, not the other way around."

"Atheists, agnostics."

"I think not." He took in a deep breath. "Since the beginning, man's predisposition has always been to believe in a higher power, a divine being if you will. This natural instinct soon manifested into chants and simple appeals, eventually prayer. As the human race evolved, billions upon billions of prayers ascended into the ether, forming a tangible repository of hope, love, and eternal life." The Mystic smiled. "Voilà: God."

"Nonsense." Gorgeous stood and slipped on her

sandals. "If humans created God, then who created us?"

"Ah, excellent question. Humans think in very narrow terms, don't you find? Attempting to explain what they can't possibly understand." The Mystic laughed—a short snicker with a dazzling smile. "Humanity has always positioned itself at the center of the universe, and one must consider the question: without evil, then what is good?"

Her mask, the constant grin, faded just a bit before returning with a vengeance. "You're nothing but a senile old man. Worthless human fears did not create me. Bah. This is pointless. I came to you for answers and you give me vomit." She spun and marched away.

His voice trailed after her, "You want to know if you will succeed."

She stopped, silent as a ghost.

"You want to know if you'll receive praise."

She turned, gliding back to the armchair.

"You want to know if you'll be punished."

She sat down. Who *was* this man? He seemed to know her every thought as it popped into her mind. She'd heard so much about him. Was it all true?

"Praise and punishment," he said. "Success and failure, they're all the same."

"How can they all be the same thing? I don't understand."

"Point of view. One man's dream is another's nightmare."

"Stop talking rubbish. I don't want to hear definitions from Webster or fairytales from The Bible or theories about humans, for Hell's sake. Tell me, in plain English, what you mean."

The Mystic smiled. "Very well then, how about a

story? I love stories, don't you?" He continued, not waiting for an answer, "There was a remote village where the people lived mainly on rice and fish. One day a stranger arrived, promising a better world for the villagers: medicine, technology, progress. He built hospitals, modern houses, and office complexes over the rice fields. The construction polluted the stream. No more rice, no more fish. Soon, the people died of famine. Was the man successful?"

Gorgeous snickered. "That's an outrageous comparison. I'm talking about real change and lasting peace."

"Peace for whom? You?"

"Of course for me—and my kind."

"Then you will be successful, and you will be praised—by your kind."

The fire in the pit flared up, producing an amber glow. The sheets of water cascading down the glass wall projected shimmering images throughout the chamber.

"I don't know why I came here in the first place." She stood. "You talk a good game, Mystic. Well, I play a better one. I don't know what you are: Human, Daemon, Devil, or Saint, and I don't care. But when the time comes, and it will come, you'd better be on the right side."

"That is a time I do not fear. Right and wrong are the same."

"Bah. You'll soon learn what true fear is."

"And so, we come to the truth."

"What do you mean by that?"

"We've already concluded fear is a wasted emotion. One cannot lead by fear. I am tempted to quote the saying 'more flies are caught with honey than with vinegar,' but you seem to have a distaste for The Book of Proverbs."

"That's not from Proverbs."

"Ah, you truly do know your Bible. Perhaps, then, something from The Quran, or Tao Te Ching, or—"

"Enough. You've made your point." At last, the man, or whatever he was, had given her a smidgen of sound advice. "Leading by fear is all I've ever known. However, at your urging, I will try another approach. There's someone else I must visit today; someone who might respond more favorably to pleasure than pain." He'd known enough of the latter from his father.

The blue mist enveloped her, and she vanished.

****

Pounding echoed in Maxwell's brain, not from the inside—from somewhere else. He moaned and rolled over. The thumping continued as his eyelids opened. His surroundings appeared through a booze-colored fog: the dump at The Wild Joker. He tried to put the past few hours into focus, but gave up. The memory had something to do with the bottle of bourbon he killed before passing out.

Another knock on the door rattled him, this time followed by a soft, feminine voice, "Maxwell."

Gorgeous. He squinted, glancing at the clock on the nightstand. The red digits blinked 12:00, as they had since he checked-in—like they, no doubt, always would. Dim yellow light penetrated the skeletal remains of the so-called window curtains suggesting either early morning or late afternoon, he didn't care which. The room tilted a few degrees when he crawled out of bed and stumbled to the door.

Her presence here, far from their usual tribal-ground meeting place, meant only one thing: she'd come for her pound of flesh for yesterday's debacle.

"Coming, my sweet," he growled through parched lips. He cracked open the door and his hand flew up, shielding his face from the brightness.

Gorgeous's gaze ran down his unclothed frame, lingering a few moments below his waist. She strode inside wearing a salacious smile. "Well, well, well, very nice; a pound of flesh you say?"

Maxwell shut the door and faced her, his hands clasped strategically in front of him.

"You're going to need more than two hands to cover that up, but then, why would you ever want to?"

He lifted his arms, put his hands on his hips, and grinned. The thought of having Gorgeous sometimes crossed his mind—more than a few times. "Are we mixing business with pleasure now?"

Her gaze moved down again. "You're tempting me—a family trait, no doubt." Her grin widened. "Do you realize how old I am?"

Despite a wicked hangover, he felt the welcome tingles of excitement. "I prefer the word experienced, don't you?"

She glided toward him, reached out her hand, and took hold. "This may be more than even I can handle."

"You'll never know until we—Christ! Let go."

She tightened her grip and pulled down. He bent at the knees, trying to ease the pain. Her smile grew when she released him. "I thought you liked it rough."

"Fuck you."

"Perhaps later, my love. For now, why don't you pop into the shower? You stink."

He marched past her into the bathroom, turned on the water, and slipped under the cold stream. With his voice straining above the deluge, he asked, "Why are you here?"

"I merely wanted to thank you for a job well done last night, that's all."

A compliment? She was up to something.

"I want you to know I trust you."

"What's that supposed to mean?"

"Look, I know the Hell you've been through in your life."

"Very funny."

"What I'm getting at is this. We're so close to achieving our goal, in large part thanks to you. I just want to make sure you know your hard work is appreciated."

No threats? "What's the catch?"

"Ha. At one time, you were all powerful, doing as you pleased, sitting at his left hand, until you angered him. He couldn't stand the sight of you; the main reason he agreed to loan out your services. But if you continue to do as I say, if my plan is successful, you may yet gain favor in his eyes."

"Point taken." Maxwell shut off the water. True, dear old dad entrusted the services of his only begotten son to Gorgeous. Also true, he'd consented to serve her, a legally binding agreement. For whatever reason, though, she offered him another chance. Oh well, gift-horses, mouths, and all that. He cleared his throat, "I acknowledge your power and willingly accept your rule."

"Oh my," Gorgeous said, "using the formal oath? How impressive. Your father will be so very proud."

"My father be damned—I may as well be a bastard. My allegiance is to you."

"Very well, then. I have much to do, and your allegiance is accepted."

"One question first," he said as he put his hands on the sink and glanced at his reflection in the mist-covered mirror. "The humans are nothing more than a nuisance to my father, something he can't rule, so it bugs him—that's all. Why are they so damned important to you?"

"Because we were first. God had no right replacing us with the abomination of man."

"Obsess much?" Maxwell mumbled. He wrapped a towel around his waist and combed his hair. "So how do I, killing a few dogs, play into all of this?"

"It keeps the good little Daemons busy and out of my hair."

"So I'm just a diversion?"

When no answer came, Maxwell stormed out of the bathroom and into the empty bedroom. Gorgeous had vanished, a blue mist dissipating in her wake.

"Fucking bitch. What do you want me to do, bow in your presence?" Maxwell bent over in a low, respectful bow—and farted. "I honor your grace from the bottom of my bowels."

When he straightened, his eyes widened. The treasures on the sullied pillow lifted his spirit: car keys, a room card reading "Wynn," and a large stack of hundred dollar chips.

"Forgive me, my queen." He waved his hand over his nose. "The gas was nothing more than a little tomfoolery to lighten the mood. I see now just how much of an ass I've truly been. You can surely count on me. I won't let you down."

He threw the towel to the floor and jumped into his crumpled clothes from the day before, their foul odors attacking his nose. Like a beggar picking at scraps, he scooped up the gifts from the pillow, stuffed them into his pockets, and began to whistle. With a final glance back at the horrid accommodations, he flung open the door and grinned.

A midnight blue Ferrari 458 beckoned. He jumped behind the wheel and started the engine. He shivered at the sound of its power. Recently buried instincts told him to gun the engine and roar out of the parking lot, but remembering his promise, he pulled onto Fremont Street like a nun with a secret.

Turning left onto Las Vegas Boulevard, he grinned. Keeping a vehicle like this at the posted speed limit was a crime. He pressed the gas pedal down. When he spied the red and blue lights in his rearview mirror, he winced. "Shit."

He pulled over, slipped the smooth stick into park, and shut off the engine, exactly six blocks from the Wild Joker Motel.

"Afternoon," the Metro patrolman said as he approached the driver's side.

"Good afternoon, sir." Maxwell looked into the officer's reflective sunglasses and smiled a sheepish grin.

"Do you know why I pulled you over?"

Maxwell had no intention of returning to the rattrap he'd just vacated. He used his best apologetic voice, a voice he seldom employed. "Going a little too fast? I am so sorry."

"That's right. This car was built for speed, but not

on this street. Keep it low and slow."

"As you wish."

"Let's see your license, registration, and proof of insurance."

Damn. He reached into the glovebox, hoping Gorgeous had seen to the little details. He grinned as he pulled the documents from the box and handed them to the officer.

"Richard Pate," the officer read, "from Perdition, Indiana, huh? Bet it don't get as hot there as it does here."

"Oh, you'd be surprised."

The officer handed back the documents. "I'm gonna let you off with a warning, Mr. Pate. Remember now, low and slow."

The patrolman returned to his motorcycle. He pulled up alongside Maxwell's open window and yelled over the rumble of the engine, "Sometimes we give the tourists a free pass. You have a safe visit." He kicked the bike into gear and roared away.

Maxwell glanced at the driver's license. "Richard Pate?" He chuckled as the obvious synonym dawned. "Dick Head."

Chapter Fourteen

The amazing aroma of freshly baked bread fills me with happy and familiar thoughts. Aunt Rose always seems to have something incredible cooking in the kitchen. It doesn't matter the time of day; the sweet-smelling scent is always...wait. My thoughts scatter like roaches caught in a light. I force my eyes open. I'm in Dixie's bedroom, lying on the bed we shared just a day ago—was it one day, or two? Pounding in my head makes me reach up and feel for the source of the pain: a large bump square between my eyes. The pain is genuine, sharp, and relentless. Everything else is blurry.

Somebody touches my arm. "Welcome back. Take it easy." Marco Ramirez sits on the bed next to me, his eyes staring straight into mine. "You took quite a knock."

With his assistance, I manage to sit up, my back propped against the headboard. It takes a few moments for the room to stop spinning. "What happened? How did I get here?"

He laughs. Why would he laugh? "Next time, you might want to buckle up nice and tight before you decide to let a palm tree stop the car for you. I'm surprised you drove all the way across town by yourself without—"

"Dixie's in trouble." A flood of memories crowds my head and dread grabs me by the throat. I try to stand up, but feel dizzy, and plop back down on the pillow. Squiggly lines of white light race across my eyes like little Tasers. I yell out, "We've got to go back to The Lakes and get Dixie."

"Whoa, take it easy." He pats my shoulder. "Everything's okay, just try to relax."

"Relax?" I use what little strength I have to throw my legs over the side of the bed. Marco grabs me around the chest and helps me stand. Without his support, I'd fall right over onto the carpet face first. "Dixie's being held prisoner. I tried to get her out, but that house was under some kind of spell or something. We gotta go back right now—"

"Did I hear my name?" Dixie hurries into the room and throws her arms around me. Marco steps out of the way, and Dixie and I stumble back onto the bed. She sits up and smiles. "What made you think you could drive? You know you don't know how to drive." Her face is happy, but her words scolding. "I was worried sick about you. I wanted to take you to the hospital, but Marco insisted you were okay. So did Aunt Rose."

Marco sits back down on the bed, patting my arm again. "You took a nasty knock from the steering wheel when you clobbered that tree. I didn't think it the wisest move to take you to the hospital, too many questions." He glances at his watch. "In any case, it's getting late, and I've got to make an appearance down at the station. They probably think I quit."

My memories are like a jigsaw puzzle, minus a few pieces. "How did I get here? Somebody tell me what happened."

Dixie puts her hand on my forehead, on the epicenter of my pain, and I wince. "Sorry." She props up my pillow and moves her hand to my chest. "I know you did your best to get me out of that house. I can only guess, in the end, you figured you'd drive my car back here to get help."

"I drove your car?"

"Not only drove it," Marco says as he puts on his coat and straightens his tie, "you totaled it. But then it doesn't take much of a hit to total cars nowadays; they're basically made of sheet metal, plastic, and rubber. The main thing is you're okay."

"Thank goodness my palm tree survived." Aunt Rose appears and puts a glass of water in my hand. She reaches into her pocket, bringing out two little white pills. "Take some ibuprofen and keep still. You really should get some rest; for a bang on the noggin, that's really the best."

I pop the pills into my mouth and gulp down the cold water.

Dixie rubs my chest before she slips out of bed. "You get some sleep. I'll check on you in a little while. Promise."

"But what about Colonel Dayton? What about Cutty?"

"What do you mean what about us?" Glancing toward the sound of the voice, I smile at the sight of Colonel Dayton and Cutty standing by the door. Cutty laughs. "Get some shuteye; you'll be good to go after some sleep. Man, you should see that car—it's a total mess." Yuk-yuk-yuk.

I prop up on my elbows, my head banging like a kettledrum. "I don't understand. The last I heard, you two were dead."

"Hardly," Colonel Dayton says. "C'mon, old boy,

lie down. You've hit your head pretty hard, but don't go making a meal of it. We're fine."

"I wish I could say the same for my contact," Aunt Rose says. "Oh well, I'm sure I'll hear from her soon."

"Get some rest," Marco says with a wave of his hand, "I'll see you tomorrow."

Once again, Dixie eases me down on the pillow, this time curling up next to me, warm and soft. "This room is too crowded. Everybody out. I'll make sure he gets some rest." She takes a wet washcloth from the nightstand and drapes it over my forehead. "Go on, now. All of you—out."

Footsteps shuffle across the carpet, and the door eases shut with a soft click. The room is dark, and the washcloth soothing. I close my eyes, feeling Dixie's warm touch on my chest. My head is heavy and my breathing soon falls into an even rhythm. Now that I know where I am, and Dixie, the colonel, and Cutty are safe, I can truly relax. When I speak, my voice is small, almost like talking to myself. "They all looked so worried."

"Of course they're worried about you, silly," Dixie whispers. "They're your friends, they care about you."

I manage a short laugh. "I've never had friends before."

She rubs my shoulder. "Well, you do now."

"I'm sorry about crashing your car."

"No, I'm the one who should apologize. I didn't know The Sufferings would take so long. I already scolded Aunt Rose. She should've warned us what to expect, but she said it's different for each individual."

Did I say something? Did I answer? The bed is soft and inviting, and Dixie feels good beside me. The hammering in my head eases. "How long have I been here? I don't remember—"

"Shhh, go to sleep."

The bed jostles as she settles next to me. Her breathing drops into a soft pattern in line with mine. From now on, this is how I want to end every day of my life—minus the headache, of course.

****

Dixie crawled out of bed just after midnight, making sure not to disturb the mattress and comforter. She paused, listening to Adam breathe—an even rhythm, calm and serene—then slipped out of the bedroom and wandered down the hallway toward a light shining from the kitchen. Aunt Rose sat at the table, her head propped in her hands.

The hypnotic aroma of freshly baked bread lured Dixie to the table. "Sourdough?"

Aunt Rose glanced up and smiled. "No, not quite. It's just white. How's he doing?"

"He's sleeping. I feel so bad. He has no idea what's going on, and it's all my fault. Now, he has a concussion."

"He took a hard knock, but his head's as hard as a rock. I'm sure he'll be quite all right by morning light."

"How can you be so certain?"

"You can tell as well." Aunt Rose motioned for Dixie to sit down. She reached across the table, covering Dixie's hands with hers. "Close your eyes and think about Adam. Truly concentrate on everything about him. Run your thoughts across his body, around his mind, and deep into his heart. You know how to do this; you learned during The Sufferings. Relax your breathing. Now, tell me what you see."

Dixie did as told. She visualized Adam, his dark eyes and boyish smile, chiseled frame and ruddy complexion. As her thoughts focused, she set aside his physical form and entered his mind. His thoughts were calm, no doubt because he was asleep, but active and dreaming. His heart beat to a perfectly timed rhythm, strong and sure. Pain coursed through his body, but it was a fleeting tenderness and promised to heal quickly. "I feel him, Aunt Rose," Dixie said, her eyes still shut tight, her lips smiling. "He's going to be fine, just like you said."

"Well done, my dear. Affinity is a skill of The Sufferings, difficult to master, but you picked it up, just like that. I'm so proud of you."

Dixie straightened up and gazed at Aunt Rose. "I wish you would have told me."

"About The Sufferings?"

"About everything: The Sufferings, being a Daemon…about The Pit."

"The Pit?" Aunt Rose ran her eyes across Dixie's face. "Why do you ask about The Pit?"

"Charlie Nguyen. She said I should ask you."

Aunt Rose sighed, rubbed a trembling hand across her brow, and closed her eyes. "The knowledge has been passed to you during The Sufferings. You know all about—"

"I want *you* to tell me. I want to hear it from you."

After a long pause, Aunt Rose opened her eyes then waited a bit longer as the grandfather clock in the entrance hallway struck the hour. "In the beginning, the Lake of Fire at the bottom of The Pit held all Daemon souls. Satan alone possessed the key to freedom. The only escape was to join The Legion, which every

Daemon did, of course. I mean, The Lake of Fire, or freedom, not much of a choice. After achieving freedom, and after hundreds of years, Daemons formed two groups: those who followed Satan, and those who did not."

"And you, do you follow Satan?"

Aunt Rose blushed. "Certainly not, how can you think such a thing?"

"I'm sorry, I just thought—"

"Be quiet and listen. Those who broke away from The Legion, over time, aligned with human design. We lost eternal life, and the ability to visit the other side."

Dixie's eyes widened. "But we gained something in exchange, right?"

"Oh my dear, we gained so much. The ability to bear children, to raise families—"

"And to love."

A large china plate materialized in front of them filled with slices of freshly baked bread.

"Have some, my dear. You'll feel better."

"I don't feel like eating anything."

"No? I find a little something before sleep is good for the body; good for the soul."

Dixie picked up a slice, still warm from the oven or wherever it came from—she glanced over Aunt Rose's shoulder and saw the "bake" light off. She took a bite. It tasted like Christmas morning.

"Now then," Aunt Rose said, "you've learned so much in the past two days—everything, really. Practice it, use it, make it part of your daily life. The better you get at using what you now know the more power you'll have over the evils, the more at peace you'll be with yourself."

"But I am at peace. What makes you think I'm not?"

Aunt Rose gave her *the look.* "I've known you your whole life, Dixie Mulholland. You've always been driven, searching for something, examining, exploring. Now you know what it was. Don't be apprehensive about being a Daemon. Enjoy it."

Dixie took another bite of bread. "You're right. I am apprehensive, but not about what I am. I'm worried about telling Adam what we have in mind. He'll feel betrayed."

"Don't be concerned. Use what you've learned." Aunt Rose beamed. "Explain it to him using the powers you now have."

"You mean a spell? No. I'm not going to make him do anything he doesn't want to do. I'm simply going to tell him the plan, and hope he makes the right decision. It's up to him."

"Fair warning, my dear, Adam may not accept his role in our plan."

"Why do you say that?"

"What I'm saying is he doesn't reason like a typical human because he's not. He's not fully human, nor is he fully canine."

Dixie took another bite of bread. "You lost me. What the hell are you saying?"

"Language, my dear." Aunt Rose stood up. "What I mean is he may be a combination of all three."

"All three? You said, not fully human, and not fully canine. What else is there?"

"Daemon...but not fully." Aunt Rose trundled to the refrigerator and grabbed a butter dish. She placed it on the table and took a knife from the silverware drawer. "Here, my sweet. Everything tastes better with butter."

"Tell me what you mean."

"Well, when the bread is warm, the butter soaks right in and—"

"No. Forget about the bread." Dixie tossed the slice back onto the plate. "Forget the butter, too. Tell me what you mean about Adam."

Aunt Rose sat down. "He and his kind were created by spell, a Daemonic spell. When spells are cast, traces remain. He was born a Giant Irish Wolfhound with the ability to transform into a human, but behind it all, there lies the residue, the slightest creational hint, of a Daemon. You know this; you've known since The Sufferings."

Dixie did know, deep down inside, but convinced herself otherwise. Her eyes misted over. All Adam ever wanted was to leave his canine ways behind and live as a normal human being. Should she tell him he might also be part Daemon?

"No, my dear," Aunt Rose said, invading Dixie's thoughts. "He needs to live his life as he sees fit. Why confuse the boy with speculation? It is, after all, only a slight possibility." She buttered a slice of bread and offered it to Dixie. "Here, you'll like it."

"I'm not hungry."

"No, you're angry."

"Of course I am. All the plans, the hopes Adam has, may not be possible."

Light footsteps sounded from the hallway. "Why?" Adam said, pacing slowly into the kitchen while yawning, his plaid robe tied snug around his body. "Why isn't it possible?"

Chapter Fifteen

"Come. Sit down, my boy and I'll tell you all about our little plan."

"No, Aunt Rose. You can't tell him just like that. It will—"

"Hush. He's a big boy, he can take it."

I'm a little shocked, but certainly relieved somebody has finally decided to tell me the reason everyone's been tiptoeing around. In a way, I'm glad it's Aunt Rose. She has a way of explaining things so they make sense—not perfect sense as in logical, orderly, and valid, but common sense as in understandable, clear, and sound. I pull out a chair and sit at the table next to Dixie. My hand closes over hers.

"Here," Aunt Rose says, pushing a plate of bread in front of me. "Take a slice. It's nice and hot, straight from the oven. Try it with butter."

"I'm not hungry."

She shakes her head. "Doesn't anybody eat anymore? Ah well, maybe it's just another lost art, like reading books, or owning encyclopedias—"

"Aunt Rose," I say in a quiet voice. "The plan?" I grab a slice of bread, swab it with butter, and take a bite. This seems to make her feel better.

"Ah yes, the plan. Every night for the past four, a survivor on Claremont has been killed by gunshot. This is no random act. Somebody is murdering the Giant

145

Irish Wolfhounds one by one. I've done my best to keep an eye over them, so has Colonel Dayton and Cutty, but to no avail. It's time we get to the bottom of this. Now, it's up to you. You, my boy, must take up residence on Claremont."

I almost choke on the bread. "Live on Claremont? Why?"

"We need somebody—we need *you* on the inside. Don't worry. You won't be alone. Charlie Nguyen will accompany you."

"Oh, that makes me feel better."

"Absolutely, my boy. She can communicate with me."

First of all, I have no intention of living with the wolfhounds. Second, I wouldn't trust Charlie Nguyen with my socks. This isn't a plan; it's a joke. And I tell both Dixie and Aunt Rose exactly that. "Where did you come up with this hair-brained scheme anyway?"

"Major Ransom," Dixie says. "It's her plan. I agree with you, it doesn't sound very workable. I've tried to tell her, but—"

"Major Ransom came up with this nonsense?" I turn to Dixie and take her other hand. "How do you know you can even trust her? How do you know she's even real?"

"She is real." Dixie squeezes my hands. "Something is luring the wolfhounds to their death, and she says you are the logical choice to find out who it is so we can stop it. I know the plan doesn't sound very—"

"Sane? Rational?" I stand up, feel a bit dizzy, and sit right back down again.

"Are you okay, my boy?"

146

"Fine. Just a little woozy. Can I get a glass of water?"

"Of course." Aunt Rose grabs a glass from the cupboard and shuffles to the kitchen sink.

I turn to Dixie and whisper, "Is this why you got me out of prison?"

"No. Yes. I don't know. Listen, I had no idea where you were. I didn't even know if you were alive or dead. Major Ransom told me all about your plight. She suggested Colonel Dayton break you out."

"So I can live with the wolfhounds?"

"Not just live with them, but help save their lives." Dixie's voice grows louder, as if trying to convince herself of the plan. "I felt the same way when Major Ransom told me, but now it makes sense. We don't need eyes on the packs; we need eyes *in* the packs. You're the only one who can see the world through their eyes. Somebody on that hill must know something, but is afraid to come forward."

"Or afraid to be found out."

"Exactly," Aunt Rose says. "The murderer could be one of them. You and Charlie Nguyen will join the survivors on Claremont, find out what's going on, report back to me, and I'll catch the culprit."

"Just like that?"

"Easy-peezy."

If Aunt Rose can't even catch my sarcasm, how is she ever going to catch the culprit? "Why Charlie Nguyen?"

"For whatever reason, I seem to have a strong connection with her mind; yours, not so much. She'll be your direct link to me."

"I don't like it. Nothing about it feels right. First,

I'm not a spy or a detective. Second, I don't even know where to begin. I mean what do I do? Walk up to each one of them and say, 'Excuse me, you don't know me, but can you tell me if you've killed anyone today?' No. This is a bad plan, and you've got the wrong guy."

"You don't need to be a spy. We've got one: Colonel Dayton," Aunt Rose says.

"And we've got a detective as well," Dixie chimes in. "But they can't be what you are—"

"And what's that?"

"A canine." Dixie is quiet for a moment, as if listening to something outside. All at once, she snickers.

"What's so funny?"

"Major Ransom wants to know if you see the irony in all this."

"Tell her, no, but I see the insanity of it."

"We first met because you thought Giant Irish Wolfhounds were hunting humans. Now, the wolfhounds are being hunted…ironic."

"Yeah, tell her good observation, but count me out."

Aunt Rose stares at me. "This is not something you can walk away from, and you know it. I see it in your heart. If you turn your back on us, you will never forgive yourself. Knowing you had the chance to stop a tragedy, but did nothing, is not in you. You must help us; if not for the sake of the wolfhounds, then for the sake of your own peace of mind."

Her speech hits the bullseye. Even though I don't want any part of this plan, it's something I have to do. She's right; I would never forgive myself if I walked away.

****

Slivers of light snake in through the kitchen window, crawling across the linoleum floor like the fingers of an invisible creature. I watch the fingers inch toward the table. A quick glance at the clock confirms 6 a.m. Dawn in downtown Las Vegas.

Dixie's gone to lie down before the others come over to discuss the logistics of the plan. I stay seated at the kitchen table facing Aunt Rose; the same chair I've occupied all night. We've been small talking ever since Dixie traipsed off to the bedroom about thirty minutes ago.

I can't explain why, but I feel comfortable being with Aunt Rose in her house; in her kitchen surrounded by all her things, the aroma of fresh baked goods filling the air. It's like I can talk to her about anything, and she'll listen—really listen—and not judge me or advise me or dismiss me. It's like we share some kind of a connection I can't explain. It feels so good to be accepted by someone this way.

The morning birds begin their chorus of chirps and whistles just outside the window in the backyard. The world is peaceful and calm. I speak to Aunt Rose, informally, like I'm sharing time with an old friend, "Dixie told me you've been looking for my sister. She said they never found her body at Claremont the night before the Convergence."

"That's true. The next night...well, that's a different story. They found dozens of wolfhounds, and dozens of humans, too. It was all quite a mess. But the night before, the night Marco was called out to the house, the only thing they found even close to canine were paw prints in the backyard. I'm certain your sister did not die that night. I wish I had as strong a connection to her as I did your brother, Ivan. In any case, it only makes sense she escaped the house alive. I'm certain of it. I feel it here, in my heart."

My optimism is not as strong. I recall Lucy and Bane fighting that night, and the awful yip Dixie and I heard as we drove away. I am positive Bane killed her.

"You mustn't think negatively, my boy. We Daemons have a saying: the universe rewards optimism."

Maybe she's right. "Another reason for me to follow your plan and snoop around Claremont. Maybe I can find a clue that'll lead me to her."

"That's the spirit." She places her glasses on the table and rubs her eyes.

"Are you tired?"

"No. I don't sleep much these days. Getting old, I suppose." She picks up the plate of bread and carries it to the counter. Even though we munched on the delicious white bread all night long, the plate looks full, as if it hadn't been touched at all. She turns around and smiles, her eyes lighting up in a bright glow. "Do you want some toast?"

"No thanks, I'm stuffed to the gills." It's a lie. I'd eaten my share of the bread, maybe more than my share—three, four slices at least, but I still had room for more.

"Nonsense." She puts four slices in the toaster and pushes the lever down. "Take a slice and don't forget the butter. Everything is better with butter. I've even got some strawberry jam in the fridge." She zips to the refrigerator, opens the door, and rummages around for a moment. "Aha, there you are, you rascal. You can't hide from me."

She returns to the table with a plate of toasted bread and a jar of strawberry jam. Before I know it, I'm slapping butter and jam on the hot toast and shoving it into my gullet. "Your food is like a drug, and I admit, I'm addicted."

"Are you two doing drugs in here?" Dixie eases into the kitchen and wraps her arms around me. She kisses the top of my head. "I shouldn't have left you alone with my aunt. She's corrupting you." Her white cotton robe is loosely tied at the waist. She's sleepy eyed, her blonde hair tousled in every direction. I'm aroused by her scent.

I pull the lapels of my robe snug around my chest, my gaze wandering away from Dixie, my mind trying to focus on anything but her. "Try this toast. It's amazing."

Dixie takes a bite of toast and jam as she settles into the chair next to me.

Aunt Rose grins. "Wait till you see what I've planned for lunch. Surprises in store for everyone."

Dixie grins. "I can't wait."

"Until then, I'm going to lie down for a little while. You were right, Adam. I am tired. Please be kind enough to wake me in an hour or so." Aunt Rose saunters down the hallway to her bedroom. "Don't bother about the dishes," she calls back to us, "I'll clean up later."

The bedroom door clicks shut, and I glance at the clock again. "It's only eight. They won't be here for another couple of hours. What do you think we should do until they—"

Her mouth is on mine, tasting like warm strawberry

jam. I lick the crumbs off her lips and run my hands around her waist. She trades her chair for my lap and sits down facing me, her legs straddling mine, her arms dangling over my shoulders. She giggles.

"What's so funny?"

"I was afraid you wouldn't be up for this because of the bump on your head. I was so wrong."

She bunches her robe up around her hips. The sun has crawled onto the table, melting the butter into a golden pool. I dip my fingers into the dish and run them across Dixie's lips.

"What are you doing?"

"I've heard everything is better with butter."

She reaches back and rubs an open hand in the melted puddle. Her palm caresses my face followed quickly by her tongue. "I've heard the same thing." She loosens her robe and runs a slippery hand across her breasts. "Let's find out."

The scent of her sex mixed with aromas of freshly baked bread and butter send me over the edge. Nothing in the world matters except the smell, taste, and touch of Dixie Mulholland. Butter covers our faces as we nuzzle. I gather her close, my body matching the rhythm of her movement. She opens her mouth and grips my shoulders in a silent scream. I follow her lead with a shudder, my feet braced on the floor, my calves tightening. For several moments, afterward we hang onto each other, panting in exhaustion.

She slips off my lap and collapses back onto her chair, smoothing her robe around her body. I readjust my robe and let out a measured breath, trying to regain a normal rhythm. Sweat, mingled with butter, drips down my face. Dixie swipes a finger across my cheek and slips it into her mouth. She grins. "Yum."

Our mouths press together in a slippery butter kiss.

"What's going on in here?"

We turn and face Aunt Rose.

She strolls to the middle of the room. "I forgot my glasses." She puts them on and inspects us like a detective looking for clues. "What have you got all over your faces?"

Chapter Sixteen

Dixie turned off the hair dryer and stood in front of the full-length mirror, examining herself from head to toe. In spite of all that had happened in the past two years, or more likely because of it, she was the happiest she'd ever been and it showed; content with whom she was, committed to helping the wolfhounds, and in love with Adam Steel. She picked a strand of hair from her shirt, tossed it to the floor, and joined the others in the living room.

Colonel Dayton sat on the couch next to Cutty. He stood as Dixie entered the room. Cutty nodded and gave her a big, toothy grin. Charlie Nguyen and Aunt Rose huddled in conversation near the rocking chair. Adam and Marco Ramirez both broke into smiles.

"Well," Aunt Rose addressed the group, "we're all here. Shall we proceed to the kitchen? Adam has been kind enough to help me prepare quite a feast for you all. I know it's really lunch time, but as some of you know, my favorite saying is: dinner is served." They filed into the kitchen where six places were set on the table, each plate loaded with a different item. "Please find your seat, it won't be difficult, it's what each of you commonly eat."

Colonel Dayton laughed. "Fish and chips. Really, Aunt Rose?" He glanced at the other plates on the table. "The selections are all a bit...xenophobic, wouldn't you say?"

"Racist is more like it," Charlie Nguyen mumbled.

Aunt Rose smiled. "I prefer the word diverse. Quickly now, find your seats."

Cutty settled into a chair behind a plate overflowing with hot dogs and French fries. He grabbed the bottle of ketchup and squirted it over both. Marco Ramirez eased into position behind a plate of burritos, beans, and rice. "Is that a glass of *horchata*?"

Aunt Rose nodded. "Homemade, I hope you like it."

Dixie spied a plate of pork chops and applesauce, her favorite, and claimed her place at the table. Aunt Rose pulled out a chair and sat down to a steaming chicken potpie.

Adam and Charlie Nguyen glanced at each other as she hurried around the table to a plate of noodles and egg rolls. That left the plate brimming with raw hamburger for Adam. He shook his head. "I don't remember helping you with *this*, Aunt Rose."

"My boy, you've got to get into the habit of changing, and changing quickly, in order to join the survivors on Claremont. This meal will help you do just that."

While the others sat down, he remained standing. "A grilled steak will do, or meatloaf with plenty of ketchup. Even beef stew might—"

"Sit down, please. You know fresh meat, red and raw, is the best diet for you now."

Adam eased into the chair, all the while glaring at the plate of meat.

"Aunt Rose," Dixie said, "how about a nice porterhouse for Adam? Or filet mignon? That would work equally as well, wouldn't it?"

"Of course," Aunt Rose said. "You're right, how thoughtless of me." The raw hamburger evaporated as if it were never there, replaced at once by a big, juicy steak, red and raw. "Now let's all eat up and discuss what needs doing.

"Colonel Dayton informed me another survivor was shot last night," Aunt Rose said. "Murdered. He and Cutty did their best to patrol the hill, but it's quite a task."

"I helped keep watch for a few hours as well," Ramirez said, "but like she said, there's just too much area for three men to cover."

"For three humans," Aunt Rose said. "But tonight will be different. We'll have three humans, two wolfhounds, and two Daemons on patrol." She turned to Adam. "You'll remain with the survivors during the day—getting to know them, that sort of thing—and we'll return again at sundown. Should anything happen during the day, just inform Charlie Nguyen, and she'll report to me.

"She will shape shift into a wolfhound and accompany you to Claremont. Colonel Dayton and Cutty will present you as two survivors they located. Of course, during the day, Nguyen must transform back into her normal skin. But then, the survivors often transform as they please from wolfhound to human, so there won't be any suspicion about her." She turned to Nguyen. "A word of caution, Nguyen. Remember the rules: shift for one day—shift for all days."

"What does that mean?" Adam asked.

"Why it's quite plain, my boy. If a Daemon takes another form for more than twenty-four hours, the form becomes permanent."

"I know, I know," Nguyen said. "Do you think I'm stupid? Who would want to be a dog for the rest of their life? They sniff poop and lick their own privates."

Adam grabbed her attention by lifting the steak up over his head, bringing it down to his mouth, and taking a bite. He chewed with purpose, swallowed, and raised his glass. "Well then, here's to sniffing poop."

Dixie choked back a laugh.

The mood in the room lightened a bit. Charlie Nguyen held an egg roll with her chopsticks and took a sip of green tea. Cutty had already devoured two hot dogs, his cheeks bulging. Ramirez showed little interest in his food as he pushed a burrito around his plate. Colonel Dayton took a sip of tepid beer and ignored his meal altogether.

Dixie cut a piece of pork chop, dipped it in applesauce, and gave Adam a quick smile before gobbling it down. In short order, the sound of knives and forks clinking against china plates filled the kitchen.

Aunt Rose stood, glass in hand. All eyes turned to her. "I would like to propose a toast." The others put their utensils down and raised their glasses. "To Adam Steel, who will soon risk life and limb to bring peace to the survivors. We all know what he will sacrifice. Adam, we thank you for your courage."

"What about me?" Charlie Nguyen said. "I'm going, too."

"Will you risk life and limb?"

"I'm going."

Aunt Rose raised her glass higher. "To Adam."

The others repeated her toast. "To Adam."

****

I feel like some kind of a celebrity, sitting at the head of the table with everyone toasting to my good health. I'm not, of course. I'm here for just one reason: I'm a human who happens to transform into a Giant Irish Wolfhound, and Major Ransom (from the other side) saw the viability of using me in an effort to stop the murders at Claremont. Nothing more, nothing less. At least the raw porterhouse tastes good, and fills me with more than simple nourishment. It gives me strength, confidence, and power.

"Adam," Aunt Rose says, "do you want to try a few transformations? From what I hear, you may be a bit out of practice. Two years is a long time."

"Aunt Rose," Dixie chides, "he'll be fine."

"No. I'm good. It's like riding a bike."

Aunt Rose turns to Charlie Nguyen. "What about you?"

"No. I've never ridden a bicycle, but I'm sure if he can do it, it's not that difficult."

I can't help myself. "You're so arrogant."

"Thank you," she says, as if it's a compliment.

"Okay, everybody, settle down." Aunt Rose clinks her glass with a fork. "Let's go over it one more time. We leave for Claremont soon, and I want everybody clear on their roles."

I place what's left of my steak back on the plate. "Colonel Dayton and Cutty will escort me and Nguyen to Claremont and introduce us as recently found survivors."

"That's correct. When they finish getting you two settled in, they'll meet Dixie and me at the bottom of the hill. They will patrol near the base, and Dixie and I will hover near the top. Dixie," she says, leaning over, "you are good with hovering, aren't you?"

"Well, never having done it before...sure. Why not?"

"That's the spirit. Now remember, I want everyone to be safe. I will stay in contact through Nguyen."

Marco, silent up until now, clears his throat. "And what do you suggest we do when we find the one responsible?"

"Why, a simple binding spell, of course."

We all look at each other. What the heck's binding?

"It's easy," Dixie says. "The subject is frozen, their memory erased, and they're transported to another city. Simple."

Marco lowers his brow. "You can do that?"

Aunt Rose giggles. "It's done all the time. You'd be surprised; a Daemon's version of catch and release."

"Aunt Rose, the lunch was great," Cutty says. "You got any dessert?"

"I think it's time we get on with it." Colonel Dayton scoots away from the table and puts his plate on the counter near the sink.

"Leave it, please." Aunt Rose stands up and smiles. "I'll take care of all the dishes. Please, all of you into the living room. I'll join you in a bit."

She puts a hand on Cutty's elbow, holding him back while the rest of us march into the living room and sit down. Before I leave the kitchen, I glance back. The table is already cleared of all dishes, glasses, and utensils. Aunt Rose hands Cutty a small plate: a piece of pumpkin pie smothered in whipped cream. Cutty's eyes gleam.

"Now then," Aunt Rose says, her hand on Cutty's back, easing him into the living room, "we all know what to do, so there's nothing left but to see it through."

Cutty wipes his sleeve over his mouth. "Nice rhyme, Rose."

"Thank you, my boy. I try. Now, be safe out there. When we get back tomorrow, I may have a reward for you."

His eyes light up. "More pie?"

"Even better."

Cutty is at the door in three large steps. He pulls it open. "What are we waiting for? Let's get this party started."

Colonel Dayton steps out followed by Marco and Aunt Rose. Charlie Nguyen parades past Dixie and I, giving me a sideways glance as she passes. "C'mon, boy, wanna go for a ride in the car? Your kind likes that sort of thing, don't you?"

Dixie puts her hand on my shoulder. "Don't listen to her. She just wants to get a rise out of you." She gives me a soft and warm embrace. "You be careful out there. When we get back tomorrow, *I* may have a reward for you."

I put my hands on her cheeks and give her a kiss. "Pie?"

"Even better."

We step out into the remains of the late afternoon. Dixie closes the door, grabs my hand, and we stroll toward the waiting SUV where Aunt Rose approaches us. "What could be better than pie?"

Dixie blushes. "You heard my thoughts?"

"I should have told you before," Aunt Rose whispers. "I've been able to read your mind clearly ever since you returned from The Sufferings. Butter, young lady? Really?"

Now it's my turn to blush. "Aunt Rose, it's my fault, I can explain—"

"No need." She gives us both a wry smile. "I was young once." She turns around. "I need a quick word with Nguyen. Now then," Aunt Rose leans into the backseat where Charlie Nguyen has settled in for the drive, "let me see you transform."

"What? Right here? In front of the whole neighborhood?"

"Yes. In the backseat of this car. No one will see anything. I want to be sure of your powers. Do you even know what a Giant Irish Wolfhound looks like? I don't want our plans to fall short because of a careless oversight."

"You have to be joking." Nguyen grins and raises her eyebrows. "Charlie Nguyen can do anything. Watch and be amazed."

Nguyen's eyes flash yellow and she dematerializes. In an instant, she rematerializes and stands on all fours in the backseat, gray and white fur covering her body. She barks and jumps out of the vehicle, pushing past Aunt Rose. She's obviously showing off.

She runs around the SUV, barking and snapping at the wind. She spins around on the front yard and goes back to take another lap around the vehicle. Cutty opens the driver's side door, and Nguyen smacks into it head first. We all rush into the street.

"Oh my God," Cutty says, "I'm so sorry. Is she all right?"

Nguyen lies in the street, unconscious.

"Well," Aunt Rose says, "that's that. We have to

postpone."

"Can't you fix her?" I say.

"I'd like nothing more than to have her fixed."

"We can't heal people," Dixie says. "We can do a lot of things: move objects, tele transport, cast spells—"

"But we can't *fix* stupid." Aunt Rose steps back, allowing Cutty and Colonel Dayton the room to lift Nguyen and carry her back to the house.

Marco grunts. "We can't just stand around and wait for her to wake up. If we do, another canine could die tonight."

"What do you suggest?" Aunt Rose waits for an answer.

"I'll take her place."

All eyes turn to Dixie.

I shake my head. "That's not the plan. We'd better wait for—"

"We can't," Dixie says. "Marco's right, we're out of time. If we don't go tonight, another wolfhound will die. Leave Nguyen here. I know what to do."

Chapter Seventeen

"Witnessing a double murder for the sake of art is quite entertaining," Gorgeous said, visiting Lucas in his small dressing room after the performance. "I must confess, however, I did hope for something a little different—more meaningful."

Lucas broke away from her gaze and turned toward the mirror. Keeping Gorgeous out of his thoughts took a tremendous amount of energy lately. He decided not to bother her with the Execution mix-up. After all, it was his mess to clean up, and he had. Funny, the audience seemed to enjoy the new ending to the katana illusion, the one where Gwendolyn did not reappear. *Humans are such bloodthirsty creatures.*

"Yes," she said, "the guillotine was a delightful addition to the performance—thank you for thinking of me."

He twirled around and faced her, steeling his thoughts against her constant probing. "I hope you enjoyed it, my queen."

"I already told you it was delightful, didn't I? Or is your mind on something else?" Gorgeous shifted her gaze to the wardrobe. She placed her hand on the latch.

"My queen, there's nothing on my mind."

Gorgeous pulled open the door. The katana gleamed from the corner of the closet. She stared at Lucas. "In any case, when you see your assistant—

Gwendolyn, is it?—be sure to tell her how much I enjoyed the performance." She reached into the closet and fondled the handle of the sword. "Especially the final act."

Did Gorgeous suspect something? "As you wish."

"Now if you'll excuse me, I have another performance to attend tonight, one which may hold a little more substance." With that, Gorgeous vaporized into a blue mist and disappeared.

"Bitch." Lucas snapped his fingers, and Gwendolyn materialized in a cloud of pink mist. The scent of cinnamon and roses faded at once, replaced by the sickening scent of cotton candy. She stood motionless in front of him as if fossilized. Her eyes focused on his every movement. A thin red line ran horizontal across her stomach.

"My dear, sweet Gwen. You've become quite the challenge. The two humans—that colonel and his young friend—have disappeared. I intended Gorgeous to witness their execution as a surprise from me, but it seems I'm the one surprised. Let's see, who recommended you to me? Ah yes, I remember. Miss Charlemagne Nguyen. It seems I, too, have another visit to make tonight."

Gwendolyn closed her eyes. A tear snaked down her cheek and fell to the carpet. Her breathing came in short, labored bursts. More tears.

Lucas ran his fingers along Gwendolyn's stomach, raised the hand to his mouth, and licked at the blood. "Quite the predicament you've found yourself in. Working with the other side against me. Why would you ever do that? To help the humans? Ha." He placed his hand in front of her face. "I could end you with one push of my little finger. You know I have the power to kill."

"You're sick," Gwendolyn's face contorted. "You will never win this war."

"A war? Is that what you think this is? No, sweet girl, this is something much more personal. Not to worry, though, the war will come." His eyes turned black as he placed a finger to her forehead. "You know, I would love to end you on stage this way, but the humans would call it murder. Ah well, tomato, tom-a-to." He thrust his finger forward. The top half of Gwendolyn's body toppled back, separating from the lower. Both halves collapsed to the ground.

He reached into the closet and drew out the katana. With a sure and steady hand, he dug the sword deep into her stomach, scooping out her bowels. He raised the sword and slashed down across her neck, a clean cut, severing her head. The scent of cotton candy faded from the room. Lucas reached into his pocket and brought out a lighter. Touching the fire to her costume, his assistant ignited in a rush of pink flame.

In an instant, Gwendolyn was gone.

Lucas straightened, slipping the lighter into his pocket. He grabbed tissues from the box on the dresser in front of the mirror, wiping clean the katana blade before placing it back into the wardrobe and closing the door.

His reflection in the mirror remained calm and cool. He opened the door to the hallway, letting the odors of burnt Daemon escape the confines of the small dressing room. Returning to the mirror, Lucas ran a hand across his hair, smiled, and straightened the lapels of his coat.

"Sebastian," he said. A moment passed. "Sebastian," he yelled.

Heavy footsteps clomped down the hallway and stopped at the open door. A large man clad in black stuck his head in. "Yes, sir?"

"It appears I have an opening for a new assistant, so spread the word. Gwendolyn had to leave us quite suddenly." He glanced down at the blackened outline burned into the light blue carpet. "And see about new rugs for my dressing room—something a bit darker."

****

Cutty navigates Claremont Drive at a steady speed, the wheels of the SUV digging deep into the crunchy gravel. A strong wind sends the pine trees into a sort of back and forth wiggle dance. Nobody says a word on the way up.

When Colonel Dayton brought me here a few days ago, I was apprehensive. Now I'm flat out nervous, another human emotion I can do without. I know what lives on this hill; I know who they are—what they are—which makes me think about what I am. In prison, I'd resigned myself to living out the rest of my natural life as a normal human being. Claremont Estates reminds me of the fact I don't have a natural life, and I'm anything but normal.

Tina and another man wait outside my old house at the top of the hill. She waves at us as Cutty parks and shuts off the engine. The other man wears a scowl and avoids eye contact. I don't trust him.

Cutty is first out of the SUV. He marches straight toward Tina and gives her a quick hug. Her face brightens and they stand together, shoulder to shoulder.

Colonel Dayton introduces Dixie and me as two

survivors found near downtown Las Vegas, like the countless others they've brought to Claremont. Because many of them have already met Dixie, she transformed into a Giant Irish Wolfhound on the way up the hill. Her gray and white coat is remarkable. She has little flecks of white in her beard, her eyes are wide and alert.

Marco Ramirez stays in the vehicle as Aunt Rose suggested. His face has not been seen at Claremont; no need to stir up any awkward questions. My face is a different story altogether.

"I'm glad you decided to give us another chance, Adam." Tina is nice. I like her. "And who is this with you? Such a splendid coat."

I give Aunt Rose an awkward glance. I know from her expression we made a mistake—we were in such a rush to get here after Nguyen passed out we forgot to invent a cover story for Dixie.

Aunt Rose wings it without missing a beat. "Her name is Jenny. She convinced Adam to give Claremont a second look. He trusts her."

That last part is the truth. My skin crawls as I glance at my old house. I have to fight the instinct to run off. Being here brings back so many awful memories. Getting as far away from this place was all I ever wanted. Glancing at the rundown house with its faded paint and chipped stucco brings back the same emotion.

"Why is she in canine form?" the scowling man says. He sniffs the air and grunts.

Tina offers a thin smile. "I'm sorry, this is Marques. He's always overly cautious of new arrivals."

I improvise and the words come quickly. "She's weak, and can't stand the pain of transformation. She needs to rest and eat, in that order."

"Then follow me," Tina says, "most of the pack is out and about, stretching their legs before the sun goes down. I'll show you to one of the bedrooms."

Cutty gives his customary yuk-yuk-yuk. "Just stick with Tina. She'll make sure you feel right at home, won't you Teen?"

"Tina," Marques growls. "Her name is Tina."

"Whoa, don't mean nothing by it. You wanna help me with some supplies, big guy?" He presses the key fob and the trunk pops open. "We got plenty of water, some crackers, and a few jars of peanut butter."

"And meat?" Marques says.

"Sorry, man. Not this time."

Marques shakes his head and strolls away.

"Thank you," Tina says. "I apologize for Marques. I'll get some of the others to help you with the supplies. Don't leave without saying goodbye." She turns to us. "Come with me and I'll show you around."

Tina leads us into my old home. The door squeaks and rubs against the framework as she closes it. "This is the living room, stairs to the basement, over there's the kitchen. Follow me down the hall to your room. Each of the six bedrooms has its own bath."

I hear Cutty making small talk with those helping him lug in the supplies. Laughter follows them into the house as they come in the back door and stomp around the kitchen.

We've done it—we've been accepted as two more survivors rescued by Aunt Rose and Colonel Dayton. Once Tina shuts the door to our room, we're on our own.

In a flash, Jenny transforms back into Dixie.

There's a tear in her eye.

"What's wrong?" I whisper.

"Aunt Rose gave me the name Jenny…my mother's name—Jennifer. I'm not sad, I'm happy." She plops down on the futon in the corner of the room.

I join her. "Just be sure to remember the shape-shift warning."

"What do you know about that?"

"Aunt Rose told me all about it when you left us alone in her kitchen last night. 'Shift for one day—shift for all days.' "

She giggles. "You worry too much. But I'll be extra careful, just for your sake."

"Good. What's on the agenda now?"

She gives me an odd stare. "There is no agenda. It'll soon be dark. We wait a little while, then go and talk with a few of our roomies—try and get some information."

"But they know your face."

"Good point. Let me shift into something a little more comfortable." Silver light blinds me for an instant. When I focus on Dixie, I see Charlie Nguyen.

"God, please, no. Can't you do better than that?"

She pauses then smiles. Another silver light. "There, how's that?"

I stare at the woman next to me on the futon, telling myself this *is* Dixie, so there's no real harm in finding the form she's taken so damn attractive. Her curly brown hair, deep blue eyes, and full smile take my breath away. "Haven't I seen you someplace before?"

"Adam Steel, using pickup lines?"

"No," I say feeling a quick blush crawl across my face. "I mean, I really have seen you somewhere, but I can't remember—"

"The picture on Aunt Rose's mantel." Dixie laughs.

"Of course, your mother." I think about it for a moment. "You're your mother?"

"Why not? My name is Jenny. Do you want me to try something else?"

"No, I love the choice." I stick out my hand. "Pleased to meet you, Jennifer Mulholland."

She shakes my hand and gives me a quick kiss. "This isn't too weird, is it, I mean, you know, you and me and my mom?"

I hadn't thought about it. Now I do. "No, nothing to worry about. Let's go out there and meet the pack. I'll help you if you get stuck with anything."

"Stuck? What do you mean by that?"

"Well, for starters, you don't smell very canine. I'm pretty sure Marques noticed, maybe Tina, but she's too nice to say anything about it. Can you take care of that?" After a moment, I sniff the air and detect the fresh, musky scent of hound. "Good. Remember, wolfhounds are curious by nature, and very suspicious at first sight. They'll probably have lots of questions for us. To blend in, we've got to answer naturally and without hesitation."

"Sounds like you've given this a lot of thought."

"Yeah, I have. I don't want either of us to get hurt. Remember, like Aunt Rose said, the plan is to get to know them without raising any alarms."

"Don't worry. I'm sure we'll all get along swimmingly." She gets up, but I pull her back down to the futon. "Hey, what's wrong?"

"Not to stereotype, but we generally don't use

words like swimmingly. Most of the wolfhounds don't have a very well-rounded vocabulary. It's not their fault, just the way they were raised."

"Of course, there are exceptions," she says, giving me a hard stare.

I nod. "Most of them learned how to kill humans while I learned how to blend in with them. Remember, wolfhounds are extremely territorial. They're aggressive, and quick to act, especially the wolfhounds on this hill. Keep in mind they were bred as killers, not scholars."

"What do you suggest?"

I furrow my brow. "Better let me do the talking. Many wolfhounds have trouble with the English language. They have difficulty expressing themselves."

She gives me a sour look. "Gee, thanks. Maybe you've forgotten, but I used to go on the air every night and speak to thousands on TV. I think I can handle a few—"

"That's just it. Most of them are quiet, introspective. They're not really word people. Do you think you can handle that?"

She glares at me and points a finger in my chest; a spat is about to start.

The door creaks open and Tina appears. "Jenny, if you need something to eat...oh, I see you've already managed to transform." She glances around the room and furrows her brow. After a quick twice over, she says, "Well, come and get something to eat anyway, if you want." She peers around again then eases the door shut.

"I see what you mean about not being word people," Dixie says. "What in the world was she looking for?"

"Leftovers. If you had just transformed, you would have left something behind."

Dixie covers her mouth. "I didn't even think about that." She waves her hand and a pile of flesh, blood, and clothes appear on the floor. She puts her hand on mine. "Maybe you'd better do the talking. I've got a lot to learn about being a dog."

"Canine. If you say the D word, it'll stand for dead."

Chapter Eighteen

Enamel paint on the kitchen walls had once gleamed a brilliant yellow as evidenced in the nooks and crannies behind some of the cupboards. The current muddy-beige pallet gave the room a worn-out and decayed feeling. With no electricity, the only light flickering into the kitchen this early in the evening came from the living room fireplace.

I stroll, hand in hand, with Dixie (under the guise of Jenny) into the kitchen, waiting in silence behind Tina as dishes are tucked away in open-faced cabinets.

Tina turns to us and nods. "Have a seat," she says, waving to the large oak table in the center of the room, "Meal time is over, but I'll get you two something to eat. Are you hungry?"

"Famished," Jenny says.

Tina narrows her eyes. "Such a human word. You must have done well out there."

"Out there?"

"She means with the humans," I say. "We got by, but we never stayed in one place for too long. We ate scraps, and kept moving. Hard living." Tina stares at me as I speak, enough to make me feel uncomfortable.

She sniffs at the air, then turns her back to us and opens a drawer. After placing two clean plates on the table, she pulls another one from the icebox. This one is heavy with bits of sausage, pieces of chicken, and strips

Rick Newberry

of beef jerky. She needs two hands to move it about.

"You have refrigeration?" Jenny asks.

"Sure," Tina scoffs, "like the humans did a hundred years ago: blocks of ice from town thrown onto the top of the box. We don't exactly live like kings, but we get by. Every day gets easier, you'll see. Still..." Her words hang in the air, seemingly for any takers.

Jenny bites. "Still, what?"

"We're not going to be here forever, you know. Cutty says we're all going to be fine. He says it won't be long now. So we eat what they bring us, and take lessons when we can."

"Lessons?" I have to ask. "What sort of lessons?"

"With speaking and human customs. Colonel Dayton and Cutty share what they can, when they can. We learn human ways—we learn fancy words like famished, which means hungry, or starving." She grins like a schoolgirl showing off her new found knowledge. "We listen to the radio and learn current customs—how to act. Some even learn about laws and countries and science. I'm content just to speak as one human does with another. Cutty is a wonderful teacher." She blushes.

I wolf down my food. In a few seconds, my plate is clean. Dixie nibbles at the sausage, and takes small bites of the chicken, leaving the jerky alone.

"I thought you were *famished*," Tina says.

Jenny stops nibbling and glances up.

Tina's voice raises, "Sorry it's not meat, red and raw. Not much of that around here. They bring us enough to last a day or so then bring more. It's like they were...I better keep my thoughts to myself."

"Like they were what?" Jenny asks.

Tina glances toward the living room, sits at the table next to Jenny, and whispers, "I mean no disrespect, but it's like they're weening us off meat, giving us less every day so we're forced to stay in human form. I don't know, maybe I'm wrong, but I sometimes think that way."

"But that would be smart, wouldn't it?" Jenny smiles "When we eventually live in the human world, you know, when we learn how to assimilate, we'll have to remain in human form all the time, right? We can't change back and forth as the mood suits us. I think—"

"Sorry," I have to interrupt, "but Jenny speaks out of turn." I carry my plate to the sink. "Thanks for the food."

Curious eyes stare into the kitchen. Three forms stand just outside the door within range of our conversation. A large human pushes away from the three and scampers into the kitchen.

"And what if being human all the time is not our choice?" Marques says. "I've been here longer than most, but I remember not being here. We were born to hunt, to eat meat. Why don't they just take us someplace where we can do that and leave us alone?"

"Where?" I ask.

Marques sits down. "Someplace." He stares at the table.

There's a strange accent in his voice—some of my brothers had the same inflection. The only way I've been able to describe it is canine-burr, but I think I made that word up. It's like some of the words he uses are not completely formed, and it's not noticeable unless one is really listening for it. I feel sorry for him.

He's doing his best to assimilate, but it's harder for some, almost impossible for others. I want to help him.

Marques closes his eyes as he speaks again. "When my Alpha was killed, during the war, I escaped into the desert. I hunted; I ate. I should have stayed there."

"Why are you here then?"

"The colonel. He found me in the desert. He said he watched me hunt and transform. He told me he would teach me how to live in the human world. He said there are some—both humans and Daemons—who would track me down and kill me and it was only a matter of time until they did. He said I would be safe here."

"Are you safe?"

Marques opens his eyes and grins—a moment of innocence gone; the rebel returned. "Like a pet in a cage."

Murmurs of support come from the living room.

"That's so unfair," Jenny says. "They're doing their best to help you."

"Help you?" Marques said, standing up from the table.

"She meant help us," I hope I covered her mistake. "Once again, thanks for the food. We're going to go outside and stretch our legs."

"Go wherever you want," Marques says, "just don't leave the cage...I mean hill."

"Marques." Tina scowls at him. She turns to Adam. "What he means is don't wander too far, especially at night. It's safer that way."

"Haven't you heard?" Marques says. "The hunter has become the hunted. We are being killed each and every night, one by one. The big, bad, wolf found its way to our door."

"That's enough," Tina says. "There have been some accidents, but Rosalyn, the colonel, and Cutty watch over us every night. We'll be okay."

"Accidents?" Marques says. "Seven accidents in a row?"

Jenny reaches for the back door. The rusty hinges shriek into the night. "I need some air. Can we go outside?"

I hold Marques's gaze for a moment, then turn and follow Jenny down the three wooden steps to the backyard, all the while straining to catch his next few words, "I don't trust them. They ask too many questions. Especially the female. Would any canine ignore this?" I can only imagine he's holding up Dixie's unfinished plate for inspection.

****

"And now ladies and gentlemen, The Sterling International Resort in Las Vegas, Nevada is honored to present: The Mystic." A simple, yet haunting melody echoed through the cavernous theater: *Le Portrait De La Petit Cossette*, track four, "Sadness," from the original soundtrack of the Japanese anime series.

The stage was unlit, silent, and still. The sold-out audience stood as the music played, waiting in the dark for the arrival of The Mystic. The music stopped and small, intense points of white fiber optic lights twinkled in the background.

Wild applause—an ovation—cheers and whistles descended upon the empty stage. A spotlight clicked on, pointing stage right. The Mystic appeared from the wings, greeted by an even louder round of applause. He strolled toward center stage, a humble figure dressed in white robes, standing no more than 5' 3" tall. The spotlight followed his slow and steady progress across the massive stage. He stopped near a plain wooden stool and picked up a glass of water placed there earlier.

As he took a slow sip of water, the audience settled back in their seats and the star light effects faded away. The Mystic wore a wireless headset microphone allowing full use of his arms and free range of the stage. He waited until the complete silence felt uncomfortable.

"Greetings and peace. All are welcome in this place." Another short round of applause rang out. "You are here tonight for a reason. The reason may be well known to you, or the reason may dawn on you later in life—sometimes it takes many years to fully understand why you are here. For those of you who *have* been here before, welcome back. For the newcomers, let me begin by giving a small demonstration of what I call, perfect balance." Nervous applause greeted the words.

The Mystic raised his hands to the side. He stood in this position for a few moments, his gray eyes washing over the crowd. The beginning of his ascent was almost imperceptible, except to the members of the audience who had "been there before." They applauded almost at once. As The Mystic levitated higher, the entire audience joined in a constant and deafening ovation. The Mystic rose three feet off the ground and hung, as if caught in a still frame photo, for well over a minute. The audience continued its applause until The Mystic descended. When he touched down and opened his eyes, he did not bow, nor did he smile. He simply waited until the roar died down.

"Perfect balance. Nothing is impossible. Nothing is beyond reach. Perfect balance." Another smattering of applause welcomed his affirmation. "You are here tonight because you seek truth. Truth about yourselves, truth about the world. You have questions. You have concerns. Let me assure you," he snapped his fingers and a large bowl of blue flame came to life behind him, "questions will be answered tonight."

Another track from *Le Portrait De La Petit Cossette* started to play: track three: "Moonflower." The Mystic ambled to the left, speaking slowly, softly, "The world we inhabit is a dangerous place full of crime, wars, and disease. Some would say the world, our Earth, our home, is on the verge of self-annihilation." He stopped and held up his right index finger. "With one push of a button, the world as we know it will end." The blue flame billowed and turned orange. "How is this possible? What led us to the eve of destruction? Was it technology? Politics? Rage?" At last, The Mystic smiled. "My friends, the answer is simple. It was us. We are the reason. Human nature. You, me, the person sitting next to you right now—we have all had a hand in this destructive cycle."

The Mystic turned and ventured to the right of the stage. "And now that we know what the problem is, we know, too, what the solution is. Perfect balance." He levitated again, this time rapidly, as if shot from a crossbow. He flew to the left, to the right, then hovered motionless, center stage. "My friends, what is the solution?"

The audience roared its answer as if with one voice: Perfect balance.

"Again."

Perfect balance.

The Mystic drifted down and touched the stage.

The audience went wild. The blue flame grew and billowed upward, then went out. "Perfect balance, that's right. What a smart audience you are." Laughter and applause echoed across the theater.

"And now that we have solved the problems of the world, my friends, let's dive into the truly difficult questions. Earlier, you were given a blank index card and asked to write your full name and a personal question. As you were told then, no last names will ever be used." He waved to the backdrop where the word USED sprang to life in large, blue, neon letters. The letters drifted apart, floated, and rearranged themselves into another word. "Because we don't want this to happen." The letters now spelled SUED. The crowd chuckled. The letters shifted position again. "And now it's time to earn my..." The audience shouted: DUES.

"The first question is from Roger. When will I find the right person?" The Mystic closed his eyes for a moment. "Her name is Debra. She will dine at the Bellagio buffet tomorrow at one o'clock. Don't be late, Roger. Oh, she'll wear a yellow dress.

"The next question is from Denise. My mother is very sick. Will she get better?" Again The Mystic closed his eyes. "She will regain her strength and live for seventeen healthy years. Make those years count."

The questions and answers went on for another thirty minutes, the crowd applauding each time The Mystic answered.

"And now we come to the final question." The audience expressed their sorrow with a collective, "Aww."

"This question is from...uh, just the letter G. G asks for guidance." The Mystic closed his eyes.

"Tonight, you must personally take charge."

Five blue flames appeared on the stage behind The Mystic. The tiny star lights sprang to life and twinkled across the backdrop as the music grew. The Mystic spread out his arms and smiled. "You are always welcome in this place. Thank you and peace be with you. Namaste." He vanished. No lighting effects, no loud bangs, pops, or whistles. The man simply disappeared into nothing. The house lights came up.

By the roar of the crowd, The Mystic's Tuesday night hour and a half show was another huge success. Especially for G.

Chapter Nineteen

"That Marques is a strange one, isn't he?" Dixie says with certain conviction as if I'm supposed to agree without comment.

"What do you mean by that?"

She snorts. "Sounds like he hates everything about this place."

"So do I. Does that make me a strange one, too?"

"No, of course not," she says, slipping her hand in mine, "you have every reason to hate Claremont, believe me, so do I. But Marques knows we're trying to help him, doesn't he?"

I'm not a Daemon. I can't crawl into other people's minds and know their thoughts. I can only guess how they feel by what I think. "Canines, especially males, like to be in control. We like to be in charge of our own destiny. Sure, we defer to The Alpha, but we still want our own way. You heard him. He lived on his own in the desert, and now his world is out of control. I think I know just how he feels."

I lead her down the side of the house and away from the backyard. A heavy wind continues to rush across the valley, and the last rays of the sun feel good on my skin. "I'm just being honest; there are just too many memories here: Sonny Russo, Bane, and Mikael—"

"And Lucy." Dixie squeezes my hand. "There are

some good memories here, too."

She's right, of course. I remember playing in the woods with my pack when we were just pups, long before the Werewolf Killer business. I smile. "So many nights, I'd stand right over there and watch the sun go down." I lead Dixie by the hand to the spot I pointed out. "Right here, mostly by myself, but sometimes with Lucy, or Ivan, or all three of us. We wondered about the world and our place in it. We had a lot of expectations then. We always thought great things were in store for us."

She puts her arms around me. "The sun's gone down. We should get back."

"Just a few more minutes."

Dixie and I sit down on the side of the road. With no electricity on the hill, the stars put on an amazing show. They look as if they're just a few inches over my head. I raise my arm and stick a finger out.

"What are you pointing at?"

"I'm not pointing. I want to touch that star—that one over there, the brightest one."

Dixie laughs and cuddles next to me. "You know, Daemons believe when you die, your essence reappears as a star in the heavens." She glanced up. "I wonder which one is my mother."

"And you believe that? Life after death? The other side?"

"I learned this during The Sufferings. Besides, I don't doubt the words of Major Ransom. She's the one who brought you back to me."

I stare into her eyes. "Then maybe that star *is* your mother. Maybe she—"

A quick movement off to the side grabs my

attention. My heart pounds as my natural hunting instincts spring to life.

Dixie pulls back. "What is it?"

"I saw something—two somethings—running down the hill. That way." I stand and help her up. "I'll follow them. You go back to the house."

She scowls at me. "Not on your life. I'm sticking with you."

There's no time to argue, so I take off at a sprint. I trip on a dead branch and fall flat on my face. Whatever's moving down the hill is much faster than I am. I sniff the air, but can't catch a scent. "I have to transform." I turn to Dixie. She already has.

It's been two years since I changed into a Giant Irish Wolfhound. Lucy taught me the secret of rapid transformations: plenty of meat, red and raw, along with a strong desire to change. I have the desire, not to mention a raw porterhouse and a few strips of beef jerky under my belt.

The tingle in the back of my neck tells me the change is coming. I start to wonder how much pain will come along with that change. Dixie gallops down the hill, no doubt catching the scent of our prey. I fumble with my shirt and pants, letting them fall to the ground. My jaw aches as it elongates. Tiny pins scratch at my skin from the inside. I ignore the pain and concentrate on the desire. That does the trick. In a few moments, I stand on all fours. I shake off the blood and bits of loose human skin remaining on my coat and sprint down the hill.

Dixie is just in front of me, racing at a good clip. I know Claremont better than she does and soon dart past her. The raw earth under my paws feels good, natural. I pick up a scent and slow down. My vision is now in canine mode, and I make out two forms at the bottom of the hill, just short of the paved road. Dixie sidles up next to me.

Who is it? A voice enters my mind. It doesn't sound like her, in fact, it doesn't even sound like speech—more like images forming in my mind—but somehow I know it's Dixie.

I can only hope she'll receive my thoughts: *Marques and another wolfhound; I don't know who.*

Something smells so good. What is it?

Fresh kill—smells like deer. Follow me. I sneak down to the base of the hill, sidestepping past branches and clumps of brush. I stay as far downwind from Marques as I can without losing sight of him. *Stay close and keep quiet.*

What are they doing?

Another figure appears behind them—a human walking in from the road. He's carrying a rifle. Marques and the other wolfhound eat the carcass on the ground. They don't notice the human approaching.

Contact Aunt Rose. We've got our killer.

In an instant, a green light floods the area. Marques and his friend scamper off. The human fires a shot after them and a yip cries out. The green light surrounds the human, and the weapon falls to the ground.

Dixie and I scurry down to the road. I latch onto the human's leg, biting into the soft flesh and crunching through bone. He screams. Aunt Rose waves a hand over the man's head, and he freezes in place. Dixie has already transformed back into human form. It'll take me a bit longer.

"You two stay here," Aunt Rose says. "I'll get the

others, and we'll take this one away. I won't be long."
She closes her eyes, then pops them open and stares at
me. "Good job, my boy. Take good care of Dixie; she's
my pride and joy." She closes her eyes again and swirls
away in a green mist.

It takes me a minute or two to transform back into
human form. "Stay here and keep an eye on this one," I
say, pointing to the man I bit. "He won't be any trouble.
I'll go see if Marques is all right."

I should have stayed with Dixie; held her so tight
in my arms she'd never get away. But I couldn't have
known she'd be gone when I came back—or that we'd
never see Aunt Rose again.

****

"The fucker bit me."

Gorgeous ignored Maxwell Sullivan's complaint,
keeping her eyes trained on Dixie Mulholland instead.
The evening started quite inauspiciously—another
wolfhound murder at Claremont Drive. It ended,
however, better than she ever imagined with the death
of Rosalyn Chase. The sudden demise of *that* bitch
would keep the Daemons of Las Vegas distracted for
days; too concerned with their own safety to worry
about the humans.

"You truly impressed me tonight," Gorgeous said,
a sinful grin twisting her lips. "I've never witnessed
anyone kill quite like that before...so much passion."
She gazed upward, into the heavens. "Poor Rosalyn. Oh
well, we all make choices in life; yours came to its
natural conclusion. I must remember to thank The
Mystic for suggesting I take a personal interest in
Claremont tonight."

"Fuck The Mystic," Maxwell said. "That damn dog

186

almost chewed my leg off." He pressed an ice pack to the back of his calf and downed a swig of tequila from the bottle. "Can't you put a magic spell on me or something—you know, do some hocus pocus to stop this pain? Son of a bitch, it hurts."

"Poor Maxwell. Would that I could, but you know the rules. I cannot heal your wounds. Keep the ice on it and be quiet."

"It hurts like hell. I swear, the next time I see that fucking mutt I'm gonna tear it apart with my bare hands, just like I did that crazy old lady."

"That's the spirit. Now, do me a favor, please direct your venom toward this little morsel sitting next to you."

"Fuck her." He winced. "I was in shock when I killed that old hag, nothing but adrenalin. I can't even stand up now, and it's getting worse. Do something—anything—or my father will hear about this."

"Listen to me." Her expression remained calm as her voice rose. "I had to put you and this little Daemon into your car and drive us all back to town. Do you understand what I'm saying? I've never been so humiliated. We don't drive—that's what humans do. Daemons ride the wind like eagles; we soar through the night on—"

"I'm serious, this leg's killing me. Shit, you have to do something."

Gorgeous stared at him for a moment and nodded. "Of course, I will."

"Then hurry up."

She held her hand over Sullivan's head. "*Dormendum*." He slumped back against the couch and passed out. "Peace and quiet at last. I've never heard so much whining in all my days. What a crybaby."

Dixie lay unconscious on the couch next to Maxwell, her breathing calm and even. Maxwell, on the other hand, twitched and groaned, his mouth hanging open as if in a silent scream. Each, in their own way, was dead to the world.

Gorgeous narrowed her eyes at Dixie. After a calming breath, she snatched up a cushion from the couch. She knew the rules, better than most, but they were still worth testing every now and again. She placed the cushion over Dixie's face and pushed down with all her weight. Almost at once, her hands felt red hot as she clutched the pillow in a white-knuckle death grip. She yielded to the pain and squealed, throwing the cushion against the wall.

Gorgeous raised her eyes to the heavens. "You're demented, you know that? What good is it being a Daemon if I can't kill anyone. I mean, what's the point?"

Her hands ached, and she rubbed them together as she trudged to the window. The suite at the Wynn Hotel and Casino offered a spectacular view of The Strip. She lingered for a moment, surveying the exquisite string of neon running the length of the boulevard. The beacon at the top of the Luxor pyramid shot a steady beam of brilliant white light straight up into the heavens. Gorgeous clenched her fists and gazed upward. "I hope it keeps you up at night."

She closed her eyes, trying her best to contact Lucas Knight, the only Daemon she knew with the power to kill. As usual, his thoughts were blocked. She tried the telephone. No answer. "This is ridiculous."

Gorgeous raised her hands and evaporated in a

swirling haze of blue mist.

Almost at once, she rematerialized in Lucas Knight's tiny dressing room and noticed the burn marks on the carpet. "Foul play?"

"Excuse me, miss," a man's voice sounded from the opened door to the hallway. "You can't be in there."

"Oh, but I can, and not only that, it would appear I am." Gorgeous spun around, faced the man in the doorway, and raised her right hand. "*Obstructum.*"

He grabbed at his throat, his dark eyes rolling back. His face turning scarlet.

Gorgeous released her spell with a wave and he fell to his knees, drawing in big gulps of air. "Quickly now," she said, "who are you?"

He coughed as he took in big gulps of air. The words came out in short, raspy, shrieks, "Sebastian. I'm the stage manager for the show."

"Very well, Mr. Stage Manager, do you know who I am?"

He nodded.

"Then stand up in my presence, and tell me where I might find Mr. Knight."

Sebastian staggered to his feet, but kept his mouth closed. Gorgeous raised her hand toward him again, bringing a rapid response. "Lucas took off a little while ago. He's hiring a new assistant for the act. He went to see Charlie Nguyen."

Gorgeous glanced at the burns in the carpet once again. "A new assistant? How interesting. Tell me, was it Miss Nguyen who recommended Gwendolyn?"

The stage manager nodded.

"Charlie Nguyen shows her hand; ah well, we all make choices in life."

189

Sebastian backed toward the door.

She waved her hand. "*Imobili*." He froze in place. "Before you rush off, tell me where I might find Miss Nguyen and Mr. Knight."

"She has a room at the Trop."

"Ah, the Tropicana, old Vegas. Nguyen always was a bit of a nostalgic. Perhaps she longs for the good old days when she understood the difference between right and wrong. What do you think about that, Mr. Stage Manager?"

"Please don't kill me."

"Calm down. You know I'm unable to kill. But causing you endless pain, that's quite a different matter altogether." Her grin widened as she brushed a strand of hair from her eyes. "Now then, shall I remove a few bones from your body, or turn your skin to glass? Which would you prefer?"

"What do you want from me?"

She tapped his head, and he regained the ability to move. "There you are, good as new. Now tell me, and be honest, how is your telepathy?"

His lips quivered as he answered. "Fair, I guess; better than most."

"Has Mr. Knight allowed you to intuit his whereabouts?"

"Yes, ma'am." A deep breath. "As stage manager for the act, we must be on the same page. Please Miss Gorgeous, don't hurt—"

"Excellent. Then here's what you can do for me: simply keep me informed of Mr. Knight's movements. Can you do that for me, Mr. Stage Manager?"

He nodded, staggered across the room, and collapsed into the settee. A tear dripped down his cheek followed by a full-blown whimper.

She sent her thoughts marching into his mind as she vanished. *It's a strong man who can show his true feelings. Be strong for me, dear Sebastian. Be strong.*

Chapter Twenty

I jog down to the bottom of the hill where Colonel Dayton, Cutty, and Marco Ramirez gather around the remains of a deer. A dozen questions pop into my mind, but I get right to the top of my list. "Where's Dixie?"

Colonel Dayton shakes his head. "What do you mean? I thought she was with you."

"Where's the man I bit? Where's Aunt Rose?"

"No one else is here," Ramirez says. "Slow down and tell us what happened."

They listen to my account without interruption. I explain in detail how Dixie and I transformed and scented a carcass at the bottom of the hill; how we saw two wolfhounds—Marques and another, feasting on it. "That's when we saw a man with a rifle sneak up from the road behind them. Aunt Rose arrived as soon as I took a bite out of the rifleman's leg. He went down fast, but still managed to get a shot off. I climbed up the hill and found Marques, shot in the back. He's dead."

"You left Dixie alone with the killer?"

Bringing me back to my original question. "Where is she?"

Colonel Dayton shakes his head. "I don't know. Aunt Rose appeared out of nowhere and told us to follow her. Cutty must have been doing about fifty on that one-lane road trying to keep up with her."

"Yeah man," Cutty says, "I was booking, but she

soared like an eagle. Man, you shoulda seen her fly. We came zippin' around that curve, and I had to hit the brakes 'cause of this deer. That was like a minute ago then you showed up."

My gut churns. I sniff the air, picking up Dixie's scent farther down the road. Earlier, we'd discussed this very scenario—getting separated, unable to locate someone. We'd agreed to meet back at Seventh Street. "Let's get back to Aunt Rose's, now."

We pile into the sedan, and Cutty hits the gas. It takes only a few minutes to jump onto the I-15 heading north. On the way, we discuss what might have taken place. I'm certain Dixie and Aunt Rose "airlifted" my bite victim back to Seventh Street. I don't know how Daemons tele transport, but I want that to be the explanation. Any other alternative is too distressing to think about at this point.

"We have to consider the alternatives," Colonel Dayton says.

"No." I can't get the word out fast enough. "We don't."

The neon of the city is a blur as Cutty hustles around slower traffic and barrels toward the Charleston exit. He brakes hard, almost skidding off the freeway. Stoplights don't seem to bother him; we race down Seventh Street in no time at all. Cutty slams against the curb and shuts off the engine as the rest of us jump out. The house is quiet, deserted.

I'm in a dead sprint for the front door with Colonel Dayton, Cutty, and Ramirez not even close. They catch up to me on the porch as I turn the doorknob. When we break through the door, my heart sinks. The entrance way is dark and quiet, the only noise coming from the tick-tock, tick-tock of the grandfather clock.

The creaking of the back door sends us racing into the kitchen. I flip on the light as Cutty darts across the linoleum and reaches for the door.

"Be gone." The voice is loud, frightened, and familiar. Charlie Nguyen.

"Where's Aunt Rose?" Cutty yells at her.

Charlie Nguyen shrieks. Her eyes are wide, her mouth opened in terror. "Don't come any closer." She raises her hands at him, fingers spread, is if she's about to cast a spell.

"Stop." I step in front of Cutty. "Calm down and come back inside."

"Adam?" She squints at me, recognition dawning on her face. "What are you doing here?"

"Come inside."

Cutty shuts the door behind her and repeats his question. "Where's Aunt Rose?"

Charlie Nguyen closes her eyes and says in a whisper, "Her light is gone."

"What does that mean?" Colonel Dayton says.

She ignores him and continues speaking in a soft, unhurried tone, "Aunt Rose is gone, and now I'm Gorgeous's target."

"For the last time, where's Dixie?"

She turns around in slow motion and steps to the back door. "I must leave."

Colonel Dayton and Ramirez take hold of her arms and lead her back to the table. She's compliant, pliable, as if sleepwalking. She allows them to place her in a chair.

"Tell us what happened," Dayton says.

"I have a strong connection to Roselynn," she says

in her trance-like state. "The connection is broken. Roselynn Chase is dead."

I lean down and shout, "Tell us where Dixie is."

Charlie Nguyen closes her eyes and lowers her head. "I have no connection whatsoever with Dixie." All at once, her eyes spring open and dart about the room in a classic fight or flight type of behavior.

I put a hand on her shoulder, a reassuring touch to try to calm her down. "Can you contact Major Ransom? We need something, anything, to go on."

Her breathing settles down, and she closes her eyes again. Time drags by as we wait for an answer. Even though her appearance went from turbulent to tranquil, I sense she's still distressed. In fact, for whatever reason, I feel empathy for Charlie Nguyen. She's scared to death.

Her words come out choppy. "Major Ransom says Dixie is at the Wynn Hotel. She's being held in room 1711 against her will."

My heart thumps in my chest. Now *I'm* scared to death.

Nguyen's next words frighten me even more. "Major Ransom fears for her life."

****

Dixie, wake up. You wake up this very instant, do you hear me, young lady? We don't have much time. Dixie Mulholland, wake up.

The voice invading Dixie's mind pleaded, screaming to be heard, the voice of Major Jean Ransom. Despite the major's urgency, Dixie couldn't react. Her legs and arms felt like wet noodles; her body weak and sluggish. She used every ounce of strength to raise her eyelids to half-mast. Nothing came into focus, as if viewing the world through a pane of glass seared by smoke. Her head ached, the thud-thud-thud of her heartbeat pounding away like a bass drum inside her ears. She felt sick to her stomach.

She managed a rough thought, hearing it rumble around in her mind. "Where am I?" Major Ransom did not answer, so she tried again, this time concentrating on each word, "Where-am-I?"

You have to get out of this place right away.

Major Ransom may as well have asked her to jump up and run a marathon. Not going to happen. Feeling the presence of someone else close by, Dixie concentrated on shifting her gaze to the right. It took a world of effort, but she got it done. A man sat limp on the couch next to her. *What the hell's happening? Who's that man?*

He and Gorgeous overpowered you. She put you into a submission spell. It can be broken, but you have to do exactly what I say.

Where's Aunt Rose? Where's Adam? I can't remember anything.

Save your questions. Let's concentrate on the spell. Listen to me. Close your eyes tight—c'mon, squeeze them shut.

That was easy. Step one complete.

Good, now draw as much air into your lungs as you can. That's right. Now I want you to concentrate on—

Dixie rummaged through her thoughts, sifting through what she'd been taught during The Sufferings. No actual lectures, lessons, or tests existed, per se. The whole thing entailed a compressed mix of knowledge force fed into her memories for later recall. *Wait, I know how to break the spell.*

The submission spell wasn't the easiest to overcome, but not the toughest either. It had to do with decontaminating her respiratory system. The science was sound, like a vacuum cleaner running in reverse, but the application a challenge.

She drew in a large gulp of fresh air, forcing her lungs to expand fully. When she exhaled, she concentrated on pushing out every last ounce of air. She repeated this cycle again. Then again. Finally, after another large breath, a small puff of light gray smoke drifted from her mouth as she exhaled. Her next breath forced out a murkier stream of smoke. On each successive exhale, the smoke turned darker. She continued the procedure until the smoke lightened, eventually clearing altogether. Her vision improved, and she regained movement.

Good job.

Dixie examined the man passed out on the couch next to her. *Who's that?* His right leg featured torn flesh and dried blood. All at once, she remembered: this was the man Adam had bitten, the man with the rifle on Claremont. Visions of green and blue light flashed through her memory. *Where's Aunt Rose?* The question came with apprehension. The man sitting next to her groaned. *Who's this man?*

I have no idea who he is. His identity is masked from me, like he's been Photoshopped from my vision. C'mon, you have to get out of here.

No. Tell me where Aunt Rose is.

There isn't time to explain. Gorgeous could come back any minute.

The door to the suite flew open. Dixie did a double

take as the man next to her moaned. She sat up and leaned away from him.

"Dixie." Adam's voice sounded just like music on Christmas morning. Colonel Dayton and Marco Ramirez ran into the suite after him, guns held at their sides. Adam crouched down, taking her in his arms. "I was so worried about you. Are you okay?"

She nodded. "We gotta find Aunt Rose and get out of here. Major Ransom says Gorgeous is on her way back. Where are we anyway?"

"The Wynn Hotel," Ramirez said. He pointed his gun at the man on the couch next to her. "Who's that?"

"No time to find out," Colonel Dayton said. "Let's take him with us."

"Right. Cutty's waiting downstairs with the car."

"Look at his leg," Adam said. "He's the guy I bit at Claremont."

The man's eyes sparked to life. They were bright red, the kind of eyes that ruin a family photo. In an instant, he jumped up from the couch, screaming as he put his full weight on his injured leg. "You're fucking dead." He lunged at Adam, and they tumbled to the floor in a heap. The man lashed out and punched Adam square in the eye. "I'm gonna rip you apart."

Adam rolled over, sending a fist to the man's windpipe. The man staggered back, spitting out a stream of black phlegm. Dayton and Ramirez trained their revolvers on him.

"No," Dixie yelled, "don't shoot. We need answers."

The man vaulted to his feet, screeching at the top of his lungs, an ungodly noise filling the room. He pounced at Adam again. Adam clobbered the man with two quick uppercuts. A black light flashed in the room, blinding everyone for a moment, accompanied by the ghastly scent of rotten eggs. Dark ooze poured from the man's mouth as he glared at Adam and crumpled to the floor, his eyes turning black. He was dead.

Oh my God. Major Ransom's thoughts entered Dixie's mind. *His identity has been revealed. This man is the Devil's son. He killed Aunt Rose. I'm so sorry, Dixie.*

Dixie rushed into Adam's arms, tears streaming down her face. "Get me out of here."

Chapter Twenty-One

Charlie Nguyen materialized in her suite at the Tropicana Hotel and Casino. Her yellow vapor vanished, slowly dissipating in the darkness. She kept the light off and rummaged around in the closet, the only illumination provided by the steady glow of The Strip outside her window.

She tossed a few dresses onto the bed then stooped down, gathering an armful of sandals, pumps, and boots. They, too, thrown willy-nilly, on the bed. She knelt on the carpet, pulled open her suitcase, and rifled through the dresser drawer. She flung panties, bras, shirts, and jewelry into the case. A buzzing noise from the hallway caught her attention. *Damn ice machine. How annoying.*

"I couldn't agree more." The lamp by the bed flicked on.

Nguyen spun around. "Gorgeous."

Gorgeous couldn't help but broaden the steady grin she wore as she approached Nguyen. "Leaving Las Vegas so soon? What's your rush? Noisy ice machine bothering you?"

"You will allow Charlie Nguyen to leave this room at once."

Gorgeous scowled and choked back a cackle. "Such brave words, but I will not."

"But you cannot kill Charlie Nguyen, and I cannot

kill you; it's a stalemate." She stood up and plopped the open suitcase on the bed. Her movements were quick and nervous. Clothes went into the suitcase, brought out, and tossed back in again.

"I smell your fear," Gorgeous said. "It's true, I may not be able to kill you, but you will never leave this room alive."

Charlie Nguyen marched to the door and tried the handle. It would not budge. Her hands rose into the air as she whirled around.

"*Excurato*," Gorgeous said. She always deciphered Nguyen's feeble attempts at casting spells. "There, your powers are useless to you. You can't even fly away in your urine-colored mist."

"It's yellow." Charlie Nguyen held her chin up. "The color of the sun."

"The color of piss, if you ask me. And your scent is quite nauseating."

"Sunflower. You know that, bitch."

"Oh my, how defiant. And from one whom I used to consider such a close associate. Why you chose to leave our cause and join such a bungling band of do-gooders is beyond me, it really is. Rosalyn Chase is dead, you know. And her little mixed-breed tribe is next on my list, after you."

"You talk-talk-talk, always talk. You tried to eliminate the humans forever. If you want to know why I switched sides, I'll tell you: you. It occurred to me, after your last failure, the human race will never be destroyed, not with your ridiculous plans. You're a joke."

For just a moment, the grin faded, replaced by a vicious glare. Gorgeous raised her hands, directing them at Nguyen. "*Imobili.*"

Charlie Nguyen froze, a living statute, unable to move.

"There, that's better," Gorgeous said as she paced the room. She took a casual tone. "I understand you're familiar with Lucas Knight. You recommended an assistant to him for his act, Gwendolyn. Poor girl. Apparently, Lucas was not very happy with her work; he fired her." She approached Nguyen, fixing her eyes on the immobilized Daemon. "You see, Mr. Knight possesses an ability which, I must confess, leaves me quite envious. Even though I may not be permitted to kill you, dear friend, Lucas Knight can."

Charlie Nguyen's eyes shut tight, her face turning white.

Gorgeous stepped away and continued wandering the room. "How or why he was bestowed with such a gift, I haven't a clue. One thing I'm certain of, however, is he'll arrive any minute. Then we'll see who the joke is."

A double knock sounded from the door.

"Ah, Mr. Knight has arrived." She stepped around the motionless Nguyen and pulled open the door.

"What are you doing here, Gorgeous?" Lucas Knight's voice filled the room.

"My, my, haven't we discussed your greetings before?" Gorgeous closed the door behind Knight as he stepped into the suite. "I'm here because I have a slight problem with Miss Nguyen. In fact, Miss Nguyen *is* the problem."

Lucas Knight eyed Nguyen. "How interesting." He turned back, staring at Gorgeous. "In that case, there seem to be two problems in this room."

"What do you mean by that?"

"Oh, you haven't heard?" He grinned and lifted his arms at her.

"You dare raise a hand to me? My Devil will end you, you worthless—"

"Your Devil is dead. *Imobili*." He waved his hand and Gorgeous became still, her eyes staring straight at Knight.

She concentrated all her powers on him to no effect. Tangled in his trap, seized by his spell, she became nothing more than a silent witness to events as they unfolded.

She glared at Nguyen as the Daemon soon fell out of the immobilization spell, raised her hands, and evaporated in a yellow mist.

Knight grinned at Gorgeous. "Alone at last, as they say. Now then, Giant Irish Wolfhounds…really? And just how effective were those killer pups of yours? How many humans did they actually eliminate? One thousand—two perhaps? Far shy of the desired goal, give or take six billion. And your current plan…let's see, what is it exactly? Ah yes, to possess the mind of the President of The United States, is that it? Brilliant, over the top, how creative. Then what? Make him push the little red button—start a nuclear war? Then what? Rule over the charred remains of a decimated planet?" He clucked his tongue. "Please. I'd say your tactics have missed the mark completely. The purpose is to regain dominion of the earth, not destroy it. This isn't a game to us."

Us? Who are you talking about?

"Come now, Gorgeous, certainly you know…you're perplexed by my ability to kill. You can't enter my mind, but I can easily enter yours. Use your thick head for once, if that's possible. What type of Daemon is able to kill?"

Gorgeous trembled as the thought gripped her mind and spilled out, *Sangre di Real, but that isn't possible. I tested you.*

"Oh, you mean this?" Knight struck a pose and cowered, a frightened expression covering his face. "Please don't hurt me, my queen. I'll do anything you say."

Gorgeous narrowed her eyes. *The True Bloods were eradicated—*

"Enslaved. However, now, thanks to you, everything is different. It seems one of your preposterous schemes actually worked."

Thanks to me? The Sangre di Real are locked in Hell forever.

"Forever's overrated. You see, once you secured Maxwell to help with your ridiculous scheme, I was released to watch over him. I failed. Oh well, too bad, so sad. And who do you think will be blamed for junior's demise? The very dog *you* created killed him. With Maxwell gone, no one's got your back."

He will never let you get away with this.

"He? You mean The Big Guy? He's as fed up with the human race as we are. C'mon Gorgeous, it's time to broaden your thinking; it's not just about good and evil anymore, or black and white for that matter." He laughed. "It's all dark, now. The humans have made a mess of everything, and now it's up to me to clean it up. The time has come to put an end to talking dogs and demented Daemons with foolish plans." Knight snaked toward her.

She used all her strength to raise an arm and screamed, "*Imobili.*"

Lucas continued his steady advance. "Nice try, but you'll have to do better than that. I must admit, it bothers me to kill a Daemon, especially one as pretty as you. It bothers me, but it won't stop me."

A low moan crawled from her mouth.

Knight grinned. "Now if you'll excuse me," he turned toward the door, "I must run across the hall and grab the scoop from that noisy ice machine."

Gorgeous forced a muffled cry through her paralyzed throat.

"Yes, I agree, it will be quite slow and very painful—a dull guillotine—but it'll be perfect for scooping you out." He patted his pockets. "By the way, do you have a light?"

****

The Mystic placed a hand over his cup of tea, wafting the steam of the Da Hong Pao as it steeped. Da Hong Pao: the most expensive tea in the world.

A frown played across his brow. The front page of the *Las Vegas Review-Journal* lay on the table next to his breakfast of dove's eggs and slices of pule cheese. Pule: the most expensive cheese in the world.

He glanced at the headline again, this time running his fingers over each word, connecting to the print. *Nation Mourns Passing of First Lady*

The Mystic hung his head. The most expensive first lady in the world.

The president is out of harm's way.

He sipped the tea and closed his eyes. Despite The Sterling Management Group's attempt to provide him with nothing but the finest, The Mystic would just as well have preferred a hot cup of Joe and some ham. They meant well, of course, as if exceeding his materialistic wants would somehow satisfy his otherworldly needs.

He lifted a small silver bell from the glass table and waggled it back and forth. Almost at once, the door opened and a young woman, dressed in shimmering turquoise robes, stepped into the chamber. She took a few paces then stopped several feet from The Mystic. She kept her gaze low, on the ground, as she, and all the members of the staff, had been instructed: no eye contact whatsoever with The Mystic.

"Sir," she said with a slight bow.

"I'd like some scrambled eggs, please, with ketchup, and bacon, white toast, and a cup of coffee. Thank you."

"As you wish." She bowed again.

"Oh, and not dove's eggs, or duck's eggs, or swan's—just regular chicken eggs. And get the coffee from the shop downstairs—latte, plain, extra hot. Thank you."

"As you wish."

"Oh, and when President Walker calls, please extend my condolences."

"His people have already telephoned several times. He wishes you to call him back at your earliest possible—"

"Thank you, Ayala. That will be all."

She bowed and shut the door behind her.

The sound of the water trickling down the massive glass wall set him at ease. He closed his eyes, clearing his mind of any thoughts. A blank slate welcoming random visions.

With his mind cleared, he eased back in the chair and chanted: ohmmmm. Almost at once, scenes of chaos filled his thoughts: humanity struggled for food, for water, for air—the planet itself nothing more than charred rubble.

The Mystic sat up and opened his eyes. He'd seen this vision before, many times. "Images of things yet to come or that which has already been? The Dark Ages or the New Age?"

He stood and wandered about the chamber, running a finger along the glass wall, feeling the cool water dribble over his hand. The vision unsettled him, a specter of great suffering.

He strolled back to the table and rang the tiny bell again. The door opened immediately.

"I wish to go out, Ayala."

"I will summon your staff at once."

"No, I want to go out alone—like before."

Ayala hesitated then closed the door to his chamber. Her words sounded cautious as she raised her head and stared at him. "But what about your breakfast?"

"I didn't cause any harm to the president's wife, you know. It was just a vision—a half vision really—nothing more."

"I know that, sir."

How could she? For her to guess her true purpose in his life could never happen. On this side, Ayala was merely a member of his staff. No, for her to have any knowledge of the other side was impossible.

"I'm ready to go, come on, hurry up." The Mystic pulled his robes over his head and stood naked before her. "It's cold in here."

Ayala pulled her turquoise robes off and held them out to The Mystic. They exchanged garments. Even though The Mystic and Ayala differed in age, they were the same height and similar build. The flowing robes concealed much.

"Relax child. If anyone should come in—oh, you know what to do." He kissed her on the cheek and settled her into his armchair facing the glass wall. "I'll be back soon."

Ayala bowed her head. The Mystic flipped the turquoise hood over his head and reached for the door latch.

"Please hurry," she said.

He imitated her voice with perfect pitch and tone, "As you wish, sir."

The Mystic knew the way out and gave a slight nod of his head as he passed Walter and Fabian guarding his chamber. They paid little attention to him. Their job was to prevent entry by unknown visitors, not exit by well-known staff.

The Mystic pressed on, reaching the elevator at the end of the darkened hallway in no time. The doors slid open and he stepped inside, pressing the down button as he turned to face the closing doors. Light instrumental music drifted from the speakers in the car. He recognized the song as "Solitary Man" by Neil Diamond. He absent-mindedly hummed along with the tune.

The doors slid open, and he fell silent. Another hallway greeted him, this one brightly lit and filled with people zipping by in both directions. A security guard moved aside and turned to him. "Hello, Ayala."

He nodded, stepped off the elevator, and ambled

toward the chaos of the casino. Crowds of people elbowed their way past him in all directions. At first, it came as a welcome change from the solitude of his private chambers, but soon grated his nerves.

He spied the bank of revolving doors leading to Las Vegas Boulevard and strode toward them through a maze of slot machines, gaming tables, and mini bars.

The Mystic exited the casino, feeling the full weight of the desert heat press down on him. The sun blinded him momentarily, even with the hood over his head. He stood still for a while, acclimating to this alien environment. His gaze wandered up, examining the obelisk announcing his presence to the world. He'd never seen the object in person before—quite impressive.

When he looked back down, a small woman stood in front of him—graying hair wrapped up in a bun, wire-rim glasses, and sharp green eyes. She held her ground, hands on her hips and scowl on her face.

"What are you playing at, young man?" Aunt Rose said.

The massive crowds of people hurrying back and forth had vanished. No sound, no movement—just the desert breeze rustling through palm trees, a ghost town.

Rick Newberry

Chapter Twenty-Two

It's a mad dash to leave the suite at The Wynn. The hotel corridors are nearly empty at this time of night; most people busy gambling, eating, or touring The Strip. On the way down in the elevator, I wonder how to tell Dixie about Aunt Rose. The words will devastate her.

My eye has closed up where I got punched and it's tender to the touch, but I know, given enough time, I'll heal. I don't know if I can say the same about Dixie.

We scramble through the casino, zigzagging our way around hundreds of tourists on our way to the exit. Dixie keeps lagging behind, and I have to put my arm around her to move her along. I stop right here in the middle of all the chaos and hold her, tell her everything's going to be okay. I've never comforted anyone who's lost someone they love before.

Cutty meets us at the hotel entrance with the car, and we clamber in. Dixie and I sit in the backseat alongside Colonel Dayton. Marco rides shotgun. We race onto Las Vegas Boulevard and head north toward the Stratosphere.

I don't know the right words to use, so I just tell her outright: Aunt Rose is dead. Dixie sobs, big gasping howls, and buries her head in my chest.

"I know," she whispers.

I slip my arms around her as she cries. Tears run

down my cheeks as well.

"I'm so sorry," Marco says.

She stares into my eyes. "Major Ransom told me everything. How Aunt Rose tried to protect me. How she fought to keep me safe."

"Pull over." Colonel Dayton taps Cutty on the shoulder. Cutty turns into an empty parking lot for The Sanctuary of The Desert Wedding Chapel, "Drive-Through Weddings our Specialty." He parks, kills the engine, and swivels around to face us.

"I know this is a painful time," Colonel Dayton says, "and I'm truly sorry for your loss." He shakes his head and takes a deep breath. "But the fact remains, we need to know exactly what is happening. Can you tell us everything Major Ransom said? Please. Charlie Nguyen is out of her mind with fear. She's certain Gorgeous is out to kill her. Correct me if I'm wrong but, I thought Daemons were forbidden to kill—"

"Nguyen's got nothing to worry about, Gorgeous is dead as well." Dixie wipes her eyes and straightens up. In a small voice, she continues, "The murders at Claremont were just a diversion to keep us busy. Gorgeous had all of us so wrapped up in helping the wolfhounds, we didn't focus on her real plan. I guess that doesn't matter anymore."

"Of course it matters," I say. "Aunt Rose was an incredible woman. She knew the danger at Claremont, and she did everything in her power to keep all of us safe. What wouldn't have mattered is if she knew it was a diversion and didn't do anything about it. Lives were lost, with more to come, and she was determined to put an end to it. She was unbelievably brave, and I'm so proud to have known her—we all are."

Dixie squeezes my hand. "Thank you."

I'm not finished. "Aunt Rose spent her whole life fighting evil. She knew the risks, but she never gave up. We need to remember who she was and honor that by keeping her in our hearts. We need to continue the fight. Death isn't the end. Major Ransom proved that. Aunt Rose will always be a part of our lives."

Dixie nods. There's a spark of hope in her eyes—she knows I'm right, as if Major Ransom confirms my words. She lays her head on my shoulder. "I know she's not really gone. She's just out of reach right now, on the other side."

Colonel Dayton breaks the clumsy silence growing in the car. "I know how you feel. It takes time, that's all. Aunt Rose will find a way to communicate. You'll see. Have you asked Major Ransom if she's heard from her?"

"She hasn't."

"Maybe she's stuck at the terminal or something," Cutty says. "You know, like her paperwork got all messed up. I saw this movie once where—"

Marco clears his throat. "The colonel's right, sweetheart. If anyone can find a way to communicate with you, Aunt Rose will." He looks out the window at the tourists traipsing up and down the boulevard. "But right now we have to find out if Gorgeous's plans died with her. I won't have another Convergence in this city. Does Major Ransom know anything?"

Dixie sniffles and leans forward, her hand resting on Marco's arm. "Gorgeous planned something bigger than The Convergence. She worked with a man named Maxwell Sullivan, the Devil's son."

"The Devil?" Cutty shouts out, "Like, the *real*

Devil?"

Dixie ignores Cutty's panic. "Daemons can't kill outright, like you said, Colonel. She had Sullivan do that for her. He shot the wolfhounds, trying to make it look like humans were responsible. But, according to Major Ransom, that was just a diversion to keep us out of her way. It had nothing to do with her real plan."

"And what was that?" Marco asks.

Dixie shakes her head.

Marco presses on. "Why did Gorgeous attack Aunt Rose?"

After a measured breath, she said, "A crime of opportunity. Gorgeous happened to accompany Sullivan to Claremont tonight. Sullivan killed Aunt Rose by her order." She scrunches her eyes for a moment, then straightens and speaks with renewed strength. "Major Ransom says everything has changed now because the Devil's son is dead."

Cutty attempts a smile. "But that's a *good* thing, right?"

"No, not a good thing at all. The Devil wants revenge. The Gates of Hell will soon open—something evil is coming."

"Man, what does that even mean?" Cutty's eyes bulge.

"The end times are here. True Blood Daemons will soon arrive."

"Holy shit, man." Cutty turns the key and the engine sparks to life. "Then let's get the hell out of here."

"Wait," Colonel Dayton barks.

But it's too late. Cutty peels out of the parking lot. "No way in hell can we fight something like that, right?

I mean, it woulda been tough enough to take Gorgeous down and now we got who-knows-what coming after us. I'm headed for Claremont to get Tina then we gotta get the heck outta Dodge."

Colonel Dayton shouts, "Stand down, Paul. That's an order." Cutty jams on the brakes and pulls to the side of the road. The colonel continues in a calm voice, "Listen to me. Like it or not, it's up to us to eliminate this new threat to humanity without any further help from Aunt Rose. I'm sorry to be so blunt, Dixie. You're being incredibly brave, but it's time to face this one fact: from now on, we're on our own."

"We're not alone in this," Dixie says. "We've got Major Ransom and Charlie Nguyen."

"Oh man," Cutty says. "Major Ransom's cool and all, but she's just a voice inside your head. I mean, she's not really here. And Nguyen? Man, that psycho is probably halfway to Bangkok by now. We need real help."

"Like the wolfhounds," I say.

Colonel Dayton beams. "That's the spirit. With Major Ransom giving us eyes in the sky and the wolfhounds providing the muscle, we can take down a small division of Daemons."

"Are you serious?" Marco Ramirez says. "From what Dixie described, we won't face your normal run-of-the-mill Daemon. These are Daemons from Hell."

All gazes rest on Dixie now, hoping for any glimmer of good news she can give us. She leans back into me as she answers, "It's true, they're not typical Daemons. Their formal name is *Sangre di Real*: the True Blood. Legend has it, they're the original Daemons, and they have the ability to kill. They can also block their thoughts and are impervious to ordinary spells."

"How do you know so much about them?" I ask.

"From The Sufferings, and from what Major Ransom just told me."

"You said these super Daemons were all locked away in Hell, right?" Cutty says, a ray of hope in his voice.

Dixie nods. "The Devil has the only key. Apparently, he released one of them weeks ago to watch over his son, Maxwell Sullivan." She turns to me. "And you killed Sullivan tonight."

I rub a hand over my closed eye. It burns. "But there wasn't anybody protecting him. Maybe these True Bloods aren't as powerful as everyone thinks."

"Or maybe..." Dixie straightens up. "From what Major Ransom told me, Sullivan's death pissed the Devil off to no end. Maybe *this* was the plan all along, and we played right into it."

I can't help but ask, "Whose plan? Gorgeous is dead."

She shakes her head. "I don't know, but whoever it is has the Devil on their side now."

****

"Perfect balance, my ass."

"Language, Rosalyn, please. You must calm yourself and listen to me."

"You set me up to be murdered. How calm do you expect me to be? I'll ask you one more time: what are you playing at?"

The Mystic smiled. "Death is a part of life; so it must follow, life is a part of death. You, of all Daemons, should know this. Your life on earth has been quite...productive."

"You mean long."

"In any case, you knew it wouldn't last forever, nothing ever does."

Aunt Rose huffed. "Death is overrated. For some reason, I thought it would be different. I thought I'd be able to communicate with the living, like Major Ransom does. I thought I'd still get to witness what goes on, you know? React with the world, but I can't get through to anyone. This is worse than having a dead cell phone."

The Mystic chuckled. "Death—it's a different experience for each individual."

"I thought, at least, I could speak with Jack and Jenny."

"Dixie's parents." He glanced up. "I'm afraid their essence has already been placed in the night sky." He turned away, treading through the empty casino, and stopped at a roulette table. After spinning the wheel, he sent the little white ball in the opposite direction. He turned to Aunt Rose as he spoke. "Nothing is guaranteed in life except death, and nothing at all is guaranteed in death. Life and death spin on an unavoidable collision course. Just to be clear, once and for all, I did not set you up to be murdered. How did you ever arrive at such a preposterous notion?"

"Preposterous?" She put her hand on his shoulder. "You suggested Gorgeous be at Claremont for the nightly execution. And why? You knew I'd be there." She waited a beat then smiled. "That was just a guess, but judging by your expression, it hits the mark."

The roulette ball dropped into the number twenty-two slot. The Mystic removed his finger from double-zero on the table. "Damn."

Aunt Rose shook her head. "You're sick."

"Perhaps." He turned and continued his trek, meandering back to the elevator. After pressing the call button, he faced Aunt Rose and smiled. "The wolfhounds were created by Daemonic spell. They were never part of the grand design. They're not supposed to exist."

"It's kind of late to play that card. It's not their fault they're here. They don't deserve to be gunned down like—"

"Like dogs?"

"That's a stupid thing to say. Are you trying to be funny? They're living, breathing creatures and deserve to live their lives just as much as—"

"Rosalyn, I'm afraid you misunderstand me. I bear ill will toward no one. Your niece, Dixie, her wolfhound friend, Adam—I wish them all the best. But I'm sure you're aware of the saying: happiness is not a gift; it's a goal. I do hope they reach their goal, I truly do. It's certainly not my place to say who lives or dies."

The elevator doors slid open. The Mystic stepped into the car and turned to Aunt Rose. "Please come up with me. There's someone I want you to meet."

She hesitated for a moment then entered the elevator. The doors closed, and she faced The Mystic. "I've heard all sorts of things about you. At first, I thought—"

"Shhh." He put a finger to his lips, cocked his head, and smiled. *"That Old Black Magic*…Sinatra, one of my favorites."

Aunt Rose narrowed her eyes. "It's all just a game to you, isn't it? One side against the other—good versus evil—you sit back and watch it all unfold from a front row seat. If one side gets the upper hand, you meddle. God forbid the battle should ever end, that would spoil your fun. It may not be your place to say who lives or dies, but you really don't care either."

"Everything dies. Will caring change that fact?"

The elevator opened and The Mystic led the way to the door of his chamber. He held it open for Aunt Rose and nodded her in.

"Ayala," he called, "this is Rosalyn Chase, a new arrival. She's not only a spirit, but quite spirited, as well." He turned to Aunt Rose with a smile. "I'm sorry; I actually *was* trying to be funny just then."

Aunt Rose said nothing.

"Rosalyn insists I don't care about anything. I wonder, what do you say?"

Ayala stood up and bowed. "I…uh…"

"It's quite all right, my dear. We're on the other side, now. Speak the truth."

"The Mystic cares about a great many things," the girl said. "I've never known a kinder soul in all my life. He loves everyone."

Aunt Rose set her jaw. "Then why did he have me killed? Does that sound like love?"

"I did not kill you, dear lady." His voice remained calm. "Maxwell Sullivan did that, and he, himself, is now dead. So you see; perfect balance is restored."

"And what of the seven wolfhounds shot to death at Claremont?"

"Gorgeous paid for that with her life."

"And who pays for *her* death? This perfect balance you love so much is ridiculous. Lives ruined, lives lost, and for what? To keep everything balanced?" Aunt

Rose took a deep breath. "And now rumor has it the gates of Hell will soon open. Where's the balance for that? Will the Pearly Gates swing open as well? Evil Daemons against armies of angels? Who will protect Dixie from the *Sangre di Real*? Is this part of your perfect balance?"

"Calm down, please. Would you like some tea?"

"No. I'd like some answers."

"Perhaps a story then. I like stories, don't you?"

Aunt Rose spun around and marched toward the door.

The Mystic raised his voice. "Gorgeous didn't care for stories either."

Aunt Rose stopped.

"I think you'll enjoy this one. A story of how the gates of Hell have slammed shut, of how the balance will truly be restored."

Aunt Rose turned and ambled back. She faced The Mystic and folded her arms. "Keep talking, and make it good."

"As you wish. Have a seat. Ayala, tea for our guest. Cream and sugar?"

Aunt Rose plopped into an armchair. "Very well then, two lumps—no cream. Tell me your story before I scream."

The Mystic raised his eyebrows. "Ah, a rhyme. Feeling your old self again?"

"I'll never feel like my old self again. Death does not suit me."

Ayala poured the tea and backed away a few steps. She stood with head lowered and hands clasped.

"Thank you, Ayala." The Mystic sat down next to Aunt Rose and whispered, "Funny you should mention

219

screaming. Ayala's a Banshee, did you know? No, of course you wouldn't. in the human world she does not even know herself. Apparently, she's supposed to scream, or sing, or hum or something when my death is imminent. Who makes up these crazy rules for our world, anyway?"

"You know who. Regardless, you said you've got a story about the gates of Hell?"

"Ah yes, the story. Evidently, a negotiation took place at the highest levels. The Tempter is much annoyed his son was killed and by a wolfhound, no less; a creature that should never have existed. However, even though he wanted to open the gates, unleashing the *Sangre di Real* upon the world, cooler heads have prevailed."

"The gates are locked?"

"Well, not entirely. A handful of True Bloods have been allowed freedom. They will descend on Claremont to destroy the wolfhounds. This is how balance will be restored."

"No." Aunt Rose clenched her fists. "You can't allow that to happen."

"My hands are tied."

"But the wolfhounds are innocent in all this. They must be warned."

"My lips are sealed as well."

"But something's must be done. Tell me what to do, please."

"Well," he leaned in again, "you didn't hear it from me, but Ayala reaches out regularly to her vast network of banshees. Perhaps, through some friend of a friend or whatnot, word will reach Major Ransom, and from there, who knows?"

"Social networking? Even here?"

The Mystic raised his eyebrows. "A sign of the times, my dear." He paused a moment. "Oh, and I suggest you hurry. The human world is measured by time, which is a shame. Measuring time only shows how much has been lost—never how much remains."

"What's that supposed to mean? Why don't you just tell me what you're thinking?"

"I'm late for my performance."

Aunt Rose bolted from the chair.

Chapter Twenty-Three

I hug Dixie like it's the last time—it may very well be.

"I'll call the National Guard." Marco grabs his cell phone.

"I'll call Admiral Garrison at the UN." Colonel Dayton brings his cell out of his pocket. "He'll assemble a team to—"

"No, wait," Dixie says.

"Wait for what, man?" Cutty is jittery, almost bouncing up and down in his seat. "You saw what happened last time, with The Disaster. We need all the help we can get, right?"

"Major Ransom says not to call anyone. It will only escalate the situation."

"What does she suggest we do?" Marco says. "Do nothing and watch the city destroyed again? Not on my watch. I'm with Cutty on this one." He dials a number and puts the phone to his ear.

Dixie reaches forward, grabbing the cell out of his hand. "No. You, too, Colonel. Put the phone down. Major Ransom heard from Aunt Rose."

Colonel Dayton eases the phone down. "And?"

A blue light flares. My first instinct is to imagine Gorgeous descending on our vehicle. I clutch Dixie in my arms then remember Gorgeous is dead. I glance behind us and see a Metro officer, flashlight in hand, approaching our vehicle. His motorcycle is parked a few yards back, blue lights flashing.

"Good." Marco rolls down his window. "Officer."

Cutty cracks open his door.

"Stay in the vehicle," the officer shouts.

"Marco, Cutty," Dixie says, "don't say a word about anything. Please, I'm begging you."

The officer approaches the driver's side and bends down, shining the flashlight beam directly into Cutty's eyes. "There's no parking on The Strip. I need your driver's license, registration, and proof of insurance."

Marco leans over and glances at the officer. "Do you know who I am?"

The flashlight covers Marco's face. He shades his eyes with his hand. "I'm Deputy Chief Ramirez. We only stopped here for a minute. Nobody's been drinking, and we're leaving right now. Do you understand?"

"Can I see your ID?"

Marco produces his badge and ID book.

"I'm sorry, sir. I had no idea—"

"It's okay. We're leaving now." He pats Cutty on the back. "Get us out of here."

"Have a good night, sir. Sorry for the—"

Cutty slams his door, turns the key, and hits the gas. "Man, we shoulda totally come clean with him. We need firepower tonight and plenty of it—more than that."

"Okay, Dixie," Marco says over his shoulder, "what does Aunt Rose suggest we do?"

"She said there was some kind of agreement, and only a few True Bloods have been released. They're going to Claremont to kill the wolfhounds. If the

223

military gets involved, then all bets are off. All the *Sangre di Real* will be unleashed on the world."

"Why?" My heart races. "Why kill the wolfhounds?"

Dixie squeezes my hand. "Because you killed the Devil's son. He wants revenge."

"Then why not come after me?"

"I don't know."

"Cutty," Colonel Dayton says, "how fast can we get to Claremont?"

"It won't take too long, but we should stop first—pick up some bazookas, or rocket launchers, maybe a couple of—"

"Get out, Cutty, I'll drive." I open my door.

Dixie grabs my arm and pulls me back in. "No. You should all stay here. I'll go." With that, a brilliant silver light illuminates the inside of the car and Dixie vanishes.

I know she feels terrible about Aunt Rose and revenge is on the menu tonight, but she's not thinking straight. Whether she wants to admit it or not, she needs our help. "C'mon, Cutty, in or out—right now."

He slams on the gas and weaves through traffic, running red lights and avoiding pedestrians to get to the 15. "Shit," he says, sliding a hand through his scraggily hair, "there are all kinds of bad vibes on this. I'm all for helping the wolfhounds, but this…" Once he hits the freeway, he mashes the pedal to the floor and the engine screams.

I don't know what waits for us at Claremont, and I share Cutty's apprehension. What I do know is Dixie's already there, and this car isn't going fast enough.

Marco and the colonel check their handguns and

rummage through pockets for extra clips. I only have one weapon: the wolfhound. I strip off my shirt and pants in the backseat and close my eyes, concentrating on the transformation.

"Do you have a weapon, Cutty?" Marco shouts over the roar of the engine.

"Nope. Oh, I've got a gun, but that ain't gonna do any good. You guys remember what it takes to kill a Daemon, don't you? Chop, scoop, burn. And those are the normal ones. Is that even gonna work on these super-freaks? Does anyone know?"

A brilliant yellow light flashes inside the sedan. Cutty swerves across two lanes of traffic and holds the wheel through a skid before wrestling the vehicle back to the fast lane. "Holy shit, what the hell is that?"

"The weapons are in the trunk," Charlie Nguyen says. She sits right next to me, her gaze running across my body. "Do you often take road trips in only your underwear?"

"What are you doing here?"

"Major Ransom told me everything. You could certainly use the help." She smirks as she turns her gaze to Colonel Dayton. "A pistol? Really? Against *Sangre di Real?* The weapons are in the trunk, gentlemen—six katanas ready for battle." She leans over the backseat and puts her hand on Cutty's shoulder. "And to answer your question, Mr. Ginger, there is one additional step to killing a True Blood."

Colonel Dayton leans away from her. "I thought you'd run off."

"I did, until I heard about Gorgeous and her long overdue demise. Now, do you want to know the extra step, or not?"

"Absolutely," the colonel says, slipping his gun back into its shoulder holster.

"Very well, listen carefully. Once the fire has consumed their bodies, their bones must be ground into the earth. Dust to dust, understand?"

"Got it," Cutty shouts out, "chop off their heads, scoop out their guts, light them on fire, then stomp on their bones. Got it, got it: chop, scoop, burn, stomp. Chop, scoop, burn, stomp."

"Why did you come back?" I ask over Cutty's chant.

Charlie Nguyen lowers her head, her eyes staring at her lap. "If the *Sangre di Real* win this battle and establish a foot hold here on earth, then we're all dead—Daemons, humans, wolfhounds—all of us. So, die now, or die later. Charlie Nguyen decides her own fate."

"How many of them are there?" Marco says.

Nguyen shakes her head.

"Are they already at Claremont?"

She shakes her head again.

I have to ask, "Do we stand a chance?"

She shrugs her shoulders and remains silent.

"Hang on," Cutty shouts as he cranks the steering wheel, "Claremont dead ahead."

****

A silver-colored mist flashed in the night, illuminating a small clearing in the woods. Pine, palm, and Joshua trees surrounded Dixie. Brushing herself off, she closed her eyes and drew in a deep breath of warm air. She exhaled slowly then pulled in another long breath, filling her lungs to capacity; a slow and steady pattern repeated several times.

Major Ransom's thoughts found their way into her mind. *What do you think you're doing? There's no time to waste.*

It's a meditation technique. I'm trying to relax before...

Before what?

I don't even know. Are they here yet?

Who?

Dixie clucked her tongue. *Who do you think? The* Sangre di Real.

No, and it's a good thing, too.

Well, when do you think they'll be—

"What are you doing here?" A woman's voice broke the silence in the clearing.

Dixie crouched down. She scanned the area, seeing nothing but shadows in the thick brush. "Where are you? Come out of the darkness and show yourself."

"No. Stand up and walk straight ahead, toward my voice. Hurry, do it now."

Dixie weighed her options and came up with none. Perhaps, it was a bit foolish to leave Adam and the others behind and tele transport to Claremont. She had no allies, carried no weapons, and didn't even have a plan. Stuck all alone in the middle of the woods, late at night, on the eve of an attack by the most powerful Daemons ever created had to be the exact opposite of a plan. She straightened and ambled forward. Seeing no one, she stopped after only a few steps.

"Farther," the voice commanded, "come on, hurry up."

Dixie held her ground. "I'm not taking another step, not until you show yourself."

"Come forward, or die."

Not much of a choice. Dixie took a few tentative steps toward the shadows masking the unseen voice. "This is as far as I go. Is that better?"

"Yes. Now!"

Dixie heard the sharp crack of something before her head exploded. Darkness faded to black as her legs buckled and the ground rushed up to punch her in the face.

"Wake up."

The feel of an open hand drumming against her cheek and cold water running across her forehead brought her back to consciousness. She took a mental inventory of her body. No broken bones, no strained muscles. Her breathing was slow and measured, as if she'd been dreaming, but it wasn't a dream. She couldn't move.

"C'mon, snap out of it," a voice said. "You hit her pretty hard."

Another voice said, "Is she dead?"

"C'mon now. Snap out of it."

Dixie's eyelids rose, bit by bit, as if tethered to a tiny hand crank. Candlelight flickered on the table in front of her. She knew this place, the kitchen of Adam's house on Claremont. She sat in a wooden chair pushed against the table. She tried again to move, but her arms and legs were secured by restraints. A sharp ache pounded through her head with each heartbeat, burying itself deep in her neck. "You clobbered me." Her words came out like a slurred whisper. "Why'd you hit me?"

"Ah, she's alive." A small chorus of cackles filled the room. "Somebody get Tina."

Dixie turned her head, wincing as the pain followed her movement. She'd found herself in this very same condition not more than an hour ago; definitely not something she wanted to get used to. "What the hell happened? What are you doing to me?" A hand slid under her chin and lifted her head. She stared into familiar eyes.

"What were you doing out there in the dark?" The tone firm—an interrogator's voice, hard and direct.

After a few moments, the speaker's face came into focus. "Tina? What are you doing to me? You know me, let me go."

"Of course we know you—Dixie Mulholland. What are you doing creeping around outside our house? Somebody's killing us one by one, every night." The hand under her chin squeezed tight. "Is it you?"

"What? No."

"Then tell us what you were doing out there in the dark."

Dixie closed her eyes and concentrated. The restraints binding her to the chair crumbled to dust. She brought her arms up and rubbed her wrists.

"I told you she was a Witch," a voice called out as feet shuffled across the linoleum.

Dixie stood up. "I'm not a Witch. I'm a Daemon, and you're all in danger." Probably the wrong thing to say.

"Hit her again."

"Cut off her head."

"Burn her."

A mad dash for the door followed, accompanied by blurred shadows prancing across the candlelit walls.

Dixie raised her hands. "*Imobili*." The chaos came to a sudden halt. Only the candle flickered, projecting a false movement from the mannequins in the room.

"You all know me," Dixie said. "You know my aunt, Rosalyn. We brought you here. We cared for you. We would never, ever harm you. Never."

She told them about the *Sangre di Real* and of the imminent battle soon to find its way to their doorstep. She explained how Aunt Rose died trying to protect them. As she spoke, she moved around the room, staring into the eyes of each immobilized being. The windows to their souls changed from anger to concern—some more quickly than others, but soon she knew they all understood the stakes. She tapped each one softly on the head and they stirred, reanimating, and stretching their limbs. "I don't know how many are coming, and I don't know when. But we've got to find a way to work together if we have any chance of survival."

Tina nodded and plopped into a chair at the table. Her voice waned. "We have no weapons."

The back door burst open hard and fast. Cutty, his scraggily red hair dancing wildly in the wind, stood at the entrance holding a katana sword. With a toothy grin, he said, "You do now."

"Cutty!" Tina's eyes brightened at once. She jumped up, rushing into his open arms.

Chapter Twenty-Four

Blast! He'd been granted command of just twelve True Bloods, far short of the thousands he'd hoped for. Not only that, strict orders given to exterminate only the wolfhounds at Claremont. The Armageddon Lucas Knight envisioned had been negotiated away by fools.

"They say the covenant is sealed," Sebastian said. "There's nothing you can do to change His mind."

Knight scraped his fingernails across Sebastian's face, burning the stagehand's flesh in fine red lines, sending a putrid smell into the air. "Don't ever tell me what I can or cannot do. Is that clear?"

Sebastian winced, covered his face with shaking hands, and nodded. "I'm sorry."

"Are the True Bloods assembled on the stage?"

Again, Sebastian nodded.

"Tell me, my friend, do they have any idea of the agreement made? Do they know this is a simple revenge mission on Daddy's behalf?"

"Sir, you can't call him Daddy. He is—"

Knight spun around and advanced on Sebastian. "I can't what?"

"Forgive me, sir. Please forgive me." Sebastian bowed his head and inched toward the door. "I'm so sorry."

Knight put a casual hand on Sebastian's shoulder. "I swear you are the sorriest Daemon I have ever laid eyes on. Except for that bitch Gorgeous, of course." He snickered. "She was a piece of work, that one—strutting around with that stupid grin planted on her face, and those ridiculous schemes of hers to destroy humanity. Ha! I found her repulsive, didn't you?"

Sebastian nodded.

"What's that? I said I found her repulsive, didn't you?"

"Yes, sir."

"Oh now, come, come. You've never been one of those 'yes sir-no sir' kind of Daemons; that's what I like about you. I always thought you were made of tougher stuff." Knight rubbed his hand over Sebastian's face, and the scars evaporated. "There, good as new. You see? I'm not as vindictive as that old hag. Now, things might get pretty ugly tonight, and I want to know I can count on your support."

"What...what does that mean, sir?"

Knight pursed his lips and strolled toward the closet. "The *Sangre di Real* have quite a history. We were the original Daemons, you know. True Bloods."

Sebastian nodded. "Yes sir."

"Humans brag about the freewill bestowed on them at creation. Daemons possess the very same freewill." Lucas turned to Sebastian and pointed to the floor. "The *Sangre di Real* chose to follow Him. The others, Gorgeous, Rosalyn Chase, and their ilk, did not. And what did we get for having a spine, for having the courage to make a choice? We were locked behind the Gates of Hell forever. Well, forever ends today."

"I don't understand, sir."

"What I'm talking about is a new chance, a fresh start. Command of twelve True Bloods with orders to eliminate a few dozen canine—a simple enough task. Then it's back to prison for the lot of us." Knight turned and paced the small dressing room. "No." He stared at Sebastian. "No more prison."

"But…forgive me, sir…I just don't…I don't think—"

"Spit it out. Just say what's on your mind. Have a backbone, man."

Sebastian pointed to the floor with a shaking finger. "As I said, the covenant is sealed. If you started a war with the humans, He might not—"

"Oh, fuck the humans. They're nothing. I don't want a war with the humans, and I don't give a shit about a few dogs either. I want to rid the world of all the no good, half-assed, cowardly Daemons who refused to commit their souls to the ultimate battle. I think, deep down inside, He wants that, too. He always has." Knight turned to the mirror and smiled. "I believe He'll release *all* the True Bloods, should the need arise, don't you?"

Sebastian said nothing as Knight admired his reflection.

"And it's up to me to make certain that need arises."

"I still don't follow, sir. I don't understand what you mean by—"

"You, my dear friend, are one hell of a magician's stage manager. What I'm talking about is right in your wheelhouse, nothing you haven't done before. You misdirect a thousand eyes every night during my show, don't you? Of course, they're merely human eyes, seeing only what they want, but they seek only the tricks, the gimmicks. They know magic isn't real and they want to prove it, to catch me in a mistake, but they never have. And why? Because you, my dear Sebastian, have all the angles covered. Remember this, my friend, sometimes defeat is the surest path to victory."

Sebastian's frown soon gave way to a smile, a dawn of understanding. "If the True Bloods are defeated tonight, He'll be forced to send more."

Knight grinned. "As I said, He may send them all." With eyes closed, Knight sent his thoughts to Sebastian. *Pick your team—just a handful—and tell them as little as possible. Come close, my friend, I have a gift for you.*

Sebastian took two tentative steps forward. He closed his eyes as Knight placed both hands on his head.

"*Sangre venomala converte.* There," Knight said with a wink, "the True Blood now runs through your veins—for a couple of hours, anyway. I'll be upstairs stalling, I mean instructing, my warriors." Knight reached out his hand to Sebastian. "Tonight we make history, my friend. Tonight, through defeat, we set a course for victory."

****

Cutty and Tina huddled together against the counter near the kitchen sink, their arms wrapped around each other as they speak in whispers. Every so often, one or the other giggles, followed by a quick kiss.

I glance up at Dixie while she caresses my shoulder with a gentle touch. "Those two picked a fine time to fall in love."

"So did we."

Marco clears his throat. "We really should discuss

strategy against these True Blood Daemons. They could be here any minute."

The house is crowded with wolfhounds, both in human and canine form. Colonel Dayton decided the majority of survivors at Claremont should gather here at my old home. The rest are stationed farther down the hill as lookouts at thirty-yard intervals.

"You're right, Marco," Dixie says. She sticks two fingers in her mouth and lets out an ear-shattering whistle. All eyes turn to her. Bodies squeeze into the kitchen and the rest watch from the living room, the back door, and through open windows. "Everybody," Dixie shouts, "this is Deputy Chief Marco Ramirez from Las Vegas Metro." A low rumble, mixed with growls, barks, and howls greet his introduction. "Relax, he's a friend."

Marco stands up. "And this, for those of you who don't already know, is Colonel Jon Dayton. He's battle-tested and experienced in strategy. I'm sure he has valuable advice to share with all of us."

Colonel Dayton stands up. "As the deputy chief said, most of you already know me. For those of you who don't, let me just say, I wish we met under different circumstances. But, as the Yanks are fond of saying, it is what it is. Now then, let's get started."

The colonel takes charge. He makes sure everyone is teamed up, saying he wants no lone fighters wandering the woods. He turns to Charlie Nguyen. "I want each team to have a sword—that means more katanas than we currently have. Oh, and we need plenty of disposable lighters, one for each team. Can you handle that?"

"Of course," Nguyen says, her chin raised. "It'll

take some time, but—"

"I'll help you," Dixie says. She rushes out the back door with Charlie Nguyen.

I glance through the window and watch as katana swords materialize, their curved, slender, single-edged blades gleaming in the moonlight.

"Now, pay attention," Colonel Dayton shouts, "what we're up against can't be killed like a normal Daemon. They must be beheaded, disemboweled, set on fire, and their bones crushed into the dirt. In—that—order."

"Chop, scoop, burn, stomp," Cutty says. He says it louder, "Chop, scoop, burn, stomp." Those in the kitchen repeat after him. He yells, "Chop, scoop, burn, stomp." The chant is taken up by everyone inside, including me. I hear it outside in the backyard, wailing from the front of the house, and reverberating through the woods. The chorus grows louder, "Chop, scoop, burn, stomp." One hundred voices strong.

The colonel holds up his hands and waits for silence. The intonation, both inside the house and around the grounds, fades into the night. "Good. Now, I've paired you up for a reason. I want one of you in canine form while the other is human. As a canine, you can see and smell the enemy approach. As a human, you can wield the katana to chop off heads, while your canine partner rips out the bowels. As a human, you can light the match. Once the fire burns out, both of you can stomp on the creature and mash the bones into the ground."

My stomach gurgles, like I've eaten something bad. Bile swirls in my throat, and I feel like I'm going to vomit. Listening to Colonel Dayton speak about the mechanics of combat in such clinical terms doesn't sit right with me. Although I appreciate his practical approach to fighting the True Bloods, I can't help but glance around the room at all the innocent survivors about to go to battle. They never asked for this. They're caught in the middle of a war between good and evil that centers on me. Me. *I'm* the one who killed the Devil's son. I'm the one the *Sangre di Real* want to kill. The feeling in the pit of my gut is guilt; the bile is blame.

I stand up from the table, and Marco stares at me. "Where're you going?"

"Outside for a little bit. I need some air."

He nods and I leave out the backdoor, passing Charlie Nguyen and Dixie still manifesting our weapons of war.

"Where're you off to?" Dixie says.

"To check on the lookouts." Of course, it's a lie, but the truth won't come.

She nods, and I make my way across the street into the woods. I run halfway down the hill, past a couple of lookouts, until I find a clearing. The full moon illuminates the trees around me, leaving everything else draped in shadows. True Bloods surround us; I feel it in my bones. I hope so.

"Here I am!"

Birds, panicked by my voice, tear off into the night. When the sound of their wings fade away, a deathly silence fills the clearing.

"You want me—nobody else. I killed your son."

A shadow scurries through the brush to my right. Another one dashes to the left. I can't see clear forms, only rough shapes darting back and forth. They are here.

I shout at the top of my lungs, "Come and get me!"

A figure dressed in black jumps from the thicket, arms outstretched, hands reaching for my throat. As I duck—a natural reflex—his head pops off, hits the ground, and rolls a few yards away from his body in the opposite direction. His stomach splits open and his intestines shoot out of his body.

A bright orange fire blinds me for an instant. The man consumed by flames. In a few moments, the fire dies down and the chant buzzes through my head: chop, scoop, burn, stomp. Before I realize it, I'm trampling on the corpse, crushing its bones to the earth.

Another form rushes forward. The same macabre routine plays out finishing with a red flame. Pure adrenalin races through me and in no time, I'm stomping on the corpse, making sure the bones crack into tiny shards and mix with the dirt under my shoes.

Colorful fires spark to life in the distance as more True Bloods are consumed by fire. Shouts, mixed with eerie screeches and squeals, echo through the woods. I don't have a clear line of sight through the trees, but I'm sure Daemons are dying. The air fills with the rancid smell of burning flesh.

I turn away from the clearing and sprint back toward the house on Claremont. Sweat and ash blur my vision as I race up the hill. The sound of death fades in the distance.

"Adam." I run into the arms of Dixie. She's panting, her expression filled with terror as she stares into my eyes. "Adam, what the hell happened?"

I try to answer, but my throat fills with smoke. She wraps her arms around me and I fall, dragging us both to the ground.

"What happened? Tell me."

I'm shaking, unable to speak. Others rush up to us: Colonel Dayton, Marco Ramirez, and a few dozen wolfhounds. I cough, spitting a gob of phlegm on the ground. My breathing is raspy at best.

Marco reaches out his hand, grabs my arm, and brings me to my feet. His voice is quiet, his tone apprehensive. "Oh my God, Adam, what have you done?"

Words finally come. "What are you talking about?"

"The lookouts saw everything," Colonel Dayton says. "They said you raced around the hill like a mad man, taking down True Bloods, crushing them, whilst we were busy making our plans for battle. They said you killed them all."

Chapter Twenty-Five

The heat of the night is relentless, making the journey back up the hill tough going. The wind swirls above the tops of trees sending them into an unscripted dance. More and more wolfhounds join us as we continue the climb toward the house at the top of the hill. I imagine it as a sort of reverse avalanche, growing in strength the higher we go.

Word spreads among the pack about my exploits. I listen to them talk of the battles they think I fought, their voices growing louder, the stories more unbelievable. When we reach my old house, almost all the survivors of Claremont have gathered together, slapping my back and doing their best to introduce themselves. My status in their eyes has elevated. By the time we file in the front door, I'm a legend.

I know I have to tell everyone the truth, but I don't know what that is. I did not kill even one *Sangre di Real*, let alone *all* of them. The look on their faces stops me from speaking—I can't let them down, or is it myself I can't disappoint? These poor souls have been used a pawns, beat down, and demoralized all their lives. I convince myself this is their night, in some warped sense of justification, and decide to let them share in the joy of victory.

"What's wrong?" Dixie squeezes my hand when we enter the kitchen. "You don't look like a man who saved every life on this hill."

I smile, for her sake. "Just tired, I guess. I need to get some sleep."

"Look around you. That's not going to happen."

Revelers stream into the kitchen. Tina and Cutty have the refrigerator door open and they take out everything—packages of meat, a variety of cheeses, fresh fruits, and bottles of juice and water. Marco attacks the pantry, pulling out boxes of Pop Tarts, crackers, and canned goods. A spontaneous feast is in the offing. Well-wishers shout over the din in the hopes they'll be heard.

Soon the kitchen, living room, and hallways come to life with activity. Dozens stand outside, laughing and talking in booming voices. Others come up the hill from their houses carrying plates of food—hot dogs, potatoes, sandwiches and bottled water. Each and every person wears a broad smile.

"Don't ask me where I got it," Cutty says, a huge grin on his face, "but take it, you earned it." He pushes a can of beer into my hand. "It's the only one on this frickin' hill, man!"

I pop the top and take a few gulps. Mistake. I can't stand the taste, or is it guilt rising in my throat? Tossing the can to the floor, I shout, "Dixie, I need to talk to you."

She frowns. "Go ahead."

"Not here. Let's go to the bedroom."

She slips her arms around me and nuzzles my neck.

With my hands on her shoulders, I push her back, moving her into the path of someone behind her. She apologizes to them and narrows her eyes at me.

I step back, trying to create some room between us,

and bump into a man behind me. He turns, grabs my arm, and grins. "There's the man of the hour."

Every smile directed at me, every mention of "good job," or "way to go," buries me until I feel like I'm drowning. To be honest, I haven't lied to anyone, they've made up their own truth, but my conscience is racked with guilt. "Dixie," I say, tugging on her arm to pull her through the crowded kitchen. "I need to talk to you right now."

"But everybody's here to—"

"I can't explain over this noise. Follow me." My voice cuts over the clamor, and most of those close by stop what they're doing and stare at me. I keep Dixie close as we navigate the crowded hallway.

Five people occupy the bedroom, and I keep a level head as I ask them to give us some privacy. They smile and snicker as they leave. I can't wait for them to leave, and shove the door closed as soon as the last one exits.

"What is it?" Dixie asks. She touches my hand and leans into me.

"Have you heard from Major Ransom?"

"No."

"You need to contact her. Ask her what's going on."

"What are you talking about? The fight is over, thanks to you. We won."

I jerk my hand away from her. "We didn't win."

The door opens and two strangers enter along with all the clatter from the celebrations outside. They grin at the sight of me. "Well, if it isn't the man of the hour—"

"It isn't," I yell, "get out."

Dixie furrows her brow. "Adam, what's wrong?"

I wait until the door closes. "It's all a lie. I'm a

fraud, a fake. I didn't kill one of those Daemons, not one. If I didn't know any better, I'd say the hand of God was involved."

"What are you talking about?"

"Please do me a favor, would you? Ask the colonel, Marco, and Cutty to come in here. I only want to have to tell this story once."

She gives me a look I've never seen before. Obviously, she's worried about me. While she's gone, I try to think about the best way to tell them what happened on the hill tonight. No words come because I don't know what happened. The only thing I can explain to them is what didn't happen.

In a couple of minutes, all my friends sit on the edge of the bed, Cutty on the floor. I tell them what happened as best I can.

"You never lifted a finger?" Colonel Dayton stands up. "But the lookouts swear you took them all down. They said—"

"I don't care what they think they saw. I didn't do anything but watch those Daemons get killed by some kind of supernatural force. Their heads lopped off, and they split in two. Next thing I knew, they were on fire, and I crushed their bones to the earth."

"Hey, man," Cutty says, "they wouldn't be dead if you didn't do that last bit."

"I get the feeling, if I didn't do that last bit, it would have been done for me."

Dixie slips her arms around me. "That's why you wanted me to contact Major Ransom."

I nod. "If anybody knows what happened, it's her."

"Perhaps she's unwilling to say." We all turn to the door. Charlie Nguyen sticks her head in. "Perhaps she still thinks of you as someone who's brave; who's formidable." She sidles next to me and sneers, "Or perhaps, as you say, she knows the truth."

****

Two knocks on the door. "Sir, twenty minutes till curtain."

"Yes, that should just about be enough time." The Mystic winked at Ayala who sat in the chair facing the glass wall of water. "I'll be back as soon as I can." He waited a moment, and put his ear to the door. "The coast is clear." He grinned. "I've always wanted to say that."

"Please hurry," Ayala said.

"As you wish," The Mystic, wearing Ayala's turquoise robe, called back in her voice. He opened the door and eased out, nodding to the bodyguards stationed in the anteroom.

The Mystic truly enjoyed his visits to the other side—a recent ritual: in one moment, convincing Ayala to exchange robes, in the next, greeting her as his Banshee.

He rode the elevator down to the casino level, enjoying the dulcet sounds of Perry Como's "Prisoner of Love," strode through the crowds of people and entered the Lucky Diamond Lounge. He sat down, closed his eyes, and listened as the frenzied sounds of the gaming house faded into silence.

He never knew when it would happen, or where, much less how, but his solo outings to the casino floor always brought the transition. His eyelids rose and he confirmed everyone had vanished, all but one. Gorgeous sat at his table nursing a beverage.

"Seven and Seven?" The Mystic asked.

"Uh-huh. Why don't you order one? Oh, you can't," her voice rose with each word, "because there doesn't seem to be a fucking waitress, or a fucking bartender, or a fucking anybody around. What the hell is going on?"

"Oh, my. I know it's not in your nature to mind your language, but there's no need to use those kinds of words here."

"Here? Where the hell is here?"

The Mystic smiled. "The Diamond Lounge at the Sterling International Resort."

"I'm dead, aren't I?"

"Well, technically you—"

"Just fucking tell me. Dead or alive?"

"It's true. You jumped to the other side."

"Jumped? More like pushed. That no-good, son-of-a-bitch, two-timing little weasel blind-sided me. Lucas Knight! Wait till he crosses over and I get my hands on him."

The Mystic laughed. "That's not quite how it works."

"Oh yes it will." Gorgeous gulped her drink down. "I want another drink." She drummed her fingers on the table and glanced around. "I said I wanted another drink, and when I say—wait a minute. Are you telling me manifestation does not work here? Just what kind of Hell did I fall into?"

"Oh, you're not in Hell, believe me. If you'd like another drink, I'll be glad to get one for you." The Mystic rose and strolled to the bar with Gorgeous in tow. He found his way behind the bar, grabbed a bottle, and poured the blended whiskey into a glass. After plucking up the bar gun, he fumbled with it until he found the soda button. The liquid splashed and fizzed in the glass. He held an ice cube six inches over the rim of the glass then let it drop. He smiled as he handed the drink to Gorgeous.

She took a sip. "Hmm. You missed your calling, Mystic."

"It pleases me to please you."

Gorgeous raised her eyebrows. "Well, isn't that just so fucking pleasing? Now tell me what in the hell—"

The Mystic nodded his head to the end of the bar behind Gorgeous. She swiveled around and dropped her tumbler on the carpet. Rosalyn Chase stood glaring at her, hands on her hips. Both women raised their arms and waved them at each other.

"Relax," The Mystic said in a soothing tone, "you cannot cast spells here. It is simply not allowed. Now then, let's go to a table and sit down like civilized people. Would you care for a drink, Rosalyn?"

"No," she said, "bad for my health."

Gorgeous snickered. "So is death."

Rosalyn stared at Gorgeous. "In that case, I'll have what she's having."

"Ah, excellent choice," The Mystic said. "I'll make you both a fresh drink and then we'll sit and have a little talk."

The Mystic mixed the drinks, finishing with his ice cube drop, and carried them around the end of the bar to the lounge. Gorgeous sat at one table to the left of the bar, Rosalyn at a table to the right. "Come now, ladies. We have much to discuss and I have a performance in a few minutes." He sat down at a table in the middle of the bar and waited. "Hurry now. I've never missed a performance in two years and I don't plan on starting tonight." The two Daemons stood and sauntered to a center table. "Good. Now sit down, please, enjoy your beverages. I will tell you a story."

"Not another goddamned story." Gorgeous folded her arms and refused to sit.

Rosalyn sat down at once. "I'm not afraid of stories." She took a sip of her drink, grimaced, and faced The Mystic.

Gorgeous sat. "Bring it on, old man."

"Excellent," The Mystic smiled. "Very well. Once upon a time—"

"Oh please. What a load of bullshit."

"Shut up," Rosalyn said, "I'm trying to listen."

The Mystic cleared his throat. "Anyway, there were two very powerful Daemons. They were always at each other's throat constantly bickering, arguing, and disagreeing. And what were they quarrelling about?"

"The fate of the world," Gorgeous said at once.

"The fate of mankind," Rosalyn said.

"You are both correct. Fate. They were in conflict over fate. As they pulled and tugged and fought over fate, they dropped it. It broke. Now, no one could have it. The fate each one had fought for had changed."

"Ha," Gorgeous huffed, "is this the part where we shake hands and promise never to fight again?"

"No. This is the part where you fight even harder."

"I don't follow your story," Rosalyn said.

"Do you both need another drink?"

"Just tell us what the hell you mean." Gorgeous downed her Seven and Seven.

"The *Sangre di Real* have entered into battle with the wolfhounds on Claremont. The wolfhounds killed them all."

"Good for them," Rosalyn said, taking a long pull at her glass.

"I'll drink to that," Gorgeous said, air toasting her empty glass.

"But the battle is far from over." The Mystic pointed to the ground. "He's not one to accept defeat lightly. More True Bloods are coming to earth, and this time not only wolfhounds, but Daemons are targets."

"How do you know this?" Gorgeous asked.

"I have my sources. Let's just say a blip appeared on the radar. In any case, Heaven is not likely to stop the attack—"

"No," Rosalyn said. "He's never been too fond of us."

"And Hell will turn a blind eye. Balance will be lost; fate will be broken."

Gorgeous placed her drink on the table and glared at Rosalyn. "I suppose we haven't made too many fans above or below, have we?"

"What can we do?" Rosalyn said.

Gorgeous raised her eyebrows. "How do we stop it?"

"Ah, you have already taken the first step. The magic word has been spoken."

"What magic word?"

"We. Work together to destroy the destroyer."

Gorgeous scoffed. "How the hell do you propose we do that?"

"I'm not at liberty to say."

"But you do know how," Gorgeous shouted.

The Mystic smiled, drifting into the other side, leaving the two Daemons on their own.

Chapter Twenty-Six

"The council met." Lucas Knight spoke with purpose, with passion. He felt another emotion rise to the surface—an emotion quite foreign to him: joy. He spoke fast, his tone aroused, "They found it difficult to believe a few dozen wolfhounds could take down twelve *Sangre di Real*—no, not difficult to believe...what were their words? Impossible to imagine, yes, that was it: impossible to imagine. Round one was a complete success. The council agreed to release one hundred more True Bloods. They'll arrive soon."

"Only one hundred?" Sebastian said. "I thought He would release them all—"

"He will, my friend, in time." Knight offered a glass to his accomplice. He filled the tumbler and toasted. "To the world's greatest stage manager." He held out the bottle, pouring another round for himself and Sebastian. "This is just a minor setback, call it round two. He doesn't like to appear weak, you know."

"You actually spoke to Him, face to face?" Sebastian's eyes widened.

"Well, no, not face to face. Of course not. Nobody ever speaks to Him one on one, but the council is almost the same thing. They speak on His behalf, as if standing with Him eye to eye. And, as I said, the defeat took everyone completely by surprise."

Sebastian beamed. "The logistics were kind of tricky. I'm used to a closed stage, but once I got my men in place and explained what to do, the rest was easy—a few yards of razor wire, some well-placed assegais, flash powder, and about thirteen rolls of gaffers' tape—"

"Enough details."

"Of course. But I haven't told you the best part." Sebastian laughed; a deep throated chortle before he raised his glass and took another drink. "The best part was the reaction of the wolfhounds. They were convinced they defeated the True Bloods on their own." Another cackle.

"Marvelous." Knight stood up from the small settee in his dressing room and paced the floor, a nervous journey back and forth, back and forth. "They'll be apt to engage the True Bloods in round two more aggressively, gives the battle a genuine flavor. How about the crew you chose? Did any of them question what they were doing?"

Sebastian grinned. "One."

"And?"

"He won't question anything again." Sebastian's lips curled up forming a crooked grin. "The power you transferred to me was incredible. I've never felt anything close to it before, like the world's most powerful drug. I felt like God."

Knight stopped pacing at once and rushed to Sebastian. He leaned down, grabbing the Daemon by the shoulders and whispered, "Don't ever say that name." He plopped down next to Sebastian on the settee. "Do you understand? Don't use that name— ever."

Sebastian cowered, dropping his glass to the floor. "I didn't mean anything by it."

Knight relaxed, his scowl fading, replaced by excitement. "I know you didn't. But you must know every time that name is spoken, we risk exposure. We play a dangerous game, my friend. If my plans are leaked, overheard, or even guessed the consequences are fatal. We must stay off the radar."

Sebastian nodded as he picked up his glass. "It will never happen again, sir. You have my word—and my allegiance."

"Excellent." Knight smiled and refilled Sebastian's glass. "Now then, what do you need for round two? More men, more supplies?"

"I have plenty of supplies, but I need a few more men and a lot more time."

"Two hours."

Sebastian's eyes bulged. "You mean tonight? In two hours? You're joking."

Knight stared at Sebastian and said nothing.

"But, sir, there's no way I can—"

Knight placed his hand over Sebastian's head, once again transferring the abilities of the *Sangre di Real* to the stage manager. He squeezed the Daemon's skull, sending the spell deep into his essence.

Sebastian opened his eyes, a new confidence spreading over his face. He beamed. "Everything will be ready."

"Outstanding." Knight stood up and turned for the door. "The True Bloods arrive in a few minutes. Take your men and supplies and go out the back. The attack on Claremont commences at ten o'clock."

"Yes, sir."

"And remember," Knight said as he pointed upward. "No mention of you know who." He darted into the hallway and climbed a flight of stairs to the side door leading to the main stage. He paused for a moment and closed his eyes, mumbling under his breath, "Game face."

Knight pushed through the door, marching to center stage. He smiled and shouted, "Welcome. I bid welcome to each and every one of you."

The True Bloods huddled together on stage in the darkened theater. Some nodded in Knight's direction. Most kept their eyes trained on him, watching, waiting, a warrior's mistrust.

"I don't know what you've been told—"

"We were told everything," a voice from the back of the crowd bellowed.

Knight felt his heart quiver. *Everything?*

"We were told how twelve True Bloods died in disgrace. How a pack of wild dogs took them down. We were told they were slaughtered."

Grunts and murmurs echoed in the theater.

"It's all true," Knight said; his hands rose for silence, bringing a hush to the assembly. "I asked for soldiers, for warriors." His voice rose. "Instead, I got a small band of mercenaries unsure of what to do. Of course, they were slaughtered. They took the enemy lightly. They were vain, prideful, and foolish. Do not repeat their mistake. Do not—"

"We were also told...they were led by you."

Knight moved into the band of True Bloods in search of the one who spoke so brazenly. "Reveal yourself."

A warrior emerged from the crowd—angry eyes,

chest out, ready for a challenge. "You sent them to battle while you performed, like a monkey, for the humans."

Knight fixed his gaze on the Daemon. The perfect time for an example to be made to all those of the same mind. "I played my part. I expected them to do the same. What is your name, warrior?"

"Mordem."

Knight marched toward Mordem and put his arm around the True Blood. He leaned in, whispering a curse under his breath; the secret word only he'd been given as a leader of the *Sangre di Real, "Exteritus."*

Mordem fell to the floor, unable to breath. His face turned red, then white. He wasn't dead, not quite alive. It only took a few more moments for his body to melt into a pool of dark liquid and vanish from the earth.

"My command is final," Knight shouted. "Authorized by the council. Are there any more questions? Good."

****

"What do you mean you don't know what happened?" Detective Ramirez places a hand on my shoulder. "Now, stop me if I'm wrong, but generally, Daemons are known for doing a lot of stupid things, no offense Dixie; suicide isn't one of them. Someone took those Daemons out, and if it wasn't you, then who…or what?"

"That's just the thing, I have no idea."

"Then why did you go down the hill?" Nguyen says. "To fetch a pail of water?"

"That's *up* the hill," Dixie scolds before turning to me with the same question.

"A stupid thing to do, I know." I hope my

explanation makes sense to them because it still doesn't to me. "But I'm the one who killed the Devil's son. It's my fault this is all happening. I didn't want anybody else to pay for what I'd done. And I was ready to do anything I could—"

"That's so selfish," Dixie says, jabbing me in the stomach and squeezing my shoulders. "You could have been killed. Nobody blames you for this, and it isn't your fault—none of it is. Don't you ever run off and try to fight a battle alone again, do you hear me?"

Before I can say anything, Nguyen speaks up, "I believe you did the very same thing, did you not, Miss Mulholland?" She grins. "Ah, altruism, is it an unselfish devotion to others? Or merely another nasty little STD?"

Cutty jumps into the fray. "You did the same thing, Nguyen, by coming back with all those katanas, so don't start accusing—"

"Now, listen here, little human—"

"Everybody shut up," Dixie yells. Her voice is raw, anxious, and final.

In fact, her voice is so strained, I wonder if she's okay. There's no pain on her face—no expression at all. Her eyes are closed and she seems to be somewhere else, certainly not in the room with us.

"Dixie," Colonel Dayton says, "are you all right? Do you need to lie down?"

"No, man." Cutty patters toward her, whispering, "It's that look, Colonel. You know, the look she gets when she's talking to Major Ransom. Quiet, everybody, quiet."

Marco points at Nguyen. "Dixie's not the only one."

Charlie Nguyen is silent, for once, her eyes shut tight. Both Dixie and Nguyen seem tuned to the same channel.

Dixie opens her eyes. "I just spoke with Aunt Rose."

"That's fantastic." I lean into her, but she backs away.

"Not really."

"What do you mean?"

Charlie Nguyen steps forward. "We were both talking to Aunt Rose, and someone else. A kind of party line, wouldn't you say?" She stares at Dixie with raised eyebrows. "Shall I tell them who?"

"You'd better, I don't think I can."

A frown spreads across Charlie Nguyen's forehead. "Gorgeous. The good news is this confirms the bitch is finally dead. The bad news? She's merely on the other side." At last, Nguyen has what she always seemed to want, our full attention. She takes measured steps across the bedroom, stopping near the window.

"Steel…Steel…Steel…Steel…" A chant grows outside. It picks up momentum and spreads through the house. My name courses through every room. They still think I'm a hero and the battle is over.

"Listen to the celebrations outside," Nguyen says over the sounds of the revelers. "How excited they all are." She turns around and stares at me. "A great victory tonight, my four-footed friend, a great victory indeed. But didn't you realize there's a price to pay for such a triumph? Didn't you ever wonder why—"

"Oh cut the crap," Dixie says. "It was all a sham. Adam didn't know anything about it."

My heart races. "Didn't know about what?"

255

"More True Bloods are on their way. One hundred more."

"God help us all," Cutty says.

"His bloodlust is aroused," Nguyen says in a whisper.

Cutty is visibly shaking now. "Who's bloodlust?"

"Can't you guess, my little gingerbread man?" Nguyen pats Cutty on top of the head, glances at her palm, and wipes it on her sleeve. "Satan." She sits down on the edge of the bed and lets out a mournful sigh, her eyes staring straight ahead at nothing. "The *Sangre di Real* are loose upon the world and that is that." Is a tear rolling down her cheek?

Silence fills the room. I turn to Dixie. "Is that true? Did you speak with Gorgeous?"

She nods.

"Would somebody tell me what the hell's going on?" Marco says, shouting over the celebrations outside.

Nguyen yells, "Aunt Rose made an unholy alliance with that bitch, Gorgeous. Neither of them wants to see the world controlled by the *Sangre di Real*—for their own reasons, obviously. The message was clear: if we don't do something, this is the end of days."

Cutty starts for the door.

"No place is safe," Nguyen says. "There's nowhere to hide."

Marco steps to the center of the room. "But who's behind all this? Gorgeous?"

Dixie shakes her head, letting the name fall from her lips in a hopeless tone, "Lucas Knight."

"That two-bit magician?" Marco says. "What the hell does that son of a bitch have to do with any of

256

this?"

"He's been behind it all along. Look," Dixie explains, "Knight was sent here to protect Maxwell Sullivan, the Devil's son, knowing there'd be hell to pay if anything happened to him—so he made sure it did. Remember that black light in the room tonight just before Sullivan died? Knight killed Sullivan and used Adam as a scapegoat. Soon, there'll be so many *Sangre di Real* on earth we'll *all* be put down: Daemons, wolfhounds, and humans. There's no stopping them."

"We don't have to stop them." All eyes turn to me. "We only have to expose Knight."

Dixie's eyes widen. "You're right. If we can stop Knight, get him to tell the truth, maybe the True Bloods will be called back."

"Where can we find him?" Colonel Dayton asks.

"Gorgeous said Knight wasn't here at Claremont for the earlier attack. Gorgeous doesn't think he'll be here for the next one either."

"Why not?"

"She said, for some reason, he's keeping distance between himself and the battle. He'll perform his second show tonight as usual."

Colonel Dayton asks, "How can we trust Gorgeous?"

"Because she's working with Aunt Rose. Besides, what choice do we have?"

Marco shakes his head as he glances at his watch. "We're out of time. Knight's second show starts in just a few minutes, at ten o'clock. That gives us only enough time to choose our battle: Claremont, or Knight."

Hopelessness crawls across my skin. "We can't

abandon the wolfhounds."

Almost at once, two beams, yellow and silver, illuminate the room. The light is so intense I have to shield my eyes from it. When I can focus again, panic sets in.

"Dixie and Nguyen are gone." Marco does a quick scan of the room then throws open the door. I hear him shouting over the noise in the hallway, "Anybody seen Dixie?" He turns in the threshold and shakes his head. "They're not here."

"Looks like they chose their battle," Cutty says. "Lucas Knight."

Chapter Twenty-Seven

"Let's go, we have to catch up to them." I rush to
the door. Detective Ramirez stands in my way, a human
barrier. "C'mon, what are you doing? Let's go after
them."

"Calm down." Colonel Dayton steps up and puts a
hand on my shoulder. "We'll never make it to The Strip
in time. Dixie knows what she's doing. I hate to admit
it, but so does Nguyen. They'll do their best to deal
with our magician friend whilst we protect the
wolfhounds."

"What do you mean they'll do their best? If we
leave right now—"

"He's right, man," Cutty says. "Dixie and that
psycho-Daemon can handle Knight. It's two against
one, right? Besides, we have a responsibility to the
survivors. We can't leave them here alone."

I close my eyes and breathe in slow and deep
(borrowing a relaxation technique Dixie taught me).
After another soothing breath, I nod. "What's the
plan?"

Colonel Dayton pats me on the back. "We've got
to make our way down the hill, but quietly. God forbid
we start a panic and the packs scatter, possibly racing
into harm's way. I suggest we leave this room one by
one. Of course, it'll be more difficult for you, Adam—
all eyes will be on you. You may have to stay here—"

"No way. I'm not staying behind. I'll find a way to meet you."

"Good. Remember, the katanas are in the backyard. Everybody grab one or two and a handful of lighters. We'll meet up about a hundred meters down the hill where Claremont Road makes its first hairpin turn."

Detective Ramirez shakes my hand. He checks the clip in his gun. "I know bullets won't stop those things, but they sure make me feel better."

He eases out the door and through the crowd in the hallway, followed by the colonel and Cutty. I wait a few seconds before leaving the bedroom.

"There's the man of the hour." A silver-haired survivor smiles in my direction. "I couldn't believe it when I first heard. They say you took down twelve super Daemons all by yourself?" The crowd grows around him in the hallway. He smiles as I edge my way toward the living room. "You're one helluva wolfhound," another survivor says. "Way to go, Steel."

The living room is just as crowded as the narrow hallway. "There he is. Can I get you anything? Hot dog? Water?"

"No. I'm just gonna check out the basement."

Voices hush around me.

"You don't want to go down there," the silver-haired survivor says. "Bad stuff down those steps. A few of the younger hounds went down earlier on a dare. C'mon, let me get you a plate of food."

Food is the most precious commodity at Claremont. Even though I'm not hungry, I can't appear rude. "You're too kind. I will have something to eat."

"Excellent, I'll be right back." The survivor turns toward the kitchen and makes his way through the crowded room. "Coming through, make way. Steel needs food."

After cracking open the door to the stairs leading to the basement, I put a finger to my lips, attempting to convince those around me they're in on a harmless prank. Muted laughter rises from the crowd. "I'll teach those pups to keep their tails out of the basement, be back in a few minutes." With a mischievous grin, I turn to the stairs.

The smell of pain and fear clings to the room; cruel memories of another time fill my head. The light is on and voices hush as I hit the bottom step.

"Halt. Who goes there?" A playful voice says.

"It's just me."

Two survivors rush up and reach out their hands. "It's Steel."

"I just wanted to take a look around down here."

The cages lining the back wall give me the shivers. The doors to the wire pens are open and a young girl struggles to free herself from one of them.

"What are you doing in there?" I ask.

"Just wanted to see what it was like," she says as she stands up and brushes herself off. "Hey, you're Steel."

"Yup. I used to live here."

"This is your house?" A survivor with bright green eyes says. "What's with the cages?"

"It's a long story—bad memories."

"Sorry, sir. I didn't mean to cause you—"

"No problem. Listen, do you think you hounds can do me a huge favor?"

"A favor?" the girl says, her eyes widening. "For the man of the hour? Name it."

"I want to get out of here and be alone for a little while—"

"Savor the glory?"

"No, not quite. I just want to get some air and maybe have a run through the woods like I did back in the day." I raise my eyes to the ceiling, acknowledging the noise of the festivities above us. "But they might think I'm ignoring them you know? I am, as you say, the man of the hour, after all."

"What do you want us to do?"

"I know it's a lot to ask, but if we all transformed and ran up the stairs as canines, I could make a break for it without being spotted. Safety in numbers, right?"

The young wolfhounds glance at each other. "Right," the girl says.

Clothes are tossed to the floor along with strips of flesh. A couple of the survivors moan. They aren't eating enough meat to transform without pain, and I feel terrible for having asked them. My change, on the other hand, is completed in a few seconds, free of any agony. I've eaten well, thanks to Aunt Rose.

The transformations are complete, and my young conspirators wait for a signal. As soon as I bark, they all race up the stairs and through the crowded room of amused survivors.

The front door is wide open and we sprint out into the night. I trot across the street and turn to the young pups. With a howl, I acknowledge their help in my great escape. They wag their tails and turn back to the house.

I'm now free to join the others at the hairpin turn. Five against one hundred—the odds are definitely not in our favor. I wish I'd spent more time with Dixie and

I miss Aunt Rose and I feel the wind on my fur and I curse the night.

****

Whether the silver and yellow streaks of light were visible to the audience members seated in the Lucas Knight Theater didn't concern Dixie when she arrived. She was too busy locating her main objective: Lucas Knight. Charlie Nguyen appeared by her side moments later and together they scanned the area.

Dixie pointed out the magician standing center stage, his back to them. Only a thin black curtain separated them from Knight—the curtain serving as the backdrop for his show and concealing them from the audience.

The magician's voice boomed through the theater, prattling on about the differences between his illusions and all the others in a city of so many copycats. "What I do on this stage cannot be duplicated by anyone in the world." He kept the audience engaged and laughing, a true entertainer.

Dixie felt the presence of eight hundred human souls watching Knight. So far, nobody seemed aware of the two Daemon's sudden arrival, and she hoped they wouldn't be harmed by what was about to take place.

You're in grave danger, the voice of Major Jean Ransom shouted in Dixie's head.

Dixie ignored the major, trying to formulate a plan to take down Lucas Knight. She had no idea how to go about it, but one thing was certain: she wasn't about to let this depraved Daemon destroy the world.

Charlie Nguyen whispered, "Fear not, little Daemon, Charlie Nguyen has the perfect plan." Nguyen seemed confident, exhibiting signs of why she was considered such a formidable opponent so many years ago. "While we were in transit, I devised a wonderful idea to end the life of this wretched soul." She seemed proud of herself and wasted no time explaining the plan in detail: "I'll have a katana ready. You draw him near, and I'll slice and dice. You light him up, and I'll stomp his bones. If we work quickly, he doesn't stand a chance."

That is not a workable plan. Major Jean Ransom's voice was urgent and to the point.

Nguyen tuned into the conversation. *You're being a bit negative, don't you think?*

I just don't want either of you to join me here, on the other side, anytime too soon.

Well, that's gonna happen sooner or later. Dixie thought, *whether you want it or not. Now, please, be quiet.*

Dixie faced Nguyen. "You make it sound so simple."

"Indeed. Now remember most True Bloods would rather use hands-on spells as their weapon of choice, so taunt him. Get him good and mad. Make him want to strangle you with his bare hands. That will draw him near and distract him so I can sneak up behind, undetected, and use the sword."

"Got it."

You don't have the power to kill. Major Ransom said firmly, as if explaining to a three-year-old why the plan wouldn't fly. *You're Daemons, and Daemon's can't kill.*

Dixie had no time for negative thoughts from the other side. She and Nguyen were in place behind the backdrop curtain and ready to attack.

Nguyen manifested a katana and whispered, "Are you ready?"

Dixie nodded while she caused a miniature ball of fire to materialize, keeping it aloft just over her left shoulder.

Nguyen winked then did a double take. She frowned as she stared at Dixie. "Just curious. How are you going to get him angry? How are you going to insult him?"

"Don't know…never taunted anyone before."

"Give me a preview," Nguyen whispered. "What exactly will you say?"

"How about, 'Hey, stupid idiot, get over here.' "

Charlie Nguyen winced and shook her head. "Change of plans, we'll switch roles." She edged Dixie out of the way, and handed over the sword. "Get ready." She reached down and lifted the back stage curtain over her head. In a piercing voice, "Hey dumb shit, get the fuck over here, asshole." Her voice echoed throughout the theater.

Lucas Knight spun around, facing the Daemons behind him. "Where the hell did you come from?" He rushed toward Nguyen, his black robes flying as he ran.

"Now, Dixie," Charlie Nguyen said.

Dixie swung the katana across Knight's throat, lopping off his head. Blood gushed out and splattered on the stage. The audience gasped. With a quick swirling motion, she slit the magician's stomach open. Intestines, kidneys, and lungs spattered to the floor. Nguyen grabbed the curtain and yanked it down, entangling Knight's torso in the material. She motioned toward the fireball, sending it down onto his flailing body. Black flames leapt into the air, sparked for a moment, and died quickly. Nguyen jumped up and down on the charred remains and scattered the bones of Lucas Knight.

The audience looked on in shocked silence. Cries and muffled moans swept through the theater in waves of disbelief. Two beefy security guards rushed toward Dixie and Nguyen as stagehands and performers ran for safety. Dixie easily immobilized both of the guards with a wave of her hands.

She turned to Nguyen, her smile beaming. "We did it."

Nguyen's face shined as she threw her arms around Dixie. They hugged near the smoldering corpse of the magician; the body that had been chopped, scooped, burned, and stomped.

Murmurs rose from the audience. In short order, squeals and shouts grew into hoots and hollers. The crowd applauded, cheering in a joyous celebration.

Dixie and Nguyen glanced behind them. Lucas Knight had knitted himself together, busily wiping the ashes from his body. He glared at the two Daemons.

Major Ransom's thoughts screamed inside Dixie's head, *You cannot kill!*

Shouts of "Bravo" rose from the audience. Applause exploded through the theater as cries of, "He's the greatest magician of all time," and "I've never seen anything like it before," rang out. The main curtain, heavy and black, came down, covering the stage from the audience as the thunderous applause continued. The uproar faded as the audience began filing out of the theater.

Knight seemed disoriented, a little wobbly in the knees. His tattered robes were caked with blood, smoke rising from his smoldering body. He staggered toward Dixie and Nguyen with outstretched hands. "*Imobili.*"

Chapter Twenty-Eight

The warm wind rustles through my fur, invigorating me and pushing me on. My paws crunch into the gravel as I follow the street down to the first hairpin turn and wait for a sign from the others. After a few moments of silence, I decide to venture on, following the shrubbery along the side of the road with my snout raised, sniffing everything in the air. The full moon bathes Claremont Hill in a shadowy light, and the breeze I enjoyed just a few minutes ago starts playing tricks with my imagination. Shrubs and trees sway like animated creatures.

Without warning, the wind gives up and dies. My heart thumps double-time as I scan the nearby area. It's graveyard silent, not a hint of another living soul.

The road ahead makes a sharp curve to the right, dipping down and vanishing into the night. I keep low, slinking along the edge of the two-lane highway. After negotiating the blind curve, a voice whispers, "Over here." It's Colonel Dayton.

With another sniff, I zero in on his hiding place; a small wooded area a few yards off the road. A hand sticks out from behind a Joshua tree and waves me over.

"What took you so long, Steel?" Dayton asks as I jog toward him. He should know better than to expect an answer. Tina has transformed as well, so I sniff her scent and tuck it in the back of my mind for future reference. She does the same to me; it's what canines do—nothing personal. I settle into the small group and lie down.

"Good to see you, Adam," Marco says. I like the way he calls me by my human name even though I'm in canine form. He puts a hand on my back and rubs my fur. His touch feels safe and pleasant, and I automatically arch my back against his fingers. "We haven't seen anything yet," he whispers.

As soon as his sentence ends, I hear a twig snap about thirty yards away to the right. My ears perk up. Tina has the same reaction to the noise.

"What is it?" Marco whispers.

I stand up and turn in the general direction of the sound. I don't pretend to have the skills of an English Pointer and wouldn't really want to, but any canine can sniff out trouble, especially when trouble's nearby.

Colonel Dayton, Cutty, and Marco follow my gaze and tighten their grips on their katanas. Cutty trembles, so I nuzzle at his arm to calm him down. He glances at me and winks.

A form appears in the distance. It marches toward us; head held high, arms outstretched. There's a strong smell of sulfur in the air: *Sangre di Real*.

Three more figures appear in the distance behind the first. They advance up the hill and the odor of rotten egg grows stronger; I even think the humans smell it. The lead True Blood is probably an advance scout. A solid line of *Sangre di Real* follows behind him at a distance like a thundering tidal wave

Colonel Dayton turns to our little band of soldiers and nods. He holds his katana in the air and waves it forward—a silent signal to attack.

Tina bolts up and sprints toward the lone True Blood, her dark coat blending in with the shrubbery. I do my best to keep up with her, but she's super-fast. She jumps at the warrior and latches onto its bicep, growling and biting into the fleshy part of his shoulder with all her might. The True Blood raises his other hand and points it at Tina. She yelps and falls to the ground. I leap at the Daemon's chest, knocking him onto his back. Tina gets up and chomps down on the same shoulder she'd started with. Wolfhounds are tenacious fighters.

I feel the strength of the Daemon as he struggles, knocking us both aside as if swatting at flies. He raises his hands, and I can only assume he's about to use some kind of spell against us.

The sound of metal slicing through air whizzes over my head. It ends in a "chop" as the Daemon's head flies off his body and rolls down the hill. Colonel Dayton stands over us, katana at the ready. He guts the creature like a trained *Samurai*, and shouts at Marco, "Burn him."

Marco produces a lighter from his pocket and touches it to the headless warrior's dark cloak. An intense black flame sends us reeling back a step or two. Tina and I watch as Dayton, Marco, and Cutty stomp on the remains of the Daemon, grinding its bones into the dirt.

One down, ninety-nine to go.

Another warrior races up the hill toward us, his arms pointing in our direction. I've never experienced the spell of a Daemon before, and never want to again. It starts with a buzzing in the head, feeling like a thousand volts of electricity. Images of Colonel Dayton, Marco, Cutty, and Tina coming under the same spell cross my field of vision as I howl and fall to the dirt.

The Daemon stands over us, a foul grin contorting his already ugly face. His arms come up and I shut my eyes, ready for the worst—thinking about Dixie.

A scream cuts through the night, and my eyes bolt open. A wolfhound has latched onto the Daemon's throat and blood oozes down its chest. Marco manages to get to his feet. He grabs the katana and punctures the stomach of the creature. The wolfhound releases its hold of the Daemon's neck, what's left of it, and Marco finishes the job with little effort. Colonel Dayton joins in, carving through the Daemon's belly. The wolfhound barks, turns around, and scampers off into the woods.

Cutty pulls a lighter from his pocket. His hands tremble so much it takes him several tries before bringing it to life. He tosses it onto the Daemon's body and it bursts into flames. Another flash of black fire sends intense heat into the air around us. When it dies down, Marco and Dayton stomp on the bones, grinding them to dust.

Rising, I search for the wolfhound who saved our lives. It's gone. I thought I caught the scent of the canine—a familiar trace: my sister, Lucy. No time to mull it over. After shaking off the blood covering my fur, I get ready for the next *Sangre di Real.*

It won't be much of a wait. At least thirty more True Bloods jog up the hill in formation, coming straight at us.

****

Lucas Knight stretched out his arm, forcing the two Daemons to their knees.

271

He sauntered toward them as he ran a hand around his neck, soothing the pain of his beheading. His stomach ached where he'd been gutted, and his flesh still smoldered, but all in all he was in fairly decent shape.

"Well," he coughed, expelling a puff of smoke from his throat. He tried again. "Well, well, well, what have we here? The dark and stormy Charlie Nguyen; feeling a bit under the weather, eh?" He leaned over to take a closer look at Nguyen's companion. "Ah, if it isn't Dixie Mulholland." He ran fingers through strands of her golden hair. "A ray of sunshine to brighten the dark mood."

Mulholland let out a growl, low and threatening.

Lucas chuckled. "Defiant to the end, eh? Your poor aunty would have been so proud—had she lived. Ah well, such is life. You know, Sunshine, I heard your aunt Rose put up quite a fight. But then you know how tricky those old Daemons are to kill—all the silly rules and what not—chopping and burning, yuck. Personally, I prefer a much more practical approach to the art of murder. Oh sure, I occasionally follow the ancient rituals, but only when I have a particular distaste for my victim—Gorgeous, for example. Couldn't stand that woman."

Tears fell from Charlie Nguyen's eyes, landing on the stage floor.

"Do you weep for Gorgeous or yourself? No need for tears. Your death will be quick. A simple word, I promise." He placed a hand on her shoulder and grinned. "Even though you were very naughty tonight. Downright rude, if truth be told. I'm willing to overlook your pathetic attack. The humans loved it. They thought you and Sunshine were part of the act—another glorious Lucas Knight illusion." He pressed his hands together, as if in prayer, and closed his eyes. "That being said, in order to show my gratitude, I will treat you to a quick death—painful, but quick. You deserve nothing less." He raised his arm and drew it back over his head. Nguyen's sobs grew as he shouted the secret word that would end her sniveling and begin her suffering, "*Exteritus.*"

Nguyen's weeping continued.

He frowned and glanced at his hand, shaking it a couple of times before aiming it at her again. "*Exteritus.*"

Nguyen remained on her knees, still blubbering like an idiot, but still very much alive.

"What in Hell's name?" Knight shifted his glance at Mulholland. She, too, knelt on the stage, but with her arm raised. How had she accomplished that while immobilized? *What in Hell's name, indeed?*

Mulholland lifted her head and stared at him. She raised a leg, planting her foot solidly on the ground in front of her, and stood up. Her arm remained stretched out to him, palm up—an aggressive gesture. "You will not harm another living soul."

In spite of her show of strength, he forced another grin—a sign of supremacy. "And you will shut the hell up, that's what you will do." He cleared his throat. "Haven't you realized by now? I'm no ordinary Daemon—"

"Neither am I," she said, keeping her hand at arm's length, marching toward him until she stood in his path.

"This is impossible. I can't read your thoughts. Why can't I read your—"

"But I can read yours." She cocked her head. "You're afraid of me. Funny, I thought True Bloods feared nothing. Are you really thinking of running away?"

Knight set his jaw and shook his hands in the air, reloading, and leveled them against her once more. "Listen to me very carefully, Sunshine, choose your next words wisely; they will be your last." With rigid fingers aimed straight at her face, he yelled, "*Exteri—*"

"*Imobili,*" Dixie shouted.

He felt his blood slow, his joints harden, and every cell in his body jerked to a stop. He told himself not to panic. He'd never been placed in an immobilizing spell before, and so he investigated the symptoms of the curse the only way he could: from the inside out.

First of all, his brain continued to function and that was a good thing for one as advanced as he, no blubbering for him. He cleared his throat and grunted. He could not form words, but at least some form of communication was possible. And sight remained. He saw the empty theater seats, the beam of the spotlights, and that wretched Daemon, Dixie Mulholland.

She touched the top of Nguyen's head, releasing her from the *Imobili* spell at once. The first thing Nguyen moved was her mouth, no surprise there.

"So, the great Lucas Knight, leader of the *Sangre di Real*, is caught—trapped like a little, teeny, tiny rat." She straightened and ambled toward him. "How did this happen? Who's to say?" She turned to Mulholland. "How *did* this happen?"

"Something he called me: sunshine. Something said during The Sufferings. At first, I thought it a poem, but it's not. Listen:

"*The sunshine has returned,*
In truth the secret lies.
The night it must be burned,
In love the body dies."

"A prophecy."

"About what?"

"About now."

Lucas tried to interrupt their ramblings, but all he managed was a snort.

Mulholland pointed at him. "He's the night, get it? Lucas Knight. And he kept calling me sunshine."

"Okay, yeah. But what about that other line, the one about the secret lies?"

"He lied to the council about what really happened on Claremont." She closed her eyes. "I'm in his mind. The truth is he made certain the True Bloods met a quick end. He had every one of them murdered to force the council to send more to avenge their death. Knight wants all the *Sangre di Real* released, and that was his way of making it happen."

Lucas grunted, drool sliding out of his mouth and down his chin. It left a snail track from his lips to the stage.

Mulholland turned to him, tapped him on top of the head, and said, "Speak."

At long last, the words he'd held for so long formed, "Fuck you."

"Listen to me, Knight. Stop the attack at Claremont—stop it right now or…"

"Or what?"

Mulholland twisted her fingers, balling them into a fist. He felt his insides wrench and constrict. A little boy's scream flew from his lips as tears rolled down his cheeks. "I can't"

"What do you mean? You started this you finish it. I suggest you do as I say. You know I can make this exceptionally painful for you. Just how much is entirely up to you."

"The council agreed to send the True Bloods. I can't override their decision. Don't you think I'd stop it if I could? Besides, the battle has already begun." The immobilization spell was no joke. Mulholland rummaged through his mind—gathering information, verifying his thoughts. He couldn't stand another minute of this bullshit. Time to use truth to buy some time. "But don't worry; the True Bloods will be defeated."

"What do you mean?"

"It's all arranged for them to lose. They'll be slaughtered on the field of battle."

"But, why would you—"

"Oh stop with the goodie-two-shoes. You're in my mind, you know why. The fight will look legit if you don't know what you're looking for. Wolfhounds will die, True Bloods will die, but in the end, the True Bloods will lose, forcing the council's hand—all the *Sangre di Real* will be sent to earth."

"So you're murdering your own army."

"Are you deaf? How many times do I have to say it? Yes, I manipulated the council by murdering my own army. Now get out of my mind, and put an end to this damned spell."

Mulholland frowned and stepped back from him. "I heard you that time." She raised her hand, twirling a finger in the air, spinning him around 180 degrees. "So did He."

A small orange glow appeared. Like a stage light, its shutters slowly opened. As the illumination grew, Lucas felt a hand touch his head, releasing him from the immobilization spell. Bowing low to the light, he whispered, "Your majesty, you've come to save me." With a trembling finger, he pointed at Mulholland. "This wretched creature twists my words. She tortured me."

"Only the beginning."

The hair on his arms singed as flames licked his body. From the corner of his eye, he spotted silver and yellow lights spark to life then vanish. It was the last thing he saw before his eyeballs burst and the little boy scream returned.

Chapter Twenty-Nine

Dixie and Charlie Nguyen materialized at Claremont, near the house at the top of the hill. The celebrations in honor of Adam had come to an abrupt end.

A few cheerful voices still came from the back of the house—some chattering, some laughing. Most of the survivors, however, stood near the front of the house, motionless with anxious faces, warning those in the backyard to keep quiet.

In the distance, shrieks mixed with an occasional howl or yip filled the night. Dixie cupped her hands around her mouth. "Adam!"

"Shhh." Nguyen pushed Dixie aside. "Do you want to get us both killed?"

Dixie ignored the admonishment, turned her back to Nguyen, and scampered down the hill toward the sounds in the woods. "Adam!"

Clouds blew in from the west, covering the full moon and sending Claremont into total darkness. Dixie stumbled over a thicket of undergrowth and fell, face first, into the dirt. She got up, took two steps, and lost her footing again. *This is ridiculous.*

She closed her eyes and concentrated on the change. In a few seconds, she transformed into a Giant Irish Wolfhound. Her vision improved at once. So did her speed.

Dixie raced down the hill toward the sound of the skirmish, leaping over obstacles invisible to her prior to the change. The beating of paws trampling the ground behind her filled the air, growing louder with each step she took. In a moment, she was surrounded by packs of wolfhounds galloping down the hill toward the battle.

Flashes of light and the cries of war spread across the hillside before her. The rancid smell of death filled the air.

A wolfhound came racing straight at Dixie, followed by a True Blood, his arms flailing in the air. Two wolfhounds pounced over her, attacking the Daemon head on. The wolfhound running away stopped and raced back, jumping onto the pile of canine and Daemon. Not a random attack, the wolfhounds worked together—hunting in packs.

"Colonel Dayton, over here." The sound of Marco Ramirez's voice cut through the woods. Dixie turned and sprinted toward the sound.

She caught sight of the two men at the edge of a clearing. Dayton swung a katana, lopping off the head of a True Blood. Marco gutted the creature and Dayton produced a flame, setting the Daemon on fire. They worked as an excellent team.

"Hey, man," Cutty howled, "there's another one."

Dixie turned and saw Cutty, racing alone down the hill toward a True Blood.

Colonel Dayton and Marco looked up from their stomping. "Wait for us. Stand down—stand down."

The order came too late. Cutty ran into an ambush. Three *Sangre di Real* surrounded him, immobilized him, and slashed his chest open. He died instantly. Dayton and Marco flew down the hill, katanas raised over their heads, Dixie and three wolfhounds joining them. Dixie and the wolfhounds ripped into the True Blood's flesh as swords slashed across throats and dug into stomachs. The True Bloods went down hard. Dayton knelt, cradling Cutty's head in his arms. After a moment, he laid Cutty on the ground, grabbed his sword, and dashed down the hill.

"Get back here," Marco yelled. He set fire to the True Bloods, stepped back from the intense heat, and then crushed their bones to the dirt. With a quick glance at Cutty, he flew down the hill after the colonel.

Marco's words from just a few days ago rang in her head: there will *not* be another war in this city. Dixie and the wolfhounds followed him toward the chaos. Before she jumped into the fray, Dixie surveyed the field of battle:

Sangre di Real were executed by invisible forces, their heads flying into the air and their innards eviscerated by unseen powers. Bolts of fire flew through the night, enveloping the True Bloods in flames. Survivors, both in human and canine form, jumped up and down on the remains, grinding their bones to dirt.

True Bloods slashed through the canines, cutting them down like fragile stalks of wheat. Yips and howls coursed across the hillside. Forms dashed from tree to tree, looking for cover, looking for prey. She knew there'd be no chance of finding Adam in this madness.

An ungodly odor grabbed her attention. She turned to the right and found herself face to face with a True Blood. He slashed out at her, his claws scraping across her leg. In a moment, his head flew into the air. Dixie glanced behind the creature's flailing body. Marco

Ramirez had cut the Daemon's head off and began the task of scooping out its bowels. Ramirez's face exhibited both exhaustion and fear, but his actions were determined.

He nodded at Dixie as he produced a lighter from his pocket and touched it to the fallen True Blood. She barked, but he did not acknowledge her. He could not have known the wolfhound he'd just saved was once his lover. How could he?

"*Exteritus.*"

The secret word popped into the air, shouted from farther down the hill. Dixie dug her claws into the dirt and took off in pursuit of the word. She witnessed more *Sangre di Real* being taken down by unseen forces as she galloped through the warzone. Lucas Knight arranged to have the Daemons killed, and succeeded with deft precision; his legacy from the grave.

"*Exteritus.*"

Dixie halted, scouring the nearby area. The moon cut a path through the clouds, bathing the hill in surreal glow. In the distance, perched on a small mound, Charlie Nguyen stood tall, her arms held out in front of her as she cast the deadly spell she learned tonight, "*Exteritus.*" A True Blood fell to the ground and dissolved into a pool of liquid. Nguyen took aim at another. "*Exteritus.*" And another.

Dixie felt a rush of joy at the sight of Nguyen taking down True Bloods, one after the other. The momentum of the battle shifted in their favor, the war nearly won. She took a step forward, felt something crash down on her head, and crumpled to the ground. She forced her eyes open, but the moon had disappeared behind a cloud, mudding her vision. Before she blacked out, Dixie caught sight of a small man wearing turquoise robes. A sweet, childlike smile played across his lips. She also detected the scent of rotten eggs.

****

I found Dixie in a ravine at the bottom of the hill. At first, I thought she was dead—she'd been found in the area of the heaviest fighting, survivors in both canine and human form covered the ground in numbers.

She drifted in and out of a coma for two days. Tina, Charlie Nguyen, Marco, and I kept constant watch over her, nursing her back to health with plenty of rest, and good healthy food. We knew it was best to keep the hospital and, by extension, the authorities out of it. I sat up with Dixie almost every night, reading to her, and drawing little black and white sketches. I placed the drawings I made of her while in prison next to her bed. I don't know if that helped with her recovery, but I like to think it did.

Colonel Dayton buried Cutty in a clearing near the house. Everyone on the hill attended the service except Tina and Dixie. Tina said it would be too painful to attend. She volunteered to stay back and keep an eye on Dixie.

Dayton gave a brief eulogy. "Paul Cuthbert was many things, but he was not a soldier. Even though, he hated war, he never shied from the fight. Cutty was a humanitarian, as you well know, a heroic figure, as we all found out, and my dearest friend. Cutty, I'll see you on the other side."

Charlie Nguyen held a brave face throughout the ceremony, but finally bowed her head and brushed tears away.

I felt compelled to say something. "Cutty could always make us laugh. He had a way with words...and food. He was genuine, open, and honest. The human qualities we should all hope to have when we leave this hill and join the outside world."

And as the days passed, the survivors left the hill and joined the outside world, one by one and two by two. Deputy Chief Ramirez arranged identification papers for every one of them. He grinned and told me he knew a guy who knew a guy who owed somebody a favor—a top of the line counterfeiter. He laughed. I guess it was a private joke.

Colonel Dayton negotiated a hefty bonus for his return to the United Nations Paranormal Activities Division with Admiral Garrison. He was never implicated in my escape. He divided the bonus among the survivors, called it seed money. Marco and Charlie Nguyen used their contacts in the city to find decent jobs for them all. I worked with them, teaching them how to control the urge to transform, and how to blend into the human world. It took time and patience but, eventually, we settled the remaining forty-three survivors into a somewhat normal life in the city—as normal as it ever gets, I suppose, for Sin City.

Dixie was depressed through her recovery, and nobody could blame her. However, her spirits improved over time, and she's now, what the humans call, nearly a hundred percent.

She's well enough to go for short runs around the hill. We leave the house before dawn and enjoy the cool, brisk air as we jog down the road to the hairpin turn. We usually walk the rest of the way down after that. Charlie Nguyen comes with us most mornings—

today she didn't.

Dixie keeps running past the hairpin, and that makes me feel good. It's a sure sign her strength has fully returned. She nearly makes it to the bottom of the hill before she slows and takes up a steady pace to the frontage road.

Even though no more monsters hide among the trees, I keep my eyes wide open, scanning the hill for anything and everything. Although I was born on Claremont, I can't wait to leave it behind and start a new life somewhere, anywhere, with Dixie. Charlie Nguyen insists Dixie is good to go, but I want to hear it from her.

I am good to go; as good as I'll ever get, that is. Her thoughts fill my mind like happy memories. I always want her in my thoughts; it makes me feel safe and loved. I don't know what I would have done if she'd died on this hill. I probably wouldn't want—

But I didn't die. C'mon, this is too nice a day to worry about what ifs. I'll race you back to the house.

She takes off in a sprint, ignoring the road and galloping up the steep slope straight toward the house. She's fast—lately, faster than me. I do my best to catch up to her, but it's no use. She's on the front porch waiting for me, her tail wagging.

I huff and puff across the street and join her. When I sit next to her, she nuzzles me and my tail joins hers in a steady back and forth sweep across the porch.

"Well, there are the lovebirds."

It's Charlie Nguyen. Her voice is friendly, teasing. She and Dixie bonded on the night they defeated Lucas Knight; Nguyen told me all about it. They became close friends in the weeks she helped Dixie recover from her wounds. The bond is understandable; they're made of the same stuff: Daemon.

Charlie Nguyen did her best to explain to me the rule Dixie broke by remaining in canine form for more than one day: shift for one day; shift for all days. She also told me about the prophecy Dixie received during The Sufferings, particularly the last line: In love, the body dies.

There are times when I refuse to accept the fact Dixie will always remain a Giant Irish Wolfhound. But after her episodes of dark depression lightened, she seemed to accept her form and the challenges ahead. She says she loves the fact she can communicate with me, not to mention, what she calls, her new "super powers": killer sight, an awesome sense of smell, and a keen range of hearing.

Still, I notice how she observes Colonel Dayton and Marco as they move about the house, or how they sometimes comment on the colors in the sky, and I know it has to disturb her. If anyone can understand what she's going through, it's me.

So I made a decision: I will remain in canine form. This is how I was born, and since the one I love has no other choice, this is how I'll die.

You're such a gloomy Gus. C'mon, let's go to our place and watch the sunrise. She barks. It's a joyful noise—I can tell.

She skitters off the porch, and I race after her. We settle into the spot at the top of Claremont we dubbed "our place" and sit facing east.

The sun peeks over Sunrise Mountain, filling the sky with a myriad of reds, pinks, and yellows (we make up the colors in our minds from memory). A warm breeze whooshes through my fur, and she rests her head on my shoulder as a new day begins bringing with it our new life together.

A word about the author...

Richard Arthur Newberry lives in Las Vegas, Nevada. He considers himself a person who "cannot not write" and regards Las Vegas as a unique setting for his short stories and novels. He has been published in *The Writer's Block*, an anthology, and placed second in the 2014 Las Vegas Flash Fiction competition.

Mr. Newberry, his wife, Betty, and their son, Samuel, share their home with Zady and Schnoodles, two loving rescue dogs who provided a world of inspiration for his novel, *Sin City Wolfhound*.

http://richardarthurnewberry.com